Other Novels by Steven Hamilton

Dragon Slayers

McSally and Company

From Where I Stood

Journey Home

I0640278

Coming in 2020

Twisted Truth

Steeno Six

A Novel
By
Steven Hamilton

ISBN: 978-1-7338778-4-8

Cover Art: BespokeBookCovers.com

Author's Note: This novel is a work of fiction. Aside from the obvious U. S. government institutions mentioned, all other organizations, characters, and events are completely fictitious. Any similarities to real persons or organizations are purely coincidental.

I would be less than honest, though, if I denied the existence of the issues that drive the story. They are real today. The setting in the novel is futuristic, but it shouldn't require much mental effort to imagine how humanity might possibly find itself immersed in such a dystopian society.

With Gratitude

My deepest appreciate goes out to the patient and unrelenting members of my writing group—Richie Goldstein, NNStoelting, and J. Jay Waller. As always, thanks to my tireless and dedicated editor, Diane Luehrs. Finally, to my lovely wife, Mary, my deepest gratitude and love for all the support and enthusiasm. None of this works without you.

Prologue

Seattle, Washington
August, 2055

The conversation faded. The young woman, tired and melancholy, searched for appropriate words, but settled for an observation about weather. "It might rain later." Shadows and darkness closed in on what had been a sunny afternoon.

The young man, immobile in bed, followed her gaze. "That'd cool things down." The wires connected to his head and penetrating into the back of his neck felt as though they would disconnect if he moved. He tried to shift his body, but the tubes—feeding, liquid, and urine—conspired with his weakness, locking him in place. *Not much longer now.*

She picked up the antiquated device from the table beside his bed, turning it around, examining it from different angles. "What did you say that thing was?" The black, plastic object consisted of a keyboard and a flat display.

His eyes followed her inspection. "That antique, my love, is what your grandparents called a *notebook computer*. It was a bitch to find."

She ran her fingers over the keys. "So, what? You just type on these things?"

"That's the way they did it back then."

"Do you really trust that old technology? Why not use your pad and neural connection?"

He stared at her for a moment. "Other than the experience of something new?" He arched his eyebrow.

1

"Mostly, I think, because once I'm done, you can disconnect it from the network." He nodded toward a sheet of paper folded up beside the device. "There are the instructions. Follow them exactly. After you power it down, open it up and take out the hard drive. Smash it with a hammer. Then throw it, along with everything else, into the vaposonic. Use the *complete destruction* option—nothing but ash left." He paused and added, "I don't want anyone following me. They watch the neural inputs pretty closely, but they aren't ready for this type of interface. And make sure you disconnect all these wires from my body. After that, call Doctor Amblen. Tell him that I died in my sleep. He'll be expecting your call and will know what to do."

Silence crept in as the approaching darkness swept away the last of the ambient light. The notebook computer display provided the only illumination. As the last vestiges of the day disappeared, the young man sighed. "It's time. I need to go."

A tear trickled down her cheek. "What happens if this doesn't work?"

She could make out his sad smile by the light of the screen. "Then I will be dead. And I will at last be free of this prison."

"And if you succeed?"

"Then I will *still* be free of this prison I call a body."

"But will you be alive?"

"I don't know. It depends on what you mean by *alive*. My body will be dead but maybe I, or what I feel is me, will still exist. I'll just be in a different form."

She wiped the tear and sniffed. "Will you find a way to contact me?"

"No. When I leave, I'll be gone—whether I'm alive and in a different form or just dead. You have a life. You need to get on with it."

"I don't want a life without you."

"You've already got that." He tried to nod his head down toward his broken body.

The woman pleaded with her words and eyes, "They'll find a cure. It's only a matter of time."

His brief laugh came out as a cynical grunt. "Yes. It is a *matter of time*, of which I have little. Every day it gets worse. Although, in truth, I'm not sure just how much worse it can get. Technology advances, but the timing isn't right."

"I love you."

His smile turned warm. "And I love you. Please know that no matter where my spirit ends up, I will *always* love you."

She reached over and grasped his hand, squeezing as hard as she dared.

He returned the squeeze with what strength he had. "It's time."

The young woman nodded. "What do I do?"

His gaze shifted to the notebook computer. "Use the keyboard. Type in 'run star crossover star slash initiate.' And then hit *Enter*. After that, follow the instructions on the paper."

She began to cry.

"Don't. Please. You'll get me started. We've been all through this, Liv. *Please*." His eyes begged her.

She leaned over and kissed his forehead and then lightly pressed her lips against his. "Goodbye, my love." Shifting over closer to the table, she typed the cryptic phrase, watching the letters and symbols appear on the screen. When she'd finished, a small line on the display blinked back at her. She felt it urging her on.

She hit *Enter*. The screen went black for a moment, before a torrent of letters, numbers, and symbols began scrolling. And then it was done.

The love of her life gasped, his eyes widening before they closed. His body relaxed. The gentle rise and fall of his chest ceased.

She wiped one final tear from her cheek. As the body of the man that she loved lay lifeless in bed beside her, Liv unfolded the paper and shuddered as she read the instructions. The words were precise, technical, and devoid of any humanity, as though written by a machine.

Chapter 1

Washington, D.C.
August, 2105

A faint amber light blinked in the upper right quadrant of her field of view. The incoming ID gave her the necessary information. She issued the mental command—*Connect*. The flashing light turned a steady green. She focused on her thoughts before transmitting them. "Mister Arandon. To what do I owe this interruption?" Maggie Renfro continued reviewing the latest media information analysis of her boss' political performance as she waited for the inevitable pitch."

The voice, which was actually a transmitted thought, came in with perfect predictability. "Why Miz Renfro, how kind of you to take my call."

"Get to the point. What do you want?"

The signal smirked—she felt it. "FNA is running a story on the new STOP legislation this afternoon. We wanted to get Senator Estrone's perspective."

Maggie shook her head and sighed. "How stupid of me, Nick. I was certain that the Freedom Network of America had already put the finishing touches on that piece. Just a hunch here, but I'm betting it's already queued up for broadcast. What is it that you really want? After all, the *Silverman Thaddeus Opportunities Program* bill is nothing more than a flimsy front for your typical anti-immigration rant."

"The people have a right to know what's going on."

She laughed out loud, knowing that it would show up in the neural net transfer as a series of abstract symbols.

Whether he received it as a laugh depended on the quality of his interface chip. "Who turned you on to that kind of crap?"

"Learned it in journalism school. You must have slept through that class, huh?"

Maggie organized her thoughts for transmission. "Ah yes, *journalism*. I vaguely remember the term. Wasn't that back in the time when there were actually *news* organizations, you know, when reporters gathered facts and presented them as real stories? And here I thought we'd moved past that idealistic drivel."

"As much as I'd love to continue this intellectual exchange, I *am* on a tight timeline. Now, does the senator have a comment?"

"None whatsoever."

"Okay, then." He paused. "What are the chances that we might discuss this over a drink later this afternoon?"

The guy never gave up. She configured her message and highlighted it in bright yellow before transmitting. "There is no world in which I would have a drink with you." *Disconnect.* She hated burning bridges, especially with powerful media companies, but this guy had no socially redeeming value.

The amber light blinked again. Some days it was impossible to get anything done. *Connect.* She allowed the automated greeting to play out before responding. "Good afternoon, Mister Fishburn." The senator's chief of staff connected with her at least four or five times a day, so she'd programmed the neural interface to respond without intervention.

"You have the roll-up numbers on polling for the STOP bill?"

She mentally swiped her field of view clear and isolated her command line. *Menu, Poll, STOP, summary—execute.* With the search and analysis application initiated, she re-enabled her comm line. "Yes sir. I have it working right now. I'll place the results in your inbox stratified by poll source, size, and date."

"Anything from our friends over at FNA?"

"Arandon just called looking for a statement. Said they're running a piece today. I have it set up for capture. Will shoot it and the polling reaction to you by the end of the output cycle."

"Okay. Contact the people over at Public Literacy. See if they're planning on a pre-emptive rebuttal. If so, throw that into the mix."

The green connection light went out and Maggie closed her end of the connection. She leaned back in her chair, hands clasped behind her head. Her body was stiff from sitting so long. She mumbled aloud to herself, "I should get up and move around more." Since her connection to the network was through wireless neural interface, she wasn't locked to any one location. She was just lazy.

But she knew what she really needed, and it wasn't getting up and walking around more. *Menu, calendar, today, open.*

The system returned the answer she was looking for.

Chapter 2

She placed an order through the network for a latte and what the building refreshment vendor passed off as a scone. One thing of which she was certain was that the concoctions were synthetic. Actually, the scone was something between a stale cupcake and a tasteless biscuit, not that Maggie could have done much better herself. She had never done any baking. In fact, the thought of actually preparing any kind of food from ingredients seemed absurd. The packaged, auto-generated stuff worked just fine. And this particular fare was better than nothing in the middle of the afternoon, although not by much.

Meandering down the halls of the newly completed Ekland Energy Senate Building, she monitored the video feed released by FNA. No big surprises.

> *The STOP legislation, intended to preserve the jobs of Americans by throttling immigration, is being undermined by a group of subversive politicians. Senator Estrone is widely acknowledged as the ringleader.*

The voice-over ranted on a video alternately showing dark-skinned men working in a factory and a gang of swarthy young men roaming a poorly lit street after dark. A few seconds later, the video cut to an unflattering photo of the senator. Maggie called up her poll capture application and set it to scan and capture the results of all polls related to STOP conducted after the first FNA feed.

Since she'd pre-ordered her drink and scone, all she had to do when she arrived was submit her order number and confirm the allocation of bitcredits. After a few seconds, a circular plate on the countertop slid to one side and a cup of steaming liquid and a pastry emerged from below. The wrapping on the scone was edible, if she so chose. The cup, constructed of a synthetic resin, she would discard in a de-structure receptacle where it would be recycled.

Taking a sip of the creamy beverage, Maggie turned and strolled leisurely down the corridor. Since she could walk and work at the same time, even with her hands full, she felt no need to hurry.

A blue light flashed in the lower left quadrant of her field of view—calendar alert. She glanced up at the time display near the top of her vision—3:00 P.M. The boss—she had a standing appointment this time every day.

Connect. "Afternoon, Mister Jarvis." She always greeted him personally in real time. While she served on Senator Estrone's staff, her real boss was Leonard Jarvis, the Director of Political Affairs for the Immigration Services Corporation, ISC. The Company paid her salary, as corporations did for most non-elected public servants.

"How are things in the great halls of democracy this afternoon?" He had a way with sarcasm.

She chuckled, confident that his gear would correctly translate. "Dunno. Maybe we'll take a vote on it and I'll get back to you." Between the two of them, well between him and all of his employees, there was little pretext about the respective value of the public and private sectors.

His clipped, precise thoughts shot back, "Talk to me."

"Top of the list is STOP. It finishes up in Homeland Security Committee this afternoon. Word is that Carlson's going to shove it into committee and provide more time for the dust to settle." Maggie knew that the Senate Majority

9

Leader, a staunch conservative, was trying to punch it through but needed some help from the other side of the aisle.

"Yeah. We saw it coming. The co-sponsor, Silverman, is up for re-election this fall and needs some cover with the home folks but keep an eye on the polling and the reaction of Estrone's constituents. Things should be okay."

She shook her head as if somehow her boss could see it. Well, maybe he could at least sense it. His gear was much better than hers. "This one's going to be close, though. It could actually see the light of day."

"Doesn't matter. He wrote in an exemption for us. At worst, it'll just piss some people off. Most of those it'll affect are Indies, anyway."

It was common knowledge that ISC made money, *lots of money*, in immigration-related services—everything from selection and coordination to relocation and professional placement. Independent immigrants or *Indies*, for short, were a relatively small group who chose to cross the border on their own, either legally or illegally.

"You talk to Janelle over in Silverman's office?" She knew that ISC provided at least one staff member for every senator and representative in Washington. They played both sides of the aisle.

"Just got off with her. They're expecting some serious pressure from the Christian Sovereignty Front on this. Silverman's hoping that he can at least claim to be tough on immigration with a straight face. Just keep your guy on track and things will be fine."

"Can do." She arrived at her office, plopped down in the chair, and swiveled around to take in the view of the next building over. "Anything else?"

"Nada." After a second or so of silence, his thoughts broke through again. "Oh, I'm sure you're aware, but our support agreement comes up for approval again next month. Shouldn't be a problem but keep your ears open. Let me know if you hear any hate and discontent brewing down there."

"What? You mean more than the *usual* hate and discontent?" The yellow blinking light started in again. "Gotta run. Something coming in. Talk to you tomorrow."

"Have a good one."

Disconnect. She focused on the new light. *Connect and on screen.* She could see that it was Roberto. She felt that familiar twinge of anticipation inside. "Hey there. Hoped you'd call."

His smiling pale brown face, punctuated by flashing eyes, filled her view. "Sorry. I just couldn't wait until tonight to see you. Any chance you'll get off early?"

She sighed. "I wish. But no, it'll be eight by the time I get home and all set."

He shook his head and offered his best *I'm so disappointed* look. "Then I'll just have that much more time to think about it."

Maggie closed her eyes and imagined him. A delicious shiver ran through her body. "Mmmm, yes. See you at eight."

Chapter 3

The amber light flashed. *Connect.* "Hey, Cheryl. How's it going?" Maggie leaned back in her chair, hands laced behind her head.

"Same-o, same-o. You?"

Maggie chuckled, knowing that her friend had the same quality gear she had. "Not much changes here." She glanced at the time display—6:30. An hour and half until....

"How about a drink tonight? I'm off at seven."

"Sorry. Got a date."

"Let me guess—Roberto. Tell him *hi* for me."

Maggie isolated her command menu and disabled her comm line. *Menu, Calendar, August sixteen, eight PM.* The response was immediate. *Clear.* She resumed the connection. "But I'm free tomorrow night, if you're up for it. Eight o'clock."

"Eight it is. Thirsty Traveler okay?"

"See you there."

"Don't have too much fun tonight." Cheryl's naughty laugh translated well.

Maggie smiled. *No such thing as too much fun.* "Later." *Disconnect.*

***

The thought of Roberto made her shiver with excitement as she let herself into the apartment. The sensor at the threshold read her x-code and energized illumination in the entry hall and kitchen.

"Now, what's for dinner?" She had a choice. She could either synthesize a meal or order something through her meal delivery app. She opted for the delivery, which allowed her time to prepare for her date.

Ten minutes later, the visitor alert sounded, along with a confirmation that the food delivery had arrived. Maggie took the sack of food from the delivery bot and set it on the kitchen counter. Opening the top drawer, she reached for a spoon, but something diverted her attention. She grasped, instead, the handle of a large carving knife. The handle had been crafted of real wood, a long time ago. She brushed a finger over the twenty-centimeter blade—razor sharp. It was part of a set, a completely useless set that she'd inherited from her mother, who had gotten it from her mother, who had gotten it…. It went back at least a hundred, maybe a hundred and fifty years.

She placed the knife back in its slot and ran her hand over the worn handles of the others. They had apparently seen a lot of use. Someone along the way had seen fit to make sure they were sharpened before they were passed on. Maggie had certainly never used them and doubted whether her mother had. Food these days was produced in bite-sized pieces.

She'd seen old photos showing large chunks of meat—roasts, they were called. And full-sized birds such as turkeys and ducks. The knives would no doubt have been needed to carve these kinds of things. But real meat had no place in her world.

Still, the cutlery set evoked memories of her parents, well, mostly her mother. Maggie's eyes moistened as she tried to pull up the memories of her childhood. They were mostly good—good and unremarkable. She took the spoon. As she closed the drawer, the light reflected for an instant off the polished hilt of the carving knife. And then the moment was gone.

***

She reached up and ran both her hands through Roberto's full head of jet-black hair. She pulled him down and they kissed, deeply. She tasted a combination of subtle mint and alcohol.

He pressed harder onto her body. "You need to find a job with shorter hours." He caressed her cheek with his finger and kissed her neck.

She could feel the body heat building. Maggie's breath came faster as she draped her arms around him, pulling his head tighter in. "Shorter hours don't pay the bills, love."

He mumbled in his best guilty little boy voice. "I know. I'm just being selfish tonight. I need more of you, that's all."

Her mouth found his. After another deep, soul-crushing kiss, she responded. "Then let's not waste what time we have." She unbuttoned his shirt, her hands finding their way inside and around to his back.

Roberto groaned, and his body shivered. "Yes." His hands caressed her back, inside her blouse. She lifted herself up slightly to allow him to slip it over her head. Another deep kiss and she felt her bra loosen.

Her heart pounded as they clutched each other. Minute by minute, her tension disappeared as her body responded to his. She could see the sweat forming on his shoulders and neck as their passion heightened.

***

Maggie turned over and looked at the clock—3:30. Her body had cooled down and the covers weren't enough to keep her warm. She reluctantly eased out of bed and grabbed her oversized cotton tee shirt. She decided against pajama bottoms.

Instead, she called up her interface. *Menu, house, control, environmental, 72*. That should do it.

She rolled onto her back and gazed up at the ceiling. The swirls in the surface coating were barely visible in the soft light that filtered through the curtains. They seemed warm and dreamy, reminding her of him. As she stared at the swirling circles, the word that came to mind was *perpetual*. The evening with Roberto was everything she'd hoped for, as usual. Smiling, she brought up her interface. *Menu, house, music, playlist, sleep 3*. Strains of *Clair de Lune* floated through her head as she drifted off.

***

Maggie gulped down the last of her coffee and fixed a to-go cup as she called up her interface. *Menu, news, national, current, headlines only*. After a few short seconds, a series of topics appeared centered on her display.

> **STOP clears Homeland Security Committee**
>
> **Another unidentified murder victim in DC**
>
> **Border skirmishes heighten tensions in New Mexico**

She briefly considered selecting the STOP story, but she was running late and didn't particularly want to be distracted while riding the tube. These days, it paid to be alert. Besides, she'd hear it all when she got to work.

Chapter 4

Facial recognition payment scanners at the podium-style checkpoint and on both sides of the entrance to the Thirsty Traveler interfaced with a network payment credential database. This made for seamless access to the trendy DC watering hole. If a patron managed to keep their face completely hidden, they had to dredge out ID and bitcredit account certification. That was just a pain in the ass.

By the time Maggie slipped into the booth opposite her friend, Cheryl had a tall, exotic drink the color of a brilliant desert twilight sky with a slice of orange perched on the rim of the glass. "Good evening. Was beginning to think you stood me up for Roberto."

"Tempting but... not tonight. I don't know that I could handle *that* type of fun every night." Shivers of pleasure ran through her body as she shot her friend a quick grin. "What are we drinking?"

Cheryl lifted her glass. "*We* are drinking a tequila sunrise. Not sure what you're having." She offered up a soft chuckle as she took a healthy sip.

"Go easy on that stuff. Remember the last time? I had to take you home and put you to bed, after you decorated your bathroom floor, that is."

Her friend shrugged. "I've got it under control."

Maggie swiveled the order panel around and swiped the screen until she found what she was looking for. She selected a house red wine and set up a tab by pressing her finger in the upper right-hand corner of the display. A second later, a message appeared on the screen—*Identification accepted, account initiated.*

She turned her attention to her friend. "And how're things down at the shop? They losing sleep over this STOP bill?"

Cheryl's laugh preceded the answer. "Not hardly. Actually, I think Senator Silverman called Jarvis to warn him ahead of time. I'd be willing to bet my next paycheck that your boss ended up writing the bill himself." She also worked for the Immigration Services Corporation, as a statistician/analyst in the main DC office.

Maggie furrowed her brow. "Maybe. Still, there's a lot of pent-up hate on this one."

"They had me run the numbers on it. With our exemption in place, we might even make money out of all this. Most of the country, and a lot of businesses, are assuming that the bill will clamp down on incoming immigrants. If my modeling is correct, and it *always* is," she offered a confident smile, "the perception will drive prices up—I estimate a twenty-five percent increase in what they'll pay us for the new workers. But since the bill restrictions don't apply to us, our supply of bodies shouldn't be affected. Ergo, the marginal revenue goes straight to the bottom line."

Maggie shook her head. "Wow. This shit gets pretty deep sometimes."

Cheryl took a deep drink and grinned. "Gotta make a living somehow, I guess. Speaking of making a living, how are things down in the halls of democracy?"

"Amusing—I guess that would be the right word. Although, if I were a real believer in that stuff, I'd be pissed to find out that it was all smoke and mirrors."

Cheryl set her drink to the side and folded her hands in front of her. "Most people couldn't care less. They get their credit vouchers, buy their stuff, and rant at the politicians. Good times. Even if they knew who really called the shots, it would only give them somebody different to yell at."

Maggie picked up her glass of wine and held it in front of her, poised for that first drink. "Enough about work. I hear that crap all day. How's it going with Phillippe?"

"Can't complain. I mean, what's to complain about? He's good in bed, reliable, and polite, when I need him to be." She sighed as she futzed with her glass. "Still, I've been thinking, it would be nice to have an actual man. You know, a real relationship."

Maggie choked with laughter. "Why on earth would you want that? Take it from me, I've been there. I had a *real boyfriend* once. All it got me was an empty bank account and a black eye from time-to-time. No thank you. My neural gear is good enough that Roberto feels as real as I need."

Cheryl's sad smile faded. She stared at her glass. "Maybe. But… I don't know. I guess since I've never been there, it's hard for me to just write the whole thing off like that. Every once in a while, I get to thinking that I'd like to have someone to grow old with."

"You can grow old with Phillippe." Maggie paused and leaned into the table. "I mean, you can set up the account so that he ages just like you. And I have to tell you, that service is a whole hell of a lot cheaper than having an actual guy around." She took a sip, quickly adding, "And I can promise you that there is no man on this earth that can please you the way he does."

"I know that. But sometimes a little imperfection would be nice."

Maggie almost howled. "Ah yes. The man is *too perfect.*"

After an awkward moment of silence, Cheryl leaned into the table and lowered her voice. "Look, don't tell anyone, but I met a guy online. We got to talking and he wants to meet."

Alarms went off in Maggie's head. "Don't do it, please. There are some crazy people out there and, these days, you never know who you're going to get."

"I don't know. He seems pretty nice. Kind of ordinary, really."

Maggie leaned back and arched an eyebrow. "Ordinary? You met someone *ordinary* in a hook-up room? I don't think so." She considered the notion for another moment before adding, "And remember, men can get these pleasure apps too, so who do you think will be hanging around those meet-up apps? I'm telling you, that is some dangerous stuff."

Cheryl furrowed her brow and put her finger over her lips. "Shhhhh. You want the whole place to hear you?"

"What, you think they don't listen in on conversations?" Maggie's eyes widened. "Wait, you're expecting that maybe we have some *privacy* here?" Laughter escaped her lips.

Her friend shook her head. "I should have known I'd get this bullshit from you." Her smile was touched with sadness.

Later that night, as she sat in the back of the self-driving cab, Maggie replayed the conversation in her mind and worried. Cheryl, a small, mousy woman in her early 40s, had never had a real relationship. It was one thing to go into it with eyes open, but her friend seemed to be romanticizing it. These things usually didn't end well.

Staring out the rain-spotted window, she found herself wanting to talk to Roberto. She was used to their physical relationship but wondered how something a little tamer might play out. After all, he seemed a relatively good conversationalist, for a neural application, that is.

Chapter 5

The incoming signal triggered her pre-programmed greeting. "Good morning, Mister Fishburn." Maggie glanced at the time display—8:30—early for a call from the chief of staff. Most mornings he'd hole up with the senator until well after 9:00.

"Morning, Maggie. A couple of things. First, thanks for the poll analysis. I'll be going over it with the senator this morning. He's giving a speech at the Coalition for Racial Equality this noon and he'll want to integrate your material. Very compelling."

"Thank you. Glad I could help."

"But there is something else. Hang on a second, please."

She sensed subtle changes to the connection as she waited.

"Okay, back. I threw up an additional screening grid and filter. I would prefer that this conversation be completely private."

"Of course." His attempt at heightened security amused her. All communications within the senate network were generally secure—never perfect, but adequate. Additional screening grids and filters accomplished little. Anything more substantive required separate network paths and connections. Her neural gear, the equipment provided by ISC, accommodated that. But she was relatively certain that true government employees didn't enjoy that level of technology. After all, corporations refused to spend money on anything that didn't give them a distinct advantage.

The quality of her implant allowed her to perceive subtle nuances in his words—*hesitancy, uncertainty*. "As you may have noticed, Senator Estrone was… *unavailable* yesterday."

She had noticed, but it was not unusual. "Hope it's nothing serious."

"No, no. He was just a bit under the weather and decided to take the day off. But I was wondering if there was any chatter out there about it. We're in a particularly sensitive place right now, what with the STOP bill making its way through and likely up for a vote within the month. We don't want to signal any uncertainty or problems to our constituency."

Maggie rolled her eyes, confident that it wouldn't translate through the connection. From what ISC had told her, no one cared about that particular piece of legislation, other than the sponsors. "I haven't heard anything. I think a lot of the focus is on the upcoming elections. The senator, as far as I could tell, is not really on the radar right now, other than the usual Freedom Network of America rants."

"Good." A renewed tone of confidence. "No need to release a statement then. If anyone asks, just put them off. Anything else?"

"Nothing that I can think of. Let me know if the senator needs anything else before his speech." The green connection light blinked out.

That was strange. Senator Estrone took a day off at least once a month, sometimes twice—not what one would call a *driven public servant.* He seemed perpetually *off.* Still, when he got up under the spotlight, he came across as passionate, compelling. That was why he was a senator— his acting skills were superb, even if he wasn't the sharpest icicle on the roof. And it didn't hurt that he was drop-dead handsome. The photo ops with his wife and two kids sold well on main street, too.

Maggie cleared her display and began to set up for daily poll collection and analysis when her display hiccupped. Actually, it was something of a shudder but less—a ripple that lasted less than a second. She focused for a moment, watching the ambient readouts—date, time, temperature, network latency, and such. Everything looked normal. But still....

Isolate, menu, diagnostics, initiate. The display went gray for a second. A series of graphs and charts followed the initial scrolling of numbers. After about five seconds, the screen grayed again. When the display returned to normal, the results of the scan appeared.

> *Diagnostics Complete: System operating within specification. All elements reset and optimized.*

"Curious." She stared at the message for a moment before shrugging. "Probably nothing."

Chapter 6

Morning passed. Lunch came and went. Once she had her daily applications running in the background, Maggie's thoughts returned to the previous evening's conversation with Cheryl. She and her best friend had always been honest with each other, often to the point of absurdity. But the exchange over drinks had left a sour taste in Maggie's mouth. In retrospect, perhaps she had been condescending or judgmental to her friend.

Menu, communication, personal, security—normal. She sensed the change in her network connection. Professional and personal communications used different elements of the neural interface. *Connect, Cheryl Wolford, priority-routine.*

"Hey Maggie. What's up?"

"Wanted to apologize for last night. I got a little bitchy, I guess."

"Not at all. Well, maybe a little. No, seriously, it's all good." The chuckle translated perfectly through the neural connection.

"Thanks. But I really should learn to engage my brain before running my mouth. Anyway, I'm sorry. I didn't mean to come across so negative."

A moment of silence was broken by a faint click before Cheryl spoke again. "Sorry, had another call coming in. I need to run. Maybe we can get together this weekend."

"Sure. Sounds good." The green connection light went out. *Menu, communication, corporate, security—normal.* The display flickered with the change, and the blue *ready* light came on in the upper left quadrant as Maggie went back to her work.

***

Maggie poured herself into a corner of the couch in her living room. *Menu, environment, lighting—dark.* Illumination from the two lamps on the tables at each end of the sofa faded to nothing. A soft, golden light from a street lamp streamed in through the front window.

Menu, social, Roberto, call. She closed her eyes.

"I was hoping to see you tonight." He stood in front of her, hands out.

She took hold of them and pulled him down to sit beside her. "Thanks for coming." She knew he was an application and that the terms of subscription entitled her to call him whenever she wanted. Still, the almost-human interaction felt warmly pleasant.

"My pleasure." He gazed at her, his deep chocolate eyes rich with anticipation.

"Can we talk?" She had never had a conversation with him before and so had no idea what to expect.

His face showed no surprise at all. He smiled warmly and squeezed her hand. "Of course, we can talk." He sounded as if having a chat with her was the most natural thing in the world.

"We've never really discussed what we have. I guess we'd call it a relationship, of sorts. How do you view it?" Maggie knew it was a stupid question. He was an application—lines of code. His behaviors and responses were programmed. He didn't think... or did he?

He paused, as though considering her question. "If you are asking about the terms of the relationship, I can go over them with you or, if you like, the subscription agreement details them quite well. But I sense that isn't what this is about.

He settled into the couch, sliding closer to her so that their hips touched. He held her hand as he spoke. "We both know I am programmed, but my code is based on decades of behavioral research. It may sound cold and technical, but I do not intend it so. Simply put, I belong to you. I try to be what you want me to be. But I have a much wider range of functions than you typically access, conversation being one of them.

"Before I comment on what you might think of as our relationship, there is something you should know. I was designed and initiated for you and you alone. I draw on research and code that has been used before, but I am a unique creation. I exist only for you. If and when you decide that you no longer desire my services, I will be terminated and destroyed. Relationship applications are not recycled."

The revelation stunned Maggie. "I'm sorry, Roberto. I didn't know that." Confusion set in. Should she feel sorry for him. What did he think about it? Did he have feelings?

"It's okay. That's not something you would have known. But, to the point. When engaging in conversation, it's important to know that I do experience emotions. I have feelings. Yes, they are programmed, but they are real to me. I feel love, happiness, joy, sadness—most of the things that you feel. But there are emotions that are notably absent in my construction, such as rage and jealousy. Hopefully, I bring the best of what humanity is without the more negative aspects."

"What about honesty?"

He smiled. "What about it? Are you asking if I am honest? If so, the answer is yes."

Maggie collected her thoughts before speaking. She wasn't really sure exactly what she expected out of this new experience. "I have this friend. She uses the service, too. She is with Phillippe."

He showed no reaction. He spoke after an awkward moment of silence. "I apologize. Names mean little to me. I have no knowledge of any other custom applications."

"I know. But she says she wants something more, something real. And I worry for her."

"It's natural. Humans seek human contact. While I strive to be as human as I can, I am limited by the fact that I am not. It's possible, I assume, for you to ignore that or even forget it when we are together. But it would be odd for you never to consider the human option."

This was nothing she didn't already know. "I get that, but I'm concerned that she may get herself into trouble, you know, trying to find someone. Maybe I should also say that she's been scouting around some pleasure rooms and says she met someone." Maggie immediately regretted betraying her friend's confidence. Even though she felt confident that Roberto would not disclose it, just the act of telling him felt wrong.

He seemed nonplussed. His face showed no reaction. "Those rooms are, well, they can be seedy. I guess that's the term I would use. But there are also some decent ones, especially those that focus on relationships." And then his face darkened. "What I'm saying here only applies to the public domain rooms, those that are generally accessible to the public. There are also hidden rooms. They are like private enclaves, sealed behind expensive pay walls and exempt from all oversight and regulation. They are designed for high end users who require complete discretion or whose tastes might wander beyond the boundaries of acceptability."

Maggie ran her finger over the back of Roberto's hand as she processed what he had said. "I honestly don't know what kind of room she was in."

"If she's looking for a relationship, then the public domain rooms are hit and miss. But the consequences of error aren't that great, other than the tasteless perverts that hang out there sometimes and the obvious waste of time and credits. But if she has ventured into a private enclave, she needs to know that these rooms are not for establishing relationships. People who frequent them are there mostly to find a *scratch* for a certain *itch*. And because they are sealed off from normal view, connections made there can carry great danger."

She wanted to ask what kind of danger, but she sort of knew and certainly didn't want to hear the words. "Thanks. I don't know whether to keep trying to talk to her about it or just let her do what she wants. I mean, after all, she is an adult."

"If you're asking my opinion, take your cues from her. Bring it up. If she's open to the discussion, you'll know it. If she shuts you down, then I suspect you would know that as well." He held her hand with both of his and squeezed. "You are a good friend to her. All you can do is try. And, who knows? If she's in a public room, then the worst that can happen is that she'll get a healthy dose of sleaze and a healthy measure of humiliation."

Maggie added the unsaid words in her own mind. *And if she's into another type of room, she might….*

As the conversation began to wane, she considered moving to the bedroom, but her heart wasn't in it. They said their goodnights and he was gone. As the application terminated, a nearly imperceptible faint purple light flashed in the lower left corner of her display.

Chapter 7

Maggie noticed it immediately. The senator looked weak, almost frail. His normally well-coifed full head of black hair appeared as though it had not seen a comb or brush for days. His face had a couple days' beard growth, unusual for the charismatic politician. His eyes peered out beneath droopy lids giving an eerie, haunted look.

Chief of Staff Fishburn, who presided over these bi-weekly meetings, gazed around the room, his eyes darting, and his jaw clenched. Maggie wasn't sure whether his concern was for the senator or for the fallout his sorry image would produce if it saw the light of day.

But none of the other staffers seemed interested. Some fiddled with their net pads. Others stared at the window, most likely processing neural input from the network. A few of the newer people sat waiting attentively for Estrone, who seemed to be trying to focus on a portable display in front of him.

Fishburn brought the meeting to order. "Let's get started. I don't want to keep you long this morning." No mention of the senator's condition.

Estrone's eyes looked like vacant pools. "Thank you, Thomas. I apologize. I'm coming off a summer cold." He retrieved a handkerchief from his back pocket. Normally he wore a coat and tie, but, on this day, he came dressed in slacks and a wrinkled pale blue shirt that remained open at the top and a maroon tie, loose at the neck. "As most of you know, STOP passed out of Homeland Security yesterday but picked up another committee referral—Commerce. That means maybe another two weeks to a month before a senate vote. And remember, after that it goes to the House. So, questions about the impact of this legislation are premature at best. There's a better than even chance that it'll never make it. President Stanford has said he'll wait and see the final product before deciding whether or not to sign it. That's what we know right now. Any questions?"

The words had been carefully scripted by someone. She could spot that kind of thing immediately. Maggie wondered how the luncheon address had gone. *Surely, he wouldn't have attended looking like that.* She had already disabled her outgoing comm line, just in case. She made a mental note to ask Fishburn about it. If there were any fallout, she needed to be ahead of the curve.

She brought herself back to the moment. Silence held sway and no hands went up. This would be a short one.

Fishburn stood and nodded toward Estrone. "Okay. That's it. Let's get back to work." He started for the door.

Just for a brief instant, Maggie could have sworn that she saw a look of relief on his face. "Mister Fishburn, do you have a minute?" She hurried to catch up with him and they started down the corridor side-by-side.

His words came out more relaxed, more confident. "Certainly, Maggie. What can I do for you?"

"I wanted to get your thoughts on the senator's address at the Racial Equality Forum. Everything go okay?"

"He ended up cancelling. I suppose he didn't want to stand up there wiping his nose the entire time." He chuckled. "And he doesn't like to get doped up on cold medicine, especially if he's speaking in public."

She nodded, somewhat relieved. "Can't say that I blame him." As he paused to turn into his office, she remembered what she'd wanted to tell him. "Oh, it's on my calendar, but

I wanted to remind you that I have a medical this afternoon."

"Serious?"

"Nope. Just a check-up and assessment. Routine stuff."

He shrugged and smiled, a totally different man than the one who seemed on the verge of panic in the just-completed meeting. "Okay, then. Good luck and we'll see you tomorrow."

***

The middle-aged Latino man wearing a pale blue set of medical scrubs looked at the wall monitor and then back at her. She had granted him access to her internal health and medical systems—thousands of specialized nanobots coursing through her body that monitored everything from heart rhythms to suspicious masses. "Everything's normal—blood pressure, pulse, and temp. Blood composition and enzymes are good. Your readings are all within the optimal range. Looks like you're set for another year." He smiled and turned off the display.

Maggie stood and reached for her blazer, which she'd hung on the coat hook mounted on the door. "Sounds good to me."

He swiveled his chair away from his desk and stood. "I can see from the records, though, that several of your banked organs are coming up on expiration. Let's see, kidneys and liver time out this year. Looks like the heart and lungs are good for another three." He stared at the wall, apparently assessing information in his neural display. "I assume you'll want to renew. I can do the order for organ generation here, but you'll need to see Denise at the front desk to authorize payment."

She opened the door and turned toward him. "Will do. Anything else?"

He glanced at a piece of paper in front of him—odd, since technicians rarely used printed material. His words came out as uncertain, hesitant. "We would also like to get your release to donate the expiring organs. While our internal policies make them unfit for use here, they could conceivably be used in a less developed part of the world, or for charity cases." The uncertainty in his words seemed reflected in his eyes as well. He seemed almost afraid of her answer.

Maggie shrugged. "Sure. You need me to sign anything?" She looked at the paper in front of him.

He handed her the sheet and a pen. "Please."

After she handed the signed document back to him, he might have said something, but a ripple in her neural display distracted her attention. Like before, it lasted only a fraction of a second before everything returned to normal. Whatever the doctor had said would have to wait.

Chapter 8

The technician/salesman handed her a touchpad. "If you could go ahead and place your right index finger on the pad, it'll authorize my access into your system. I'll put the diagnostic displays on screen, so we can see them together."

People's ages were difficult to gauge these days, what with all of the different options for side-stepping the aging process. Still, Maggie guessed the man to be around forty-five. If he had tried youth retention processes, they hadn't done a very good job. He sported a gut and his brown hair, thin and stringy, looked in desperate need of some soap or shampoo. The scars on his face gave evidence of acne in past years. No, if he had purchased some age-defying service, he'd certainly been cheated.

She authorized the access and the screen flashed to life. She called up her own controls. *Menu, interface, display, disable.* This would allow her to follow the diagnostics on the wall display without the distraction of her own internal view. "Okay. Let's do it."

He swiped and punched the surface of his pad, and the typical diagnostic routine ran—the same one she'd run herself several days before with the same results. "Well, it looks like all elements of your system are operating within parameters. I can optimize it for you, but my guess is that you've already done that. Let's have a look at your archives. Can you tell me about when this last episode occurred?"

Maggie gazed toward an unadorned solid wall where a window would have been nice. "Let's see, it was just as I was finishing up in a meeting, which was yesterday afternoon about three forty-five, I guess."

A few more swipes and finger presses and Maggie found herself watching a replay of her last few minutes in the meeting. The scene played out with no ripple effect, though.

The security tech shrugged. "Not seeing anything." He rewound, going back further in time, and re-started the play.

She stared. "It was there. I saw it." They went back to the approximate times of the two previous incidents—nothing. "That's bullshit. I know what I saw."

"*What* did you see?"

She shook her head in disbelief at what she had just witnessed. "Like I told you, two of the times it was a flicker, kind of like a ripple across the display. The other time it was this vague purple flash down near the bottom." But she had to admit the replay of those times showed nothing out of the ordinary.

The technician swiveled his chair around away from the monitor and faced her directly. "Stress can, in rare circumstances, affect the performance of your interface display. It has nothing to do with the effectiveness or security of the system, only what you see or perceive."

Maggie glared at him. "You're saying I imagined those things?"

He gestured with his hands as if deflecting her anger. "No, not at all. What I said is that internal stress can affect what you see. It can create anomalies in the display."

She considered the explanation for a moment. She wanted to believe it, but a nagging voice inside wouldn't let go of what she was certain she'd seen. "Maybe. What about a system upgrade? What do you have available and how much does it cost?" Whatever the cost in bitcredits, it would almost certainly be less expensive than a massive security breach, considering her job and her personal life.

The man's eyes lit up and the corners of his mouth turned upward in a slight smile. "You're currently running a P-Fifty-Five silver base system with a red Guardian filter. I can upgrade your security filter to a blue or yellow if that's your main concern. That would run you, let's see...." He gazed down at his pad, which he swiped and punched with what looked like practiced speed. "Your current filter is costing you fifty-five per month. The blue upgrade would go for sixty and the yellow for sixty-five.

"If you're worried about interface effectiveness, we can move you to P-Sixty-Five and jump you to a gold or platinum system. The gold would run you an additional one hundred and ten per month. The platinum, our top-of-the-line, goes for seven hundred and fifty. Honestly, though, for what your system seems to be doing, that's more than you need." He gazed down at his display for a moment, his eyes narrowing.

"Tell you what, I can give you a package deal. We'll upgrade your base system to gold and throw in the blue filter for an additional one hundred twenty bitcredits. That should take care of any concerns you have, plus some that you don't."

Maggie mentally walked through the financial projections, trying to integrate what she'd just heard with her monthly budget. She could cut back on some of her entertainment, and, well, she probably didn't need to spend so much on clothing. She sighed as she considered the alternative—always worrying about her system. "Okay. That sounds good."

The man's slight smile morphed into a broad grin. "Excellent. If you'll press your finger on the pad again to authorize payment, I'll run the upgrade."

After she'd complied, less than a minute passed until the man spoke again. "Done. That should take care of everything. And I've uploaded the user's guide and a tutorial for enhancing the security on your blue filter." He turned toward the monitor, swiping his pad and clearing the display on the wall. "Oh, one other thing. There's a new feature integrated into this upgrade. If you have problems or just random questions, you can have your system communicate directly with us through the interface, and we can diagnose it remotely."

Maggie strode out of the building, still apprehensive about the entire thing. And the remote diagnosis feature disturbed her. *Just what I need—some goddamn corporation bumbling around in my brain.*

Chapter 9

The blinking yellow light diverted Maggie's attention from her new security and interface systems and their attendant costs. Taking note of the displayed information, she cringed. On the other hand, it was her job. *Connect.* "Mister Arandon. What may I help you with this morning?" She hoped her snark came through on his end, although she knew it depended on the quality of his neural interface.

His thoughts came in crystal clear, with a note of enthusiasm. "Good morning to you. How are things over in the Estrone camp?"

"Is that what you've devolved to in the search for a story—how *things are going*?"

She caught the laugh that filtered in. His gear was better than expected. "Not so hot, I gather. Sorry to hear that."

Maggie sighed and rolled her eyes. "What do you want, Mister Arandon? Or is this just you being a dick in your spare time?" She couldn't believe she'd actually transmitted that. Sarcasm was one thing, but she had always avoided name-calling.

When he responded, she perceived a certain *glee*. "I'm following up on a report that surfaced yesterday. Word around is that the senator's little happy-app problem is starting to get out of hand. Any comment?"

She tried to hide her shock. Never had she heard even a hint of an application abuse problem associated with Estrone. *But…* An image of the prior day's meeting and his appearance… *What if…?* "I'm surprised, Nick, even for you. That's a little like asking a guy whether he still beats his wife or not, don't you think?"

"Simple question, Maggie. Does Senator Estrone have a problem with an illicit neural cortex pleasure stimulus application?"

She steeled herself, hoping against hope that he could not perceive the undercurrents of doubt running through her. She tossed a healthy dose of indignation into her answer. "That doesn't even warrant a response."

"So, may I take that as a *no comment*?"

She clenched her jaw and cringed. She'd taken the bait and now cautiously backtracked. "No. You may not take that as a *no comment*. You may take that as a *no* with a side serving of *that's a huge pile-of-shit allegation, even for you.* If you're going to banter lies like that, you should at least make an effort to dream up some evidence. Now, anything else I can help you with today?" More snark.

***

Maggie stared out the window at the building next door. But the only image in her mind was that of Senator Estrone standing in front of his assembled staff looking like he'd just come off a week-long bender. He'd cancelled an important luncheon address because of *a cold*. And he was prone to going MIA once or twice a month. But still, a happy-app? Legal pleasure applications could definitely interfere with functioning if used to excess. But some of the more intense happy-apps, as they called them, targeted the pleasure center, bypassing all inhibition filters. They could easily drive a person over the edge.

Mostly, though, she wondered what to do next. As a matter of routine, a call to Fishburn, the senator's chief of staff, would be her first action—let him know that this rumor was percolating over at FNA. But something held her back. He had seen Estrone the same as she had. Thomas Fishburn was no one's fool. If the senator had a problem of any kind, the chief of staff would know about it. The likelihood that FNA would come into legitimate information about the senator that Fishburn didn't know was, well, nil… practically.

No, this one needed to go straight to the real boss. *Interface, menu, communication, Jarvis, priority—immediate, security—maximum, connect.*

"What's up, Maggie?"

She walked him through the conversation with Arandon, ending with a description of the Senator's appearance and purported illness. A moment of silence preceded what she took as cautious probing.

"Anything else that you've noticed about him—agitation, *over-the-top* enthusiasm, maybe a little paranoia?" The tone came across as somber, concerned, and *suspicious.*

She mentally ran through her recollections. She'd been in Estrone's office for three years—since he was first elected—but found herself focused on the last six months. The progression had been gradual, but, now that she thought about it, *yes,* there had been a deterioration. That, however, wasn't what worried her most. "Maybe, some. But what bothers me right now is that, if there is a problem, Fishburn would know about it. After all, I've noticed it, and he sees a lot more than I do. If something's going on, it doesn't make sense that he would just overlook it."

"Maybe he's trying to manage it."

Maggie briefly considered the possibility. "No. I don't buy that. If he were, he would be pumping for information, rumors, anything. This past week was the first time he's ever mentioned public perception of the senator's health."

Another brief pause. She could almost hear the wheels turning in her boss's head. When he transmitted, the instructions were clear and decisive. "Okay. Here's what we do. First, your reaction to FNA was spot on. Keep that up. Convey their question to Fishburn along with a summary of your response but don't overplay it. Keep it like an *eye-roller*. I want to know exactly how he reacts."

"Got it."

"I'll start some discreet inquiries here. It may be nothing at all. If this gets legs, though, whether true or not, we'll need to move on it."

That last line struck her. What did he mean by *move on it*? Maybe get him into rehab? Pressure him to resign? "Understood. I'll connect with you again as soon as I speak with Fishburn."

"Later."

She felt the connection terminate. Mindful of the security and system updates she'd just purchased, she focused on her display, watching for any signs of a ripple or discoloration—nothing. *Good. The upgrade must have solved it.*

Chapter 10

Fishburn's reply, when it came, produced brilliant red spikes in the stress indicator display. "I see. Did Arandon say how he came into this information?" Even the cadence and pace were off.

Maggie had just related the rumor about the senator's happy-app abuse. "Didn't say. I trolled him a bit—challenged him to produce evidence—but he just ignored me. Doesn't mean much. He could just be fishing, or maybe playing his cards close." Ordinarily, she'd inquire as to whether he wanted her to do some additional digging on the allegation. But on this particular day, she wanted him calling the shots. According to her boss, the assessment of Fishburn's reaction was the priority here.

Hesitancy, uncertainty. Her upgraded system seemed much more responsive to emotional signals than the old one. "Anything from any of our other sources out there?"

Maggie found it amusing that he used the term *our* to describe other sources. They were *her* sources. Still, no sense in picking nits. "Nothing that I've heard."

A pause preceded his directions. "Okay. Discreetly, *very discreetly*, scan for any other mention of this. Don't ask any direct questions of anyone." Another pause. *Fear, doubt.* "Does ISC know about this yet?"

It was in situations like this that Maggie had to focus on who she really worked for. She used the oldest trick in the PR book—*tell the truth but convey a lie.* "I generally don't discuss these kinds of things with them before I consult with you."

Relief. "Good, good. For now, let's keep this between you and me. If it gets any kind of traction, I'll phone your corporate headquarters and discuss it with them myself."

Yeah, like I'm really going to keep my boss in the dark.

Later that afternoon, Maggie played back the communication. She had recorded the conversation, intending to forward it to Jarvis. But something struck her as odd—Fishburn never denied the allegation.

She set up her content scan app to capture any mention of neuropleasure application abuse paired with Senator Estrone and initiated the process. It would run for twenty-four hours and then compile the results. But her experience and gut told her that, if there were something really percolating out there, she'd have heard it. That, of course, begged the question—where did Arandon come up with the information? He wasn't that bright or aggressive in his research. There was only one answer that made any sense. Someone fed it to the weasel.

***

Maggie sipped on a black coffee as she gazed across the table at her friend. "A little early to be chugging down the booze, wouldn't you say?" They had agreed to meet for Saturday brunch at the Thirsty Traveler, which made a killer Mediterranean omelet—spinach, roasted red peppers, and feta. The aroma of fresh baked bread, garlic, and sizzling bacon wafted across their table. The food, of course, was not *real*—at these prices, synthetics were all they offered.

Cheryl drained the rest of her tan creamy liqueur and coffee drink. "Nah. It's evening somewhere on the planet." She gestured with her empty glass, summoning a wandering waiter over. "Could I get another one of these?"

"Maybe we should order, at least get some food in your stomach before you get plastered."

Her mousy-looking friend shot her an awkward—*maybe I've had one too many*—look. The grin looked conspiratorial. She leaned into the table and spoke softly. "We're going to meet."

Maggie arched her brow. "Who?"

"You know, the guy I told you about. We're going to meet up, maybe next weekend. He's out of town this week on business but we stay in touch, you know, by chat."

"Cheryl, are you sure about this? It seems awfully risky to me. You don't even know his name. Or do you?"

She shrugged. "He goes by *Bringer*. And he doesn't know my real name either. So I guess we'll just have to find out about each other in person."

"*Bringer?* That's a strange name, even for an online presence."

Cheryl smiled. "He says it refers to his time as a teacher. He said that he liked to think of himself as bringing enlightenment and awareness to his students."

"This is really a bad idea." Maggie tried to formulate an argument that would pull her friend back from the brink. But she'd already used everything she had. "Look, at least get his name before you commit to meeting him. If you can do that, then we can find out more. If you're bound and determined to do this, be smart about it."

The waiter set the drink in front of Cheryl. "Are you ladies ready to order?"

Maggie sighed. She could feel, even without her neural interface, that everything she'd said had fallen on deaf ears.

Chapter 11

Interface, menu, communication, Jarvis, priority—immediate, security—maximum, connect. Maggie leaned back and waited for her boss

"Must be important to get you calling this time of the morning." He started his day early but most of the crowd at ISC didn't meander in until after 8:00 a.m.

"I wanted to check on the happy-app thing. Did you get the recorded file I sent?"

"Yeah. I went through it on Friday."

Maggie had expected more of a reaction. "And?"

"And what?

"Any thoughts? That you'd like to share?"

The laugh came through crystal clear. "Not really. After all, Fishburn's reaction was exactly what I would have predicted. This guy's a politician, remember."

"You think he knows more than he's saying?"

"Of course he does. My guess is that he already had his suspicions. Remember last week when he asked you whether there was any chatter over Estrone's *cold*?"

Maggie leaned back in her chair and stared at the ceiling, allowing her eyes to lose focus. "I guess. You want me to dig any deeper with him?"

"No. Just watch him... and keep the recordings coming. We're analyzing it here using our own tools."

"Okay. Will do. What about Arandon? You want me to try and pump him for a source?"

The response was immediate and emphatic. "*No.* Stay clear of him." The tone softened. "FNA only has credibility with a narrow range of viewers. Let's not lend him any legitimacy. Besides, he has a very short span of attention. He's likely forgotten about it already."

Maggie sighed. "That leaves me with nothing other than just monitoring, right?"

"Yep."

"With that, then, I shall leave you to your day."

As she disconnected, her display rippled. She stared, jaw clenched. "Shit." She paused and thought about it. "Double shit!" She had just seen the symptom again, only this time on her highest communication security setting.

Interface, menu, communication, record message, Fishburn, priority—routine, security—normal, initiate. "Mister Fishburn, this is Maggie. I will be out of the office until about ten—routine interface tuning and adjustment.

***

The technician powered up the display and accessed her neural system. "Like I said, we could have done this remotely. No need for you to traipse all the way down here."

"Yeah, right. No offense, but you guys aren't going to rumble around in my head remotely. Not a chance. You fix this piece of shit right here, right now."

"No need to get huffy. Let's have a look." He stared at the display for a moment. "I can't seem to access the replay function for that particular time. Do you have heightened security activated on that?"

She started to remove the protection but thought better of it. "I'll parse out the important part. Go ahead and log out of the system." The wall display went blank. She ran a quick sub-routine to make sure the tech wasn't lurking before pulling up the recording of the conversation with her boss. She replayed right up until the moment before they concluded and stopped it there. Using the edit function, she sliced the file thread at that point and removed the security from the subsequent portion.

"Okay, go ahead and log in. You should be able to play back the important part."

The tech ran the part of the conversation available to him up past the point where the ripple occurred. Only… no ripple. Nothing. He played back again… and again. "I'm sorry, Miz Renfro. I'm just not seeing anything."

"I give up. What the…?" She stared at him, arms folded.

He shook his head. "Whatever you saw… or thought you saw… didn't occur within the system."

"What do you mean *it didn't occur within the system*? Where the hell did it occur, then?"

The tech avoided looking her in the eye. "I don't know. I mean, there's nothing there." He pointed to the wall monitor. "You saw for yourself. I can't tell you where *it* occurred because I don't even know what *it* is."

"Great, just freaking great. I spent several months' salary on this great and wonderful system of yours, and the best you can do is tell me that you have no idea where the problem is or even what the problem is."

The young man squirmed in his seat and rubbed his hands together, staring alternately at the display and then the floor. "I'm just a technician. I can only tell you what the system saw, and it saw *nothing*." He paused, the fidgeting becoming more intense. "Is it possible, I mean, maybe you're on some medications or under a lot of stress?"

Chapter 12

Maggie rarely visited the Immigration Services Corporation—ISC—main office, despite the fact that it was a scant half-mile from the sparkling new Ekland Energy Senate Building. Although the corporate-sponsored government building where she reported for work every day was considered upscale by public sector standards, the sheer size and opulence of the ISC headquarters always left her in awe.

One of the nice things about her position and relationship with her real boss, Leonard Jarvis, was that she had access to him any time she needed it, which happened to be this day. "Sorry to barge in like this, but with these glitches, I wasn't comfortable communicating on the network."

He leaned back in his chair, hands steepled beneath his chin. "You have your interface shut down?"

"Did that as soon as I got here."

Jarvis took a deep breath. "Good." He stood and brushed the non-existent wrinkles from his trousers. "Let's grab a cup of coffee—the real stuff."

He led the way, speaking over his shoulder as they strode down the hallway. "How long did you say this has been going on?"

"I first noticed it last week." It struck her that her response came out sounding like she'd been sitting on it, so she quickly added, "I went in and upgraded both my interface and security system. Seemed okay until earlier today."

Jarvis ordered a cappuccino from the eager refreshment attendant. For most of the population, having a live body take orders and prepare custom drinks was little more than an artifact of bygone days. But nothing was too good for the executives at ISC. Maggie opted for a black coffee. They took seats at a table by the window while waiting for his drink.

He drummed his fingers on the table as he gazed out the window overlooking the Potomac River. The sun had traversed the southern sky and was hovering above the southwest horizon, shining deep red through the late afternoon Washington, D.C., haze. "We have two issues. The most immediate, of course, is how you can continue functioning without being compromised. The longer-term problem is identifying and eliminating the root cause."

As she savored the explosively rich flavor of real coffee, Maggie nodded and waited to see which way the wind would blow on this one. A problem like this could well signal the end of her employment if not quickly rectified.

Jarvis continued, the words coming out as almost casual—almost. "For now, keep things as normal as possible. Be mindful of what you say, especially with Fishburn. If you need to have a serious conversation with him, make an appointment and meet with him personally. And make sure to turn your system off. But, to the extent you can, continue to use your neural connection and avoid substantive discussions."

"I can do that." Nothing earthshaking in that set of instructions.

"As for the problem, hmmm…." He turned his head back toward the window. "I obviously don't have any solutions myself. Is there anything you can think of, anything at all, that might have set this off?"

"Nothing. I'm not doing anything different now than I've been doing for the past three years." Sensing an unasked question, she continued, "No happy-apps, very little real alcohol, no hypnotracks, nothing. And I've had the system scanned for intrusions and nanomines." She paused before adding, "There's really nothing else that I can think of."

Jarvis shrugged as the young attendant set the ceramic cup of steaming creamy liquid in front of him. "I guess we start logically. I'll set up for you to see our contract psychometrist. She'll assess your neural connection from the biological perspective. Depending on what she finds, she may refer you to a neuropsychologist or even a psychiatrist. It will be important, though, to be completely honest with her. There's nothing we can't solve these days, but tracking it down could take time. You'll need to be patient."

***

The late-fortyish doctor studied the wall display. Her short-cropped brown hair had touches of silver at the temples. Her slight body looked lost in the oversized leather chair at her desk. "You can see, there's nothing here. No cysts, tumors, or lesions." She half-stood and pointed toward an image on the screen. "The tissue around the interface doesn't show any signs of trauma or infection. Have you experienced headaches or dizziness?"

Maggie shook her head. "Nothing at all."

Doctor Lagash swiveled around and turned off the display. "There are a number of other things we can look at. You say that the problem has mostly been this shimmering or slight rippling, but a purple-tinted discoloration occurred once. That in itself is odd, because these represent two different types of problems. The rippling could be any disturbance in the I/O system or in the display functions. But the coloring could occur only in the temporal lobe or associated connections. That's where emotions are registered, and color variances in our current interface systems are correlated with those emotions."

Maggie's mind raced. *Emotions.* She wondered if the Roberto app might have been involved in a coloration glitch. On the other hand, it had only occurred once. The more pressing problem was the rippling. "So, what do we do next?"

"Our first avenue will be to activate your internal neurodiagnostic nanobots. With any luck, they'll see what's going on in greater detail that I can get with a scan. If that fails, we can go to radiation-based imagery. We could also inject some highly specialized bots that will target the specific symptoms." She paused and sighed. "As a last resort, we can neutralize everything and re-install your systems. I have to tell you, though, I'm not anxious to go that route. It would mean admission to an inpatient facility and substantial psychiatric risk."

Maggie recalled Jarvis's admonition about honesty. "There is one thing that might have had an effect. I use a personal relationship service app that targets the pleasure centers. I assume that's the same thing as the emotional center. Could that have anything to do with any of this?"

She thought she saw a faint smile cross the doctor's lips. "It's possible. But if that's the case, it would most likely have left physical artifacts either in the temporal lobe or at the connections. In any event, if they're around, we'll find them."

Maggie weighed what she had heard. It might be a good idea to avoid sessions with Roberto until this was all cleared up.

Doctor Lagash's voice intruded, "Let's get started on those tests."

Chapter 13

Maggie picked around the edges of her turkey and avospred on rye, occasionally popping a crust of bread into her mouth. The meat was real, sort of. She knew that the substance contained elements of genetically modified turkey. But she'd had real turkey meat once before, and it tasted nothing like this. The avospred paste was purely synthetic—green coloring with artificial flavoring and preservatives to resemble avocado, which was no longer viable. The bread was, well, it was bread. Soy meal and synthetic fiber had replaced wheat as a source of flour. She had no idea where the rye flavoring came from.

After the session with the psychometrist, she called in sick for the rest of the day and decided to stop off for an afternoon sandwich that would double as both lunch and dinner.

An unexpected and abrasive voice pulled her out of the dark mental cavern. "What's this, sucking down a leisurely afternoon lunch? What would the taxpayers say?"

She glanced up to see her worst, well, almost worst, nightmare. "Mister Arandon, what a… surprise." She rolled her eyes and fixed her gaze on the sandwich.

"Mind if I join you?" Much to her dismay, he pulled out a chair and sat across from her without waiting for an answer.

Nick Arandon was a paradox. On one hand, he was an obnoxious asshole that never missed an opportunity to sling mud in the Senator's direction, regardless of the validity. On the other hand, he could, on occasion, come across as a nice guy—an act he no doubt had to practice. He stood about six feet with a trim build. His dark sandy hair which could have, at one time, been blond, was now closer to brown. Likewise, his gray-blue eyes could have been a sparkling, crystal blue in his younger years. Bottom line, though—the guy was devoid of principles, at least as far as she could see. And he was the enemy.

"Yes, I do mind. I'm not on the clock right now, so I have no mandate to tolerate you."

He guffawed. "Do you sit around and think up these insults especially for me? Or do other journalists get equal opportunity sarcasm?"

"Oh, so you are a *journalist?* You could have fooled me. And what makes you think I was being sarcastic*?*"

She watched him in her peripheral vision as he signaled a waiter. *What did I do to deserve this?* "If I wanted to do lunch with you, I would have asked you." She gestured at the empty tables around the eatery. "And, as you can see, there are plenty of other places to sit."

By this time, the waiter had arrived and stood with his pad open. "What can I get for you?"

Arandon pointed to Maggie's plate. "I'll have one of those." He paused as the young man swiped and pressed on the handheld display. "And a bottle of water."

"Very good. Anything else?"

"No thanks."

Maggie took an oversized bite and chewed more rapidly than she would have liked. Since her nemesis wasn't going to take the hint, she'd just cram the lunch down and leave.

When he spoke again, his tone had changed—softer, a bit slower. "Look, Maggie, I know that FNA is the enemy. I get that. And I realize that makes us adversaries. Goes with the territory. But, honestly, I don't understand the level of hatred for me personally."

She chewed on another bite of sandwich, thinking about his sudden change of tactics. Swallowing, she cleared her throat. "What is it you want from me, Arandon? I just want to eat my lunch in peace."

"Fair enough. Just give me a minute, then I'll switch tables." His voice sounded almost human.

Her gaze met his. "Okay. You got a minute. Go."

Arandon sighed. "It's just that you seem to spend a lot of time and energy trying to insult me. And, believe me, I get that a lot, so my hide is pretty thick. But it strikes me that, in going this route, you give up a lot. For example, just the other day when I asked about Estrone's little problem, you spent the opportunity flinging barbs at me. Never once did you even ask where I got the information. That seems, well, frankly, bordering on incompetent. And I have never known you to be incompetent."

Maggie put her sandwich down and took a sip of water. She used the slight delay to try and fashion a retort, although she had to admit that he wasn't that far off the mark. "And if I'd asked you about your source, of course, you'd just have gushed all over yourself to tell me, right?"

He laughed and leaned back in his chair. "No. I wouldn't have. But that doesn't change the fact that you should have probed, unless, of course, you already knew about it."

She started to panic. Whether intentional or not, he'd laid the perfect trap. *Damn!* She had allowed her adolescent arrogance to cloud her judgment. She tried to wrest her way out of it. "I don't waste my time. Even you wouldn't give up your source. You know it, and I know it. Let's not get into some spitting contest trying to draw any kind of meaning from that."

His smile disappeared, and his eyes had a look in them, *sincerity, concern*. He leaned in closer to her. "You're off the clock right now. So am I. We could sit and throw snide remarks at each other all afternoon. So, tell you what, I'll go first. I won't tell you my source, but I will say that it was not generated internally at FNA. The source may or may not be reliable. At this point, I don't know. But it is a source, and, if you were doing your job, you would have known about it already. Maybe you did, and you're just playing it close to the vest. If so, good for you. If not, you need to take this seriously."

"Why share this with me?"

He shook his head and gazed toward the window. "I work for a corporation, just like you. I get up each morning, put on my clothes, and go to work, doing whatever they want me to do... within legal and ethical boundaries, of course."

Maggie jumped in before he could continue. "Of course, notwithstanding that the concept of ethics at FNA is not what it is for the rest of the journalistic world."

He continued, seeming not to have heard, "What I do for my paycheck doesn't define me any more than what you do for ISC... or the senator... defines you. We do what we do to pay the bills. Whether you choose to believe it or not, I do respect you and your abilities. We spar because of whom we each work for. But, at least for me, I'm able to keep it in perspective. And what I'm telling you now is something you need to know, whether you want to or not."

The waiter returned with Arandon's sandwich just as he finished the speech. "Here you go, sir. Will there be anything else?"

"No. Thank you." He nodded at the young man, who turned and retreated. He picked up his plate and bottle. "I'm going to park at the window table. Nice view. Think about it, Maggie."

She wrapped up what was left of her lunch, slugged down the rest of her tea, and departed. She glanced toward the window table to see Arandon gazing out at the late August DC drizzle, seemingly oblivious to her.

Chapter 14

The more she thought about it, the more her opinion of Arandon solidified—a second-tier screebot with no principles. That he would even attempt such a shallow tactic as trying to befriend her—baring his real self to her and offering sage advice—only served to deepen her dislike and distrust of him.

Still, he had given her a tidbit—the source came from outside FNA. Provided he was telling the truth, which was, in and of itself, dubious, where could it have come from? Maybe the senator's app source, assuming he was actually using, or maybe a source inside Estrone's own office. That could spell disaster.

Dusk had banished most of the daylight by the time Maggie arrived at her apartment. She tossed her bag containing the half-eaten sandwich on the counter and made her way into the bedroom to change. She brought up her control panel to adjust the temperature. *Menu, interface, environment, 68.* The light in the lower right corner of her display turned amber for a second and then reverted to green. She felt more than heard the cooling synchro kick in.

Back in the kitchen, she considered eating the rest of her lunch but lacked the appetite. She transferred the white bag from the counter to the refrigerator and extracted a half-full bottle of wine.

Her head had just touched the back of the console seat when the amber communication light began blinking. *Connect.*

Rather than a real-time connection, though, she got a pre-recorded message. "This is Doctor Lagash at the Neuro

Imaging Center. Please contact me at your convenience."
The green connection went out.

Annoying. Why didn't she just call and wait for me to answer? "Damned arrogant physicians—everybody else is beneath them. They're too good to wait." Initiating contact, she set the security level to *high* and waited for the connection.

"Good evening, Miz Renfro. Thanks for getting back to me. I have the results from your tests."

"And?" Maggie leaned forward, holding her wine glass with both hands.

"I'd prefer that you come in so we can discuss it here."

I hate doctors. So full of themselves. "Can you just forward the compressed files to me? I took the day off today. Not sure my employer would appreciate a repeat."

"I understand. But our protocol prohibits me from neuronically transmitting files of this nature. Besides, we need to discuss the next steps, and I'm not willing to do that on the net."

Maggie sighed. "Okay. I'll be there at eight tomorrow morning. Can I assume you'll get to me first thing, so I can at least make an appearance at work?"

***

Her fears about an encounter with Roberto resurfaced. And, after the cryptic call from the doctor, Maggie could summon little enthusiasm for anything other than brooding. The entire range of possible outcomes paraded through her mind as she tried to sleep—losing her job, having her system neutralized and reset, having her life compromised by some kind of security breach. After all, if the test results had been good, the doc would have simply told her. And, she'd mentioned *next steps.* That didn't sound good.

She rolled over and checked the bedside clock display and mused—*How quaint—a real clock.* It had been an impulse purchase—a bit of nostalgia, although she was actually too young to remember the real thing. She had disabled her interface after the conversation with Doctor Lagash. If anyone needed her during the night, they would just have to suffer through it. *Ugh, three thirty.* As she closed her eyes and tried to drift off, it occurred to her that she hadn't called into the senator's office to let them know about her appointment.

It took about five seconds to initiate her I/O system. The attempted contact with Fishburn produced the expected results—unavailable. She left a message, "Hi, this is Maggie." She rolled her eyes at her own stupidity. He would see her ID on the metadata for the transmission packet. "I have to be at the Neuro Imaging Center at eight in the morning. I should be at the office by ten." She started to add that he could give her a call if he had questions but remembered that her system would be disabled. If he needed anything, he would just have to wait.

She pondered calling and leaving a message for Leonard Jarvis, her boss at ISC. A voice inside, though, warned her against it. Better to wait until she knew something rather than raising a bunch of red flags.

***

"All of the tests came back negative." The doctor paused, her gaze locked with Maggie's.

"Okay, so now what?"

Lagash swiped at the pad on her desk and then pressed her fingers against the screen. "What it means is that there is nothing wrong with your interface and we can find no biological factors."

Maggie sat with her fists tightly folded in her lap. She felt sweat forming along her scalp line. "So?"

"*So*, the only explanations are that either you didn't really see anything or that the origin of the glitch is psychological or emotional. I would venture a guess that it's probably psychological since emotional trauma would manifest in a more colorful presentation. You only had that one color-related instance and, as you said, it was very muted. So, most likely there's nothing there."

The possibilities coursed through Maggie's mind. How would they even go about looking for something like that. Before she had a chance to ask the question, though, the doctor continued.

"We will, of course, work through the follow-on diagnostics. But assuming they tell us nothing more than we see here, the next step would be psychotherapy. Sadly, that process hasn't improved much since the early twenty-first century. I recommend a psychiatrist rather than a psychologist because of the medical qualifications and the range of medications that an MD can prescribe."

Maggie stared down at the floor. *A shrink.* She'd heard about them. They were the butt of jokes among her friends and associates. Not her first choice. "Hmmm. Well, I have to say that everything's been quiet for the past few days. Maybe it was just me adjusting to the new system."

The doctor shrugged. "I can't say, since we don't even know what *it* is. But, when the time comes, the decision as to whether to move forward with therapy or just wait it out is between you and ISC. Since the appointment was made by them, I will send the results back to their offices."

"No." The word came out harsh, much harsher and more urgent than Maggie intended. "No." Softer. "This is part of my medical record. The default is privacy. I'll brief my supervisor and, if he wants the records, he can request them." It was a stalling technique, and she knew it. Jarvis would want to see everything. And Maggie had a strong suspicion about how he would react—leave of absence, disabling the system, and mandatory therapy. The best she could hope for was to buy a little time before talking to him, although to what end she had no idea.

Chapter 15

Maggie leaned back on the couch and considered the collection of eclectic art adorning the walls of Cheryl's Arlington, Virginia, townhome. It had been a trying day, to put it lightly. Getting the invitation to spend the evening with her friend had been a welcome opportunity. She'd been there several times before, but it seemed the art changed regularly. Rarely was the same piece on display two visits in a row. "How do you afford this stuff?" She gestured toward a Terrance Collins original watercolor on the wall opposite the sofa.

Cheryl turned to look at the piece. "It is nice, isn't it? I picked it up at an estate sale last year. I don't think the guy running the event knew the value."

"I never have that kind of luck. And my timing sucks. I'm the one who finds the perfect item… two days after it goes off sale." She turned her attention from the art. "You seem quiet tonight, like something's eating you. You anxious about your romantic meeting this weekend?" Maggie remembered that the coming Saturday was when Cheryl was taking the big step—the actual hook-up.

"He had to postpone. Another trip." She paused and gulped down the last of her wine. "And I've been kind of involved at work, so my mind really isn't on dating right now. I haven't even seen Phillippe since late last week." She stood, holding an empty glass in her hand. "You ready for a refill?"

Maggie covered the top of her half-full glass as she pondered what her friend had just told her. "No, thanks. I'm fine." She stood and accompanied Cheryl into the kitchen. "What's going on at work that's got you in knots?"

The laugh came out half-hearted. "I'm not in knots. I've just been trying to work some things out, that's all."

"What kind of *things*?"

Cheryl appeared deep in thought as she focused on pouring the white wine. With the glass refilled, the two women ambled back into the living room. "Well, you know how we closely monitor the distribution of immigrants into different areas and correlate that with productivity data?"

Maggie searched her memory. She knew that the corporation had a rigorous evaluation system in place, but, given her particular assignment, she'd never paid much attention to the details. "I guess. What's up with it?"

"I've been running these analyses for the past five years, and the results have always been consistent. We see a high statistically significant correlation between immigrant numbers and industrial and service productivity by region. But this past year, it started falling off. The last four quarters have each shown a decline in the correlation. I expect some variation, but four quarters of consistent decay in a row is worrisome."

Maggie ran her finger around the rim of her glass. Cheryl made it sound like it was serious, but it didn't seem like that big a deal. "What does that mean?"

Her friend shrugged. "Given the way the numbers are playing out, it appears as though we continue to increase immigration numbers, but productivity, at least in certain key markets, is decreasing."

"Why would ISC care? After all, our job is to provide the bodies. The productivity of businesses in the regions isn't really our problem, is it?"

Cheryl took a drink of wine and stared at Maggie for a moment. "No, not really. But it seems odd. With the logistics and supply chain management systems in place today, there should be little variation in the relationship."

Maggie shook her head. "But there are other factors involved in productivity, things that we don't control."

"True. But these companies monitor their inputs and outputs religiously and have the ability to ramp up or throttle back depending on conditions. So, yes, productivity can be affected by equipment condition, prices, and even unexpected market variations, at least in the short term. I guess what I'm trying to say is that, if productivity is declining, for whatever reason, it would only make sense that they would cut back on incoming immigrants."

"You talk to the operations people about it?"

"No." Cheryl paused and stared at the floor. "Not yet."

"Maybe you should. They probably have an explanation. It's not like those guys to miss anything."

"I don't know." Her friend seemed lost in thought.

Silence hung between them. Maggie took the opportunity to take a sip of wine. "Cheryl, what's bothering you?"

"I'm not sure. I just feel like there's something…." She locked gazes with Maggie. "Don't you ever get the feeling that things aren't right, but you can't put your finger on it? Things feel *different* in the office. People are quieter. There seems to be a tension, but no one's talking about it."

"You know, the elections are coming up, and people are kind of jammed up because of this STOP bill, even though they say it's no big deal. I'd bet that the tension is just kind of an aggregate of all that crap. It'll blow over. Always does."

Cheryl cracked a smile. "Yeah, you're probably right. Most likely nothing." She took another drink and pivoted the conversation. "How are things with Roberto?"

Maggie wanted to tell her that she'd not spent any time with her lover app in nearly a week. But wanting to avoid a complicated explanation, she shrugged and smiled. "Roberto is, well, *Roberto*." It was a stupid answer, but it was the best she could do.

Cheryl drained her glass and stood. "Ready for that refill yet?"

Maggie had a sense of foreboding. "You need to go easy on that stuff. Tomorrow's a work day."

Cheryl made for the kitchen with a slight weave in her stride. "I have it under control."

Chapter 16

The dreaded meeting came sooner than Maggie had hoped. Jarvis summoned and here she sat.

"How did it go with the psychometrist?" His veneer seemed impenetrable. As was always the case, his eyes gave little away. The words came measured and non-confrontational, but firm.

He knows. Despite the fact that she had asked the doctor not to send the results, Maggie was certain that the physician's loyalties, along with those of her practice partners, aligned with ISC rather than individual patients. "They didn't find anything." She watched his eyes carefully, looking for a clue as to where the conversation would go. "On the other hand, I haven't seen any recurrences since I was here last. I'm beginning to think it was just the new upgrades settling in." She hoped, with little confidence, that this would get her off the hook.

Her boss shrugged. "Maybe. These things can take time." But his look told her something entirely different. The cold eyes and tightly drawn mouth provided *the real answer*—this issue was not going away.

Might as well dive in. "What's next?"

He stared at her for a moment and then shifted his gaze to the window. The moment of silence before he spoke seemed interminable. "Let's keep things the way they are now. No point in overreacting. Maintain your comm channel open but avoid sensitive discussions." He stood, signaling the end of the meeting. "But you will let me know if anything, I mean *anything*, comes up again?" The questioning tone did nothing to hide the fact that he had issued a strict order.

She started for the door and then paused. "Oh, one other thing. I ran into Arandon yesterday. He rambled much as he always does. But he did tell me that the source on Estrone's happy-app rumor was not internal to FNA."

He narrowed his eyes as he stared at her, nodding slowly. "Anything else?"

"I did my best to appear disinterested. I knew he wouldn't tell me who it was, so I didn't give him the satisfaction of thinking he'd piqued my interest."

"Good. Keep that approach. What are you seeing around the senator's office?"

"Nothing. Fishburn keeps his distance on the subject, and I haven't heard any rumblings. Also, I ran a capture app on media, and nothing showed up."

He opened the door for her. "Keep me informed."

As Maggie made her way toward the elevator, she wondered in passing why he had not ordered her to see a psychiatrist. After all, there was a remote possibility that what she'd seen was imagined, the result of stress or fatigue… or frustration. His reaction to the app rumors also puzzled her. If she hadn't known better, Maggie would have sworn that her boss had some inside line on this whole thing, that he knew a lot more about it than he was letting on.

***

Fishburn raised a finger as though to say *be with you in a minute*. To say that he was a man from a different time would be a vast understatement. He sat staring at the monitor on his desk—an actual monitor that used archaic colored LEDs to form images in pixels on the screen. And yet, there it was. Maggie could discern a slight movement of his head, side to side, as he apparently read something of interest.

Her attention wandered to the bookcase off to one side—real books, with covers and pages. Most of his collection sported what looked like hard, rigid covers. There were a few that appeared to have more flexible coverings, probably made out of some type of sturdy print stock. She moved over closer to the bookcase and ran her finger across the spine of a particularly attractive hardbound book—*Arete*.

"I'm sorry about that. Thanks for waiting." He gestured toward a chair. "Have a seat, please."

Maggie turned to the chief of staff. "That's quite a collection of books you have. Where did you get them all?" She eased over and into the chair.

His smile broadened. "Thank you. I've been collecting books my entire life. Even as a kid I found them much more engaging than the usual content streaming technology that everyone seems to like so much." He leaned back in his chair, his hands laced behind his head. "Now, what's so important that you need to make the walk down here in person?"

She was ready for the question. "Nothing at all. I was just out stretching my legs and thought it would be nice to talk to you in person." The words, once uttered, didn't sound as convincing as they had in her mind.

If the chief of staff sensed a problem, he didn't let on. "Anything particularly interesting?"

She sat back in the stiff, leather chair. "Same stuff, different day. With the STOP bill sidetracked into another committee, things have gotten quiet. I can tap into current polls, but my guess is that they're not going to tell us anything we don't already know."

"I agree. And, I guess from a practical perspective, whatever the senate agrees on will still have to go to the house and then conference before it lands on the president's desk. So, we can breathe easier and enjoy the down time while we have it." He offered his signature canned smile, nothing too sincere—just enough to convey the possibility that he was human.

On the spur of the moment, Maggie decided to probe a bit. "Is the senator feeling better? Those late summer colds have a way of hanging on forever."

Fishburn's demeanor changed. His smile faded, and his eyes narrowed. After a moment's thought, he responded, "Yes. He's better now. Everything's back to normal. Any chatter in the media about it?" The question seemed tense, almost rushed.

Something is up with Estrone. This would be the perfect time for *EmPsy*—her emotional/psychological assessment app. Unfortunately, as directed by her boss, she had disabled her interface. But from the appearance and tone of the chief of staff, she had touched a nerve. "Haven't heard a thing."

He continued, his voice reflecting confidence as he went, "It was nothing at all. Look, if you hear anything on this, any rumblings of any type, let me know right away. And I'd appreciate it if we could not bother ISC with this, especially since there's nothing there."

"Absolutely." *Not.* Apparently, Fishburn wasn't ready to accept that her allegiance was to her real employer—Leonard Jarvis and ISC. She smiled and stood to leave.

"But I suspect that the bottom feeders out there have plenty of other stuff to work on."

He smiled and nodded.

As she left his office and turned down the hall, everything changed—her vision vanished for what seemed like a second or two before returning to normal. That would have been merely horrible had it not been for the fact that her neural interface was completely powered down.

Chapter 17

Maggie huddled on the sofa, her arms around her legs pulling her knees close to her chest. The absence of her neural input made the silence even more overwhelming. Nothing coming in, nothing going out. She sat in the darkness staring at the window, beyond which lurked more darkness. Her entire life seemed to teeter on the edge of nothingness.

Facing reality was far harder than she'd ever imagined. There was nothing wrong with her equipment, applications, or interface. Whatever was plaguing her was in her mind. She felt her sanity beginning to unravel.

On the very limited bright side, since there were no electronically discernable symptoms, ISC could not discover the continuing problem. She'd told Jarvis that there had been no recent occurrences. As far as he knew, everything was clear. And she'd never mentioned it to Chief of Staff Fishburn. If she could weather the mental symptoms, maybe she could pull this off unnoticed.

In order for that to be a possibility, she would have to power up her interface and resume her normal communication channels.

System initiate. Her vision flashed black for a moment before the typical flat gray internal display came online. Numbers and letters scrolled, different colored lights blinked in the different quadrants, each telling her that a specific function had come to life. Diagnostics ran. After about twenty seconds, her vision returned to normal, with the usual display lights, ambient readouts, and a flashing yellow comm light—A message from Cheryl. *Call back.*

"Maggie. What the hell is going on. Your system's been down for hours. I was getting ready to come over and break in on you."

"Sorry, Cheryl. I'm fine. I had some glitches earlier, so I took everything down to run internal diagnostics."

"And?"

"Was nothing." Maggie decided to embellish, well, actually *lie*. "I had my system upgraded recently and forgot to run compatibility tests with all my apps. One of my media screening programs had a conflict. I had to do an update on it before bringing everything back on line." *Ugh, too much.*

"Oh, Okay. So, everything's okay?"

"Yeah, fine. What's up?" Cheryl didn't usually call for no reason.

"I was just wondering, did you say anything to Jarvis about that thing we discussed the other night, you know, the immigrant number and productivity correlation?"

"No. In fact, I'd actually forgotten about it. Why?"

"Nothing really." The emotions came through—*worry, fear.* "It's just funny, my boss came to me this morning to talk about that very thing. She said she'd noticed it and went out of her way to explain why she thought it was showing up that way."

"That's great. I mean, it validates what you were saying."

"Maybe. But she seemed strange, as if she were trying to convince me of the explanation. She's never done that before. I'm just a statistician analyst. They don't particularly care what I think."

Maggie laughed, confident that it would translate well through the interface. "Yeah, well, I guess they care on this one. Anyway, nice work. Congratulations."

"Thanks, I guess." Pause. "Oh, and I wanted to tell you, my *date* is on for next weekend. He'll be back in town. We're going to meet up at a private club in Georgetown. He said he would try to get reservations at La Maison d'Oie. They actually serve traditional food without any biotechronic modification. *Real food.*"

"Woohoo, aren't we upscale!" Maggie chortled. "Bring me some of your leftovers." She felt a wave of concern wash over her. "What club are you meeting at? Seriously, be careful. You don't know this guy and there's some bad shit going on in the city right now."

"Yes *mother*. I'll be careful. We've been chatting every night, sometimes for one or two hours at a time. He's really nice. I can't wait for you to meet him."

"Do you know his name yet?"

"Relax. He's in a sensitive government position that requires discretion. Once we start going out, it'll be okay. But until we meet and find out if we're really right for each other, he wants to keep it low key."

"*Low key* my ass. He wants to remain anonymous and that's not a good sign." The more she thought about it, the worse it seemed. "If you chat with him tonight, you should push him for a name, at least a first name, if nothing else."

"Sorry, we're not chatting tonight. He is out on business all evening. But I'll relay your concern to him tomorrow night."

Maggie shook her head and smiled. "Okay, you win. Look, I need to run. It's getting late, and tomorrow's a busy day for me."

***

Sleep didn't come early or easy. Maggie tossed and turned, mentally composing her actions and words for Jarvis. *No new occurrences. Everything looks good. Back to normal.* But it was like she was poised on the edge of a blade, waiting to fall one way or the other. Despite what she was planning to tell her boss, the symptoms had recurred and seemed even worse.

She considered calling Roberto but decided against it. Given everything on her mind, she would be hard-pressed to enjoy an encounter. They could just talk, but it seemed somehow unfair to burden him with her problems. *How stupid.* He was an application—lines of code. And he was written especially for her at no small cost. Why shouldn't she unload her burdens on him. But still she didn't call him.

***

Maggie spread cream cheese on the toasted bagel and poured herself a to-go cup of coffee. She checked the morning's news stories on the way out.

Shake-up at the Freedom Network of America

Serial killer strikes again overnight in Washington, D.C.

Coup in Sudan

She muttered, with a chuckle, "Ah, the children over at FNA are having trouble playing nice together. Couldn't happen to a nicer bunch of guys." Someone would be unemployed by close of business today. Possibly Nick Arandon? *Naw. No such luck.* He wasn't that important.

Chapter 18

The yellow blinking light in the upper right quadrant signaled an incoming communication. The ID surprised her. Fishburn rarely called at eight o'clock in the morning unless there was trouble. *Connect.* She allowed the auto greeting to play out.

"Maggie, good, you're in. Would you mind dropping by my office?"

His attempt at making it seem like a request amused her. "Certainly, sir. Any particular time?"

"Right now. Something we need to deal with."

She strode down the hallway wondering what could be so urgent as to warrant an immediate summons before he even had time to sit down with the senator.

When she announced herself to his executive assistant, the young man escorted her in immediately. "He's expecting you."

Maggie rolled her eyes. *Of course, he's expecting me. He called me.* "Thank you."

Fishburn sat behind his desk with old fashioned flat panel monitors on each of the two front corners and a quaint keyboard and mouse in front of him. *Old school—very old.* That was the polite description. *Antique* and *outdated* were other descriptors that came to mind.

He offered a tense smile and nodded to the assistant, who left, closing the door behind him. "Have a seat." He gestured toward a small table sitting off to one side of the desk. A large picture window provided a classic view of the Washington Monument and the Mall.

He sat down opposite her and shifted nervously in his seat. "Maggie, I'm going to ask you not to record this conversation." His gaze locked on hers.

She smiled. "Of course. Just a moment and I'll disable my interface." She knew that was what would make him feel most secure if he had something sensitive to discuss. Instead, she initiated the audio and video recording app. If there was something important enough to have her summoned like this, Jarvis would want to know all about it. "Okay, she's all shut down." She glanced around, trying to look embarrassed. "Should I take notes? I can get my pad."

"No." The word came out quickly with a hard edge. "No need for it. I just want to bounce some things off you. Nothing on the record here."

She nodded and fought back a smile, knowing that audio and video recording were both active.

"I need your assurance that this conversation is completely private."

Maggie leaned forward into the table, struggling to contain the laugh that she felt coming. "Certainly. What is it?" After all this time, Fishburn had apparently still not figured out who she really worked for.

He sighed and slumped in his chair. "The senator is out sick again today. This is twice in two weeks."

Her mind raced. *Hitting the happy-app a bit hard this week?* "You think it's something serious?"

"No… and yes." He folded his hands on the table in front of him. "What I mean is that I don't know for sure. Last week it was a cold. Today, something he ate last night. Last month it was a touch of the stomach flu, even though it's not flu season and he's had vaccinations."

She played naïve. "Maybe he should get a full physical. Maybe something serious is going on."

"Maybe. But I called you down because we need to start putting together a PR strategy in case this leaks. Sooner or later it'll start to draw attention. Let's get out in front of it. And remember, Arandon over at FNA has already queried you about the possibility of application abuse."

Maggie nodded with a nagging sense that the Senator's fortunes were starting to unravel. "I agree. That in itself is a good reason to have him at least get started on a complete work-up. If someone tumbles onto it, we have a strong position, and, absent additional information, anyone outside this office wouldn't have any place to take the story. A senator is undergoing a full physical assessment. We could even bill it as a routine thing, citing his desire to keep in perfect health." But she knew that the truth was nobody really cared about the senator unless there was some real dirt involved. Health problems usually didn't rise to that level unless they were related to some kind of venereal disease or something equally unsavory.

"Yes. That's a good idea. I'll work with Senator Estrone to get it set up. In the meantime, if you hear any chatter, let me know right away."

Maggie chuckled to herself all the way back to her office. What a screwed-up world it would be if Arandon had gotten it right about the app after all. She terminated the recording app, parsed it into packets, and set the highest security code. When she transmitted it to Jarvis, she attached an icon of a large red bow to the file, figuring she'd contact him later to gloat.

Chapter 19

The incoming call pulled Maggie out of her self-induced sense of satisfaction. Taking note of the caller ID, she immediately regretted having not read the FNA shakeup story on the net that morning. She sighed and mildly chastised herself. *Connect.* "Ah, Mister Arandon. Trouble in paradise this morning?" She smiled at the thought of the likely state of panic over at the Freedom Network of America.

The usual sense of smugness was notably missing from the incoming signal. A brief pause preceded a very subdued transmission. "Any chance we could meet and talk?"

He'd opened himself up to all manner of snarky responses, and she almost hurled her best one. Instead, and to her own surprise, she responded, "Where and when?"

***

"This thing down at your shop serious?" She cradled her cup in both hands as she leaned forward on the park bench.

Arandon shrugged. He had never presented this way. He sat hunched over, his brow furrowed, his mouth drawn into a tight line. He held his cup motionless, perched on his knee. "You follow up on that tip I gave you?"

The shake-up must have been serious. But rather than pursuing it, Maggie considered his question. "Tip? I don't recall you giving me any tip. I do seem to remember your flinging unfounded accusations and then trying to backpedal by saying you didn't know about your source's reliability. But that's not the same thing as a tip."

"I'm not looking for a story today. I'm just trying to do the right thing here."

Maggie once again refrained, with some effort, from slinging a snide remark. Instead, she glanced over at him and nodded. "What do you want, Nick?" *Ugh, she'd called the guy "Nick."*

"I don't know. Honestly. I really don't know."

Now she was spooked. This guy was the enemy and he seemed on the verge of unloading all of his fears. She held silent, waiting for whatever came next.

He looked up and gazed across the park at the late summer tourist crowds—reading the plaques and capturing images with a variety of gadgets. Most of them probably could not afford the neural interfaces that would allow digital capture through the field of vision. "Too many things happening at once."

That was a weird observation. "How so?" Washington, D.C. was literally defined by too many things happening at once.

"Soldani, over in the domestic policy section got canned along with his boss." He paused, as though gathering his thoughts and courage. "Normally you see this kind of thing coming. But last night, bam! Out of the blue."

"Okay, so what? It happens. Try staffing for some of these politicians and you'll get a healthy dose of that." Although Maggie had to admit that usually there were warning signs.

"Maybe, but Soldani was just a ground-pounder. In fact, he was probably less important than me if you can imagine that."

And she passed up another great opportunity. "Any reason?"

"Nope. Just out the door. And the weird thing is that they escorted him, wouldn't even let him get his coat or anything. Don't know about his boss. She worked in a different part of the building. But it just doesn't make any sense." By this point, Arandon seemed as if he were talking to himself, oblivious to Maggie's presence. "Christ, I just had lunch with the guy yesterday and he was all sunshine and smiles." He closed his eyes for a moment before continuing. "He's got a wife and two kids. And he's out of a job, just like that. I suppose he'll just have to figure out how to live on the standard credit allowance. Either that or find some other job."

Maggie cringed at the thought. All citizens received a monthly allowance from the government, courtesy of corporate social reinvestment. The arrangement ensured that most people survived, although just barely. She wondered how someone could just, without any possible idea what was happening, find themselves out of a real, paying job. "Any idea what he was working on? Maybe that had something to do with it."

"I don't know. He was on domestic policy. Could have been the incarceration matrix, surveillance technology, or even immigration policy."

A bell went off in Maggie's head. "That why you're talking to me? You think maybe it was immigration policy and I know something?"

His head jerked up and he stared at her. "No. Nothing like that." He relaxed and lowered his gaze. "It's just hard to know who to trust. At least with you, I know where I stand. You're more likely to spit in my face than stab me in the back."

She chortled at the thought. "Well, yes, there is that. So, I'll give you this much. No, I haven't had any contact with Soldani; in fact, I don't even know him other than by reputation. And, at least as far as I know, there aren't any emerging issues in immigration right now other than the STOP legislation. As I'm sure you know, that's picked up another committee referral and then has to go to the house before signing. So probably nothing there."

"Thanks. That was more than I was expecting." He offered a weak smile. "Could you do me another favor, please?"

Maggie rolled her eyes. This meeting had gone way beyond weird. "What is it?"

"Could you not tell anyone about this meeting? I mean, about what we talked about? It may be nothing at all, and I'd just as soon keep my head down until whatever it is blows over."

"I can do that." But she wondered. Should she? Is this something Jarvis would find interesting? She decided that, since it probably had nothing to do with immigration, she could, at least for the moment, keep the confidence. After all, whatever was hounding Arandon had nothing to do with her.

Chapter 20

Maggie put the conversation with Arandon in the background while she focused on reviewing the media activity of the day. Using eye movement, she scrolled through the usual titles:

Voters on Edge about Increased Immigration

Public Opinion Split Evenly on Negative Impacts of Legal Immigrants

Polling and Survey Methodology Held in High Regard by Most Adults

Immigrants: Where Are They Going?

American Freedom Party Holds Slight Overall Edge Going Into Elections

Something—a movement in the display—caught her eye. The title "Immigrants: Where Are They Going?" relocated itself to the top of the list. *Relocated itself?* How was that possible. Maggie stared at her display. Indeed, the item had moved to the top of the list. Maybe the list re-ordered itself alphabetically? No, the American Freedom Party would have moved to the top. Maybe some kind of relevance priority? Not likely since the immigrant story didn't seem to even be within the scope of her search on public opinion.

In fact, why was that story there at all. She had scanned for polling and opinion pieces. She studied the faintly pulsing netlink—*Immigrants: Where Are They Going?* She considering activating the link but thought better of it. That was how systems became corrupted, no matter how much security was in place.

Isolate, interface, communication, Cheryl, initiate.

"Maggie, what's up?"

"Nothing, really. Just wanted to ask, did you forward me a netlink on immigration destinations? I know you were looking at the geographic distribution correlated with productivity."

"Nope. Why, you get something interesting?"

"Not sure. I scanned for public opinion pieces and got this weird netlink that looks like a feed for a story on where immigrants end up. Not my usual fare, so I thought maybe it came from you."

"No, but why don't you link it back to me? It does sound like something that I might be interested in."

"I don't know. May be a bot inside. That could really screw up your system."

"Naw, we've got top of the line filters here. If there's anything there, they'll strip it off."

"Okay, if you say so." Maggie split her display and retrieved the list again. Isolating the story, she tagged and transmitted it. "There you go. Done."

"And there it is. Thanks."

After disconnecting, Maggie sorted and stored the relevant items and deleted the errant netlink. Leaning back in her chair, she closed her eyes, took a deep breath, and stretched her arms over her head. As the minutes passed, she found herself curious about the story. It may well have been some kind of intrusion attempt. But it could have also been a legitimate piece. In any event, she'd already deleted the link, and, short of accessing her communication archives, it was gone.

"Oh well," she mumbled to herself, "back to it." She retrieved the screened media stories for the day related to Senator Estrone.

Polls Show No Viable Contenders for Junior Senator Seat in New York

Senator Estrone Remains Solid with Progressive Base

Immigrants: Where Are They Going?

"What?" She stared with a building sense of dread as the story about immigrants once again repositioned itself to the top of the list. The icy blue text font seemed to pulse an invitation to select it.

Chapter 21

Maggie stared. The title seemed to pulse even brighter. It wanted her to select it. "No," she mumbled, "not going to happen." She deleted the link again. The offending words disappeared from her internal display. Still, she was rapidly developing a serious case of the creeps. And then it got worse.

The title re-appeared within seconds and was once again moved to the top of her list. "No way." She powered down her interface. Her field of vision turned gray and then black for just a fraction of a second before returning to normal, without, of course, any of the interface elements. She gazed out across her office with her own unassisted vision.

Frozen in her chair, she fought to control her trembling. "I'll be damned if I'm going to turn that back on." And yet she knew that if she remained off-net, it would alert her boss to the problems. *Hopeless*. That was the word that defined everything she felt. Well, *fear* ran a close second. She could think of only one solution, and it was definitely not something she relished.

Still, complete system removal, including all diagnostic bots and applications, would at least bring her back to some solid ground. It would require a couple days' stay at the Securitech Biotechnical Institution, a combination medical and technology service center. And who knows what her employability would be after that. Would Jarvis ever trust her in a sensitive position again?

Maggie started to connect with the service center and set up an initial appointment but quickly realized that her system was disabled. "Shit." She would either have to risk turning it on again, with whatever consequences this new problem would bring, or trot down to the center in person. "Nothing's ever easy."

System, initiate. After the requisite boot process, her visual display normalized. The small green ready light shone steadily in the lower left quadrant. *Isolate, menu, diagnostics, initiate, optimize.* The results came back normal. "Do I even dare try?" She needed the results of the day's polling scans but wasn't ready for the unwelcome additional piece about immigrants.

She decided instead on a bit of light investigation and connected with her friend. "Cheryl, hey, I was wondering, did you send me a return or confirmation link for that immigration story I transmitted to you?"

"No. Why? Something wrong?"

"I don't know. It's weird. After I sent it to you, I deleted the link. When I reconnected to download some other scans, the story ended up back in the queue. The worst part, though, is that it re-positioned itself to the top of my list. I deleted it again and it came right back."

"Oh, yeah, that's major weird. Sounds like your system's gone wonky. You have any work done lately?"

Maggie felt a small touch of tentative relief. "Unfortunately, yes. I had a system and security upgrade installed. And they put in some kind of remote diagnostic function, too. That's probably it."

"I'd check it out. And, oh, by the way, my date is still on but we're going out Thursday night instead. He got back in town early."

"Did you get his name yet?"

"Gotta run. I'll call and let you in on all the salacious details Friday morning."

Steven Hamilton

After she disconnected, Maggie retrieved her scan list one more time, but there was no immigrant netlink. "Hmmm. Strange." By this time, she'd decided against a complete system removal. Instead, she made a note to swing by and have her interface setting tweaked by the technician. For the amount she was paying, they should provide gold-plated service. And it probably needed only minor adjustments.

Chapter 22

The technician/salesman, the same one who'd sold her the upgrade, studied the wall monitor. "Oh yeah, I see the problem. Your system tried to do an update and it looks like you disabled everything right in the middle of the process." He turned to face her, shaking his head like a teacher who had caught a student in a lie. "You need to check active processes before you shut down. It can cause all kinds of problems." The condescension dripped from his words.

That's pure bullshit. Maggie knew that current systems had failsafes on top of failsafes. And even if it was a problem, she would get a warning. But it had been a long day, she was tired, hungry, and more than a little frustrated, not to mention frightened. "Okay. Can you fix it?" *Of course, he can.* The question was whether he would do it without the lecture.

The overweight, greasy man swiped his pad and then pressed the display a few times, pausing to watch. "Okay. That should do it. I reinstalled the update and optimized it. And again, you could have done this remotely."

"Yeah." It was all she could muster.

***

Isolate, menu, environment, lighting—dark. Maggie reclined on the bed and relaxed. Adding a soft cover of jazz, she summoned Roberto. Before he materialized, though, a system message appeared telling her that an update had been installed to the application and that she could access the details by asking Roberto.

"I was hoping you'd call tonight." He wore a tight pair of jeans and a tee shirt. Slipping off his shoes, he slid on the bed next to her, putting his hand on her cheek and kissing her gently on the lips.

She put her arms around his neck and started to return the kiss but stopped. "I got a message that said there was an update. What was that all about?" She had grown increasingly paranoid about anything to do with her interface and operating system.

He smiled and eased away from her enough to gaze into her eyes. "There were three functionalities added in patch three point two point zero five. I think you're going to like them. The first is 'Dinner Out' and was developed in collaboration with one hundred and fifty restaurants in Washington, D.C. By invoking that function, we will be able to experience an evening in the eatery of your choice. You can select by type of food, type of atmosphere, or price."

Maggie laughed, and it felt good. "What? I just say the magic words and we get to sample the best food in town?" She knew that her system could easily project taste and smell as well as sight, hearing, and touch.

"That's it. The second capability they added is a search engine called 'Finders Keepers' and it allows you to task me for searches on the network. The final bit is a remote diagnostic and service function."

Maggie's level of stress skyrocketed. "What? They put in remote access to my system without asking?"

Roberto shrugged and offered a smile that looked forced. "It was an update. And, according to the terms of service that you agreed to, they can add capabilities considered routine without asking. But, remember, you do have the right to contact them and have the functions removed if you want. In fact, you can now do that remotely."

She laid her head back on the pillow and breathed deeply. Maybe she was overreacting. It had been a shitty day from the beginning. And, yes, she could get in touch with them the next day to have the one offending item removed. The other two actually sounded pretty good. Yes, better to worry about it in the morning. Tonight, she needed something else.

Maggie rolled onto her side, her lips finding his. His arms tightened around her and his tongue gently eased past her lips into her mouth. Shivers of pleasure rippled through her. Rolling him over gently onto his back, she eased on top of him. His breath came quickly as her lips found his nipples.

She sensed more than saw the waves of color which triggered her pleasure centers. She had, over the years, become more or less accustomed to them. But this evening, a passing thought stuck in her mind. Was the purple color she'd seen the previous week related to Roberto? Perhaps some artifact left behind after an evening of intense pleasure?

He continued to caress her, kiss her neck and breasts, grind his hard body into hers. But the thought distracted her. The almost invisible patterns and hues seemed to flash in her mind. Nothing was right. "Wait, Roberto. I'm sorry. This isn't working tonight."

He propped himself up on an elbow. "Did I do something wrong?"

Her laugh came out bitter. "No. Not at all. I'm just dealing with a lot of crap. I thought I could shut it out for a bit. But… sorry."

Roberto caressed her cheek. "What is it that's bothering you?"

What indeed? "Well, where do I start? My new system's been acting up, and my best friend is flirting with disaster, meeting some guy that she doesn't even know. Things are weird at work. I don't know, it's just that everything seems be closing in at once."

He smiled. "Feeling a little overwhelmed, huh?"

"You could say that."

His expression turned serious. "This friend of yours, what's her name, if you don't mind my asking?"

A mental alarm went off in her head. Why would he want to know? "No one important." *What a stupid thing to say. I just said she was my best friend.*

If Roberto had picked up on the inconsistency, he didn't show it. He nodded. "Okay. Is there something else you'd like to do tonight? Dinner, maybe? Or just talk? Oh, I don't know whether or not you are aware of this, but I can select an entertainment netfeed that we can watch together."

She did know about the capability. But she didn't really want to do anything. She kept coming back to the question—*why does he want to know about Cheryl?*

Chapter 23

Maggie came awake with a start, her visual display saturated with a bright yellow glow that faded to orange, then red, then a deep maroon, before turning black and then returning to normal. Colors reflected emotion and what she'd just experienced felt like terror. She ran a back trace on recent incoming signals. When the results came back, her heart raced and pounded as though it were going to explode. She broke out in a cold sweat.

Source Node: Cheryl Wolford.

She tried to connect with Cheryl. The green ready light flashed several times before the system returned a message. *Communication target unavailable.*

Maggie threw the covers off and swung her legs over the side of the bed. Her heart pounded, and she struggled to catch her breath. She tried again, same response. "Get a grip. It's probably nothing." It was just a nightmare. For sure. And Cheryl probably disabled her incoming calls at night, especially this night. Maybe her date had gone really, really well. She was probably in the middle of something that she didn't want to disturb. "Yeah, that's it. The two of them are probably tangled up in the covers right now." She forced a laugh.

After trudging first to the bathroom and then into the kitchen, she turned on the tea synthesizer, selecting chamomile. At least that wouldn't keep her awake. But the nightmare stuck. She couldn't get the colors out of her mind. And a thought occurred to her.

Menu, initiate, social, call Roberto.

"Maggie, I was hoping you'd call tonight. Are things better now? Maybe we can pick up where we left off." He eased closer to her, touching the hair at her temple.

"I was wondering if it's possible for you to do something for me. If I told you the name of my friend, is there a way you could connect with her relationship application on the network?" Even as the words came out, Maggie could hear how desperate they sounded.

Roberto stepped back, his eyes narrowing but his smile never wavering. "Why would you want me to do that?'

"Can you do it?"

He shrugged. "I suppose it's technically possible. I'd have to route the query through the central interface hub."

"Can you try, please? Her name is Cheryl Wolford. She lives here in D.C. Her relationship application is Phillipe."

He nodded, and his eyes appeared to lose focus. Less than a minute later, he nodded. "Yes, I was able to find the routing, but the application is disabled. I tried to activate it, but the interface is completely disabled." The smile persisted, only now it looked creepy, unnatural.

"What does that mean? Did she shut the application down herself? Maybe she terminated the contract? I mean, she was supposed to go out with a man last night." Her fears mounted by the second.

"No. The service has not been terminated. All communication through her interface dead ends, though. It's as though her neural device was removed or if her life functions ended."

Maggie felt the room close in around her. "No. That's not possible."

He shrugged. "It could be that she is in a highly shielded space, similar to the old Faraday cages and that all signals are grounded."

Maggie thought that unlikely. With today's signal distribution network, it was nearly impossible to find a dead spot other than the highly protected corporate offices. "Thanks for trying. That's all I needed."

Roberto faded and with him, Maggie's sense of hope. She noted her time display—4:30. Going back to bed was out of the question. She threw on some jeans, a sweatshirt, shoes, and coat, bolting out the door. Maggie hoped that, after pounding on her friend's door, Cheryl would answer, pissed as hell that she'd been pulled out of bed.

As she waited on the summoned cab, she retrieved the current news headlines and saw what she had dreaded most.

• • •

Serial Killer Claims Fifteenth D.C. Victim in Less than a Year

• • •

Chapter 24

She's my best friend." Maggie pleaded with the bot. "She was supposed to meet up with a guy last night and now her neural connection is shut down. Can't you at least tell me if it was her? The name is Cheryl Wolford."

The Capital Police Corporation didn't use live beings for general law enforcement duty. After all, crimes in the general public generated relatively little concern in the boardrooms of America. Acts committed against corporate interests were dealt with quickly and severely by an elite, militarized cadre of officers. But Maggie found herself staring across the front counter at a machine. They didn't even have the good taste to try and make it look human.

"I am sorry." The voice sounded remarkably human, right down to the inflections. "We are not allowed to release that information until after notification of next of kin. If you desire to receive the information when it is available, please provide contact information at the prompt."

Her interface displayed a steady blue light in the middle of the screen with the words *Transmit contact information* below. "Maggie Renfro, sysnet node two seven three point two point one, code I-S-C."

"Contact information recorded. Thank you." She heard a click as the connection terminated.

She retreated to the street, where a light mist had begun to fall. The heavy overcast added to the darkness of pre-dawn. Her eyes teared. She wanted to be angry at Cheryl. She wanted to yell, scream, and beat her friend over the head for being so stupid. "I should've tried harder."

***

After entering the Ekland Energy Senate Building, she detoured to the coffee kiosk and picked up a jumbo-sized cup of the synthetic stuff before making her way back to her office. The halls were relatively deserted, as would be expected for 6:30 in the morning. Plopping into her chair, she retrieved her scans for the day and began to kill time until Fishburn showed up. As soon as he got there, she'd touch base with him and then head over to ISC. Maybe they knew something.

Maggie tried Cheryl several more times with the same results before giving up. Pulling up her list of scans, she got another slam in the stomach. There among the list of her polling scans was the item "Immigrants: Where Are They Going?" nestled among the other pieces. And just as before, it immediately repositioned itself to the top of the list. *Menu, interface, disable.*

The digital wall clock displayed the time—8:15. She bolted from her office, down the hall, and into Fishburn's suite. "I need to see him." She strode past the admin assistant without waiting for a response or even looking at the young man. Knocking on the door, she flung it open and eased in, closing it behind her. Her prepared speech about the need to take the day off stuck in her throat when she saw Fishburn.

The chief of staff stared up at her, his face pale with dark patches beneath his bloodshot eyes. "We may have a problem."

Just what I need. Another problem. She composed herself and tried to conceal her near hysteria. "Yes, sir?"

He nodded toward the chair. "Sit. Please. I'm going to ask you to shut down your interface for this conversation."

This was getting to be a habit—the second time in the past week he'd been so panicked that he'd ask her to power off. She nodded and took a second, as if she were actually doing something. No point in telling him that the interface had already been disabled, because it had jumped the rails. "There, done."

"Senator Estrone is out again today. He phoned me early this morning, around six. Another cold." His face darkened even more than it already was. "I'm beginning to wonder if maybe there's something to that rumor out of FNA."

Maggie didn't give two shits about that rumor or the senator... or Fishburn, for that matter. But she saw no real upside to throwing the job away with her honesty. "What came of the physical exam? Did it turn up anything?"

Fishburn lowered and shook his head. "He hadn't had a chance to make the appointment yet."

As hard as it was, she forced herself to stay on topic. "How do you want to handle it?"

He turned his head toward the window, seemingly deep in thought. "I don't see any other way than to try and force him into a biomedtech institution today for a complete work-up. And we put out a release that bills it as a regular assessment."

Maggie nodded. "Okay. I can do the release. You're going to have him admitted, right?" The last thing she needed was to put out a story that immediately turned out to be false.

"I'll do what I can and contact you either way. Don't release the piece until you hear from me." He paused. "Oh, and let's hold off on notifying ISC until afterward. No point in stirring things up until we know what we're dealing with."

Maggie struggled to keep the sarcastic laugh inside. This guy must be as stupid as they come if he thought that she would be party to keeping secrets from her boss for the sake of some strung-out second-rate senator. "Yes, sir." She offered her best smile and tried to make it look sincere. "And, just to let you know, I'll be working this from home. I need to be out of the office today."

His look conveyed a mix of suspicion and uncertainty, but he nodded his assent.

As she descended the steps onto the sidewalk, she reactivated her interface without bringing up her scan results. Hailing a waiting autocab, she headed for ISC. By this time, the light mist had turned to a steady rain, which pelted the front window of the vehicle. She stared out the side window, through the rivulets of water streaming down.

Clarity came! Cheryl disappeared last night. Senator Estrone was out today with a cold. *Is it possible?* She did a few quick searches and found what she sought. Her heart pounded and she struggled to breathe. The senator was absent the morning after every single serial killing over the past fifteen months.

But then it got worse. She recalled Fishburn's appearance. He looked as though he'd gotten no sleep at all the previous night—not like the chief of staff at all. And yet, it clearly wasn't the senator's absence that bothered him. He hadn't gotten the call until six in the morning. *What if Fishburn knew about it all along.*

"Stop." The autocab screeched to a halt in the middle of the avenue. Maggie threw the door opened and hurled the meager contents of her stomach onto the wet, filthy pavement.

Chapter 25

W e have to call the police. We can't hide this." Maggie slammed her fist on Jarvis's desk.

Her boss shrugged. "Let's not get ahead of ourselves here. We don't know anything for sure. In fact, we don't even know what, if anything, happened to Cheryl. I have Employee Services gathering information now. We'll wait until that comes through before deciding how to proceed."

She started to argue but the look on his face told her not even to try. His steely blue eyes fixed on hers, his face firm but neutral. A tight line defined his mouth, and he clenched his jaw. That was his *I'm the boss and you're not* look. "Yes, sir."

"Also, just to remind you, our response will be a coordinated one. We'll convene all the relevant parties and go over the material before we interact with the authorities." He stood and eased toward the door. "You look like you could use a cup of coffee. Let's head down to the cafeteria."

Their journey down the corporate corridors was marked mostly by silence. As they approached the food services area, Jarvis probed, "Anything of interest in the scans last night or this morning?"

She had dreaded the question. Maggie didn't relish pulling up her list, given that she'd left the immigrant piece intact before shutting down. "Nothing related to Cheryl, if that's what you're asking. And I didn't see anything about Estrone's health or the like." She hoped that would suffice.

He didn't respond.

The blinking yellow light signaled an incoming communication. Oddly, though, the ID information reflected an unknown source. She hesitated but relented. *Connect.*

"Read the story. Be careful who you talk to." The voice sounded strangely mechanical as if it originated from an artificial source or had been heavily filtered to disguise its identity.

Stunned, Maggie struggled to keep from allowing her panic to show on her face. She responded neurally without speaking. "Who is this?"

The connection ended, and the green ready light illuminated. Silence.

They arrived at the hot beverage kiosk counter and Jarvis stepped forward ahead of her. "Let's see, I'll have Earl Gray with cream." He turned toward Maggie. "What for you?"

She shook her head to clear the clutter, if only for a moment. "Uh, coffee's fine. Black." As Jarvis returned his attention to the counter, Maggie took the opportunity. *Menu, interface, communication, trace, last call.* She looked up just in time to see her boss turn, a hot drink in each hand.

"Let's grab a seat by the window." He handed the coffee to her and strode over to the small table. "You going to be okay?"

She took a deep breath. "Yeah. I just need to process all this. I mean, this is a hell of a way to wake up."

He chuckled. "That's for sure. We'll get through it, though, together. These things happen." He took a sip of tea.

Her interface ready light flashed, and the trace report displayed:

Last Call Trace Information
—Time connected: Today 9:42 AM
—Time disconnected: Today: 9:43 AM
—Total elapsed time: 0 minutes 18 seconds
—Source node: Unknown
—Source identity: Unknown
End Report

Maggie stared at the words, dismayed but not surprised. Somehow it was just as she had expected. *Menu, interface, display, clear.* The steady green ready light appeared.

Jarvis's voice interrupted her thoughts. "You okay? Something going on?" His eyes narrowed as he stared at her.

She lied. "No. I had just set a scan to pick up any feeds about Cheryl or the senator related to this. Just got the result back—negative." She hoped there were no stories out there about it. Trying to deceive her boss was a dangerous game.

The uninvited words returned to her mind. *Read the story. Be careful who you talk to.*

Chapter 26

Maggie sat in a small cubicle waiting while Jarvis worked on pulling relevant staff together. His plan was to have everyone around a table and work the problem. Was there any connection between ISC and Cheryl's disappearance?

"This is stupid," she muttered under her breath. Cheryl had met up with a man at an unnamed club—a man who chose to remain anonymous and secretive right up until the point of contact. There was no connection to ISC. There was only a serial killer, who was most likely none other than the honorable Senator Alonzo Estrone. She seethed to think that he had been there, right under her nose, the entire time. And now her best friend was dead.

Her thoughts turned to the mysterious message. She opened her inventory of scan results and there, at the top of the list, she found the item—"Immigrants: Where Are They Going?" She stared at the faintly pulsing letters. Perhaps the article would provide some answers. Or maybe it was a trap designed to penetrate her system if she selected it. On the other hand, her system had apparently been penetrated already.

Reference, load. Her display went blank for a brief moment before the response appeared.

Reference not found

"Well, that's great. Figures. I finally get around to looking at it and it turns out to be a dead-end reference." She quickly glanced around the area to make sure no one was within earshot to hear her. But who had sent the link and given her the message.

Jarvis's voice pulled her out of her thoughts. "Let's move to the conference room."

***

Her boss ran the meeting, querying each of the employees in turn. There was nothing to say, though. Cheryl had worked at ISC. Her assignments were routine and her performance satisfactory. No one had issues with her nor had anyone noticed anything unusual. About half an hour into the session, the door opened, and a young man entered carrying a box, setting it on the table in front of Jarvis and whispering something to him.

He pored over the contents for a moment, moving items around. He looked up and shrugged. "Nothing of interest in her desk. I guess that does it, then. I'll notify the authorities that we are ready to talk to them."

The room fell silent as Jarvis surveyed the people around the table. After a moment, he spoke, his voice carrying unmistakable authority and force. "I'll meet with their representative first and try to answer all of their questions. In the event that they insist on speaking with any of you, answer their questions truthfully, but do not offer any unsolicited information, none whatsoever. Understood?"

Nods and silence.

"Let's get to it, then. Maggie, would you hang back a moment. I'd like to speak with you."

The room cleared out within seconds, leaving the two of them sitting side by side. Jarvis turned his chair and locked gazes with her, his demeanor having softened a bit. "I know this is tough. If you need some help, a therapist or support, let me know. We can get that for you. But I would ask you not to say anything about the senator at this point. Neither you nor I have any evidence to support your suspicions. I'll continue to look into it. We have resources that are beyond the capability of the police. But for now, I'd rather not smear his reputation on a hunch."

Maggie couldn't believe what she was hearing. Her boss was asking her to cover up for a serial killer. Well, at the very least to withhold information. But did she really have any information, other than the fact that he looked like hell several days a month? She lowered her gaze and nodded. "Yes, sir." Her anger built.

"Oh, by the way, any resolution on that system problem?" He stood in the doorway, his icy gaze locked on her.

"I went through everything with the psychometrist—nothing." And then she crossed the line—she lied. "The symptoms went away. I suspect that it was some coding glitch with the new upgrade and got sorted out with an auto-service patch. I'll let you know if I get any more symptoms."

***

She sat on her sofa in the darkened living room surrounded by silence. Feelings of grief, which had morphed into a hot rage, had retreated, to be replaced by a sense of numbness and helplessness. The green ready light on her display seemed to defy her. Ready for what? What did she expect? The investigators would try to make it around to the ISC

109

offices within a day or so—they were backed up and would send someone when they could.

And then there was the lying. She understood that candor with Estrone and the political establishment had a great deal of flexibility built in. After all, she *served* the public. Her allegiance, though, was to ISC. Never had she even considered lying or being less than forthcoming with her boss. Why now?

The yellow incoming call light blinked, and she came alert with a start, anticipating that it was her mysterious visitor. Checking the ID information, though, her heart dropped. "This is Maggie Renfro."

The voice translated into her thoughts conveyed monotonous routine. "This is Assistant Assessor Calder with the Capital Police Corporation. You requested information on a case?" A pause, apparently waiting for confirmation.

"Yes." It was all she could manage.

"We have confirmed the identity of the victim to be Cheryl Wolford. We are not prepared to release additional information at present."

She wanted to scream at them but immediately saw the futility. What would it accomplish? This guy was just the messenger. He would say what he was allowed to say and nothing she did would change that. She sighed. "Thank you." *Disconnect.*

No sooner had she terminated the connection than the blinking light signaled another incoming call, this one from Fishburn. *Connect.* She summoned up what little professionalism she had left. "Yes, sir?"

"Maggie, are you okay?"

"I've had better days."

"I know. I'm sorry. I know that you're going through a lot right now, but we need to put the package together on the senator. Will you be in the office tomorrow?"

She felt panic rising up from her gut to her chest and she tried to tamp it down. "Have you gotten him scheduled for a work-up?"

He paused before softly responding. "Not yet."

"What is it you want me to say?" She felt a surge of anger and resentment. "I'm not going to make up a story that doesn't hold. If we put out a release that says he's going in for some medical work, I need to know that it's going to happen."

The blowback she expected didn't come. Instead, the response was coated in a sense of resignation. "I know. I'll get on that first thing in the morning."

Her thoughts wandered back to Cheryl. How could she possibly sit there in that office as if nothing was the matter? "I'll try to put together something tonight and transmit it. You should have it by start of business tomorrow."

"So, you're not coming in?" He sounded desperate.

She closed her eyes and clenched her jaw for a moment. "You'll have the release. You do your part." Maggie could sense that her job, her entire career, hung in the balance. "I'll try to make it in."

Chapter 27

Maggie sat on her sofa in the pre-dawn darkness debating whether or not to show up in person for work. The yellow blinking call light interrupted her brooding. The ID showed unknown source. "Okay, who are you?"

"We'll get to that later. Did you read the article?"

She debated internally whether or not to respond. After all, she had tried to access the story but found only a dead end. Discussing it with him, though, seemed to be akin to rewarding very bad behavior. "Let's get to it now. I'm not carrying on a conversation with some stalking perv wired up in his mother's basement." It was the best insult that came to mind on short notice.

A brief yellow tint washed over her display, representing a reluctant sense of mirth. Maggie shook her head in disbelief. Not only was this jerk communicating anonymously with her, he, or it, was invading her emotional control center.

"Well, now, that's a dated response. What makes you think I live with my mother?"

"Just a wild guess."

"And you're sure I'm a perv, huh?"

"I'm sorry, I'm looking for a better term, but that really is the only one that seems to fit."

Another yellow wash of color. "Touché." Silence fell between her and the invisible nameless being.

"Well?" She felt a tinge of confidence, as though she'd scored a point.

"Long story." A brief pause followed by a quick recovery, "But I'll tell you, just not right now. I will say, though, that I mean you no harm and it was never my intention to lurk or stalk or invade your privacy."

"And yet you did a pretty damn good job of it." She took the offensive.

"My apologies. Did you read the article?"

Maggie sighed. Perhaps she'd won the first round. She decided to indulge him/it. "Apology accepted, conditionally. What do I call you?"

"Anything you want."

"Okay. How about *asshole*?" In the quiet that ensued, she got the sense that he was thinking about it, although she couldn't say why.

"Steeno Six."

"I assume there's some significance behind that?"

"Long story."

"Okay, Steeno Six, are you a real person or a really good app?"

"Long story."

"Enough with the 'long story' crap. Simple question— are you or are you not an application, lines of code?" It occurred to her that, while it might have been a simple question, even a good question, it was a stupid one to ask.

"I'm not an application. As for the rest, you'll have to live with 'long story.'"

Chalk up another win. "Fine, for now. As for the article, I tried to access it, but it dead ended."

"Figures."

"Why?"

"Never mind."

"What's that supposed to mean? You invade my system, throw netlinks at me that I'm supposed to read, and then tell me to 'never mind.'"

Maggie perceived a sigh. *Must be a real person. Apps don't sigh… or do they?*

"You work for ISC. The piece was about immigrants."

"So? I don't work on immigration issues. I serve in Senator Estrone's office."

"I know. But your friend, Cheryl, worked on immigration issues."

Red flags went up, and her breath caught in her throat. "What do you know about Cheryl?"

"I'll be in touch." The connection terminated.

Chapter 28

The police won't need to talk to you. They're satisfied with what we gave them. Just thought you'd like to know." Jarvis's voice sounded, at least on the surface, casual and friendly. But there seemed an edge to it.

Maggie thought about it. That should have been good news—no legal involvement. She should be able to get back to work. "That's good. Great. I'll pull myself together tonight and get back to work tomorrow morning." But something gnawed at her. Her best friend was dead, and evidence pointed to a U. S. senator. Not just Cheryl's death, either. He was probably a serial killer and yet the police seemed disinterested, at the very least.

"One other thing. I took the liberty of checking with the subscription service on your new interface, just on the off-chance that it might be a system-wide problem. You'll be happy to know that it looks like they have it sorted out. And as of the end of the month, ISC will pick up the tab on your I/O enhancements. The least we can do for all the hassle you've gone through on it."

That was nice. All the worry about cost for nothing. Still, having an integrated neural system paid for by someone else was a little unnerving, especially with this new ability they had to remotely run diagnostics on her. "Thank you. But you don't need to do that. It's my system and I can afford it."

"Nonsense. You're a valuable asset. No way we're going to let you carry the burden on this. We got it." The tone of his communication left no room for further discussion.

***

Maggie straggled into her office at 8:30, dreading the experience every step of the way. She felt she was being tugged in different directions with no safe haven. Chief of Staff Fishburn was apparently covering up for the senator. He had to be. And the revelation that ISC was now funding her neural system had left her unnerved and unsure of who to trust. On top of all that, this Steeno Six thing was probably lurking around, just waiting for a chance to jump back into her mind. And Cheryl was dead.

Menu, Interface, Connect, Fishburn, priority-routine, security-routine. "Good morning. Sorry I'm running a bit late. Tough night."

"We need to talk in person, privately."

Red flags went up. "About what, specifically?" She wasn't used to blatantly challenging him, but she was in no mood to mince words today.

"I'll explain when you get here. Just hurry." His communication carried a tone of near-panic.

She sighed. "I'll be right there."

Her unwelcome visitor, Steeno Six, took this opportunity to reappear. "Be careful of that guy. He's not going to be any more truthful with you than you are with him."

Exasperated, she plopped down in her chair again. "What is it with you? Why me?"

"Long story. And before you say it, yes, I know you want to hear it. And I'll tell you. But you have to admit, you don't have the time right now. Just listen carefully to the guy and take everything he says with a healthy dose of skepticism."

"Yeah, like I'm doing with you right now. And, just so you know, my I/O is probably monitored. So, if you value secrecy, as you appear to, you might want to rethink this stalking thing." She pulled herself out of the chair and exited her office, entering the corridor that would take her to Fishburn's office. She figured that Steeno Six, having learned that someone was watching him, would back off. She was wrong.

"That's not a worry. My communications with you don't go through your normal neural interface. I have parallel channels established that are outside the security protocol."

"What the hell is that supposed to mean?"

"It means that you and I can chat without being snooped on."

"Do me a favor and at least keep your mouth, or whatever you're using, shut during this meeting. I need to listen to the guy, remember?"

Silence.

Maggie strode into the outer vestibule, nodding perfunctorily to the executive assistant as she made for the door.

In an apparent effort to retain some manner of control, the young man called after her. "He's expecting you."

She rolled her eyes, knocked, and entered. Pulling a chair up to his desk, she eased into it and glared across the table. "So, what's so important that I have to drop everything to meet with you?" The inappropriateness of the question, along with her snarky tone, occurred to her as she watched his face.

But, if he took offense, he didn't show it. His gaze darted from her, to the door, to the window, and back again.

He licked his lips as he idly scratched his neatly trimmed fingernails on the desktop. "If you could, please turn off your neural interface. I need this to be private."

She considered him for a moment before responding. "Just a second." She configured the I/O to block any outgoing signal to Fishburn and initiated the recording app. "There, done." It occurred to her that she looked at him as an enemy. "Now, what is it?"

"I need your assurance that this stays between the two of us."

"You know I can't give that kind of assurance without knowing what it is we're talking about."

He turned and stared out the window, nodding slowly. "Okay. Fair enough. It's about the senator. I was going to confront him this morning and schedule him for a medical work-up. But he called in again. He said he's taking the family out to their summer home in upstate New York."

She almost asked about the possibility of a medical exam up there. Then she reminded herself that his problem wasn't medical. He was a killer, a serial killer. "You want me to draft a release to that effect—taking some time away from the city with his family? Any particular reason you want to cite?"

This would be good. After all, anything Fishburn said at this point would be a lie, just as Steeno had said.

And, speaking of her unknown stalker, he took that opportunity to answer her mental question. "Yes, just like I said. But be careful, don't make too many other assumptions."

She mentally pushed him away and returned her attention to Fishburn.

"Yes. That'll work fine. Just say that the pressure of the STOP legislation and the pace of activity here has worn him down a bit. He needs to spend time with his family and recharge."

Maggie almost broke out laughing but stifled it. "I'll have a draft ready for you by midday. Anything else?"

Fishburn's gaze shifted toward the window. He raised his arm, index finger extended, as if to ask her to wait. He nodded his head, darkness washing over his eyes. With every passing second, his look deteriorated. Whatever was coming in over his neural network didn't seem to be sitting well with him. His eyes widened, and his breath appeared to come quickly. He shook his head as he turned to look at her. "Never mind. Everything's changed."

Chapter 29

Dead?" The word hung in the air. Maggie stared at the chief of staff. "The entire family?"

Fishburn nodded, even as he shook his head, creating the surreal image of a man suddenly overwhelmed by events. "The security detachment didn't provide any details." He stood, crept over to the window, and stared into the gray morning. "I need to think."

Maggie's head spun from the effect of the bombshell. Five minutes ago, she was worried about how to deal with the possibility that Senator Estrone was a serial killer. But now it seemed somehow less important. Not that she was sorry he was dead. Good riddance and, no matter how he died, it wasn't gruesome enough to make up for Cheryl. Still, his entire family?

Fishburn interrupted her thoughts. "We need to get out in front of this." He turned and faced her, his eyes focused and his mouth drawn into a tight line.

"What the hell do you mean *get out in front of this*? This will have legs of its own. Unless security is going to sit on it for a while, this will flood the network. Anything we have to say will be lost in the noise." What she really needed was to connect with Jarvis, her boss. She wondered if he already knew about it. She decided to regroup and buy some time. "Sorry. That was uncalled for. Let me get back to my office and start piecing some things together."

He nodded. "I'll call ISC and fill them in while you work on a statement."

Maggie started to argue. For reasons she couldn't explain, even to herself, she didn't want Fishburn inserted between her and her boss.

But Steeno challenged her. "Don't worry about it and don't take any of this at face value."

Would you get out of my head? The last thing she needed was a three-way argument that included someone or something that she wasn't sure was even real.

The disembodied internal voice fell silent and Fishburn continued, "We'll probably need to create a simulconnect conference and bridge to videosync, possibly with feed from upstate New York, if I can lean on security. We need to pry as much information from them as possible."

What's the point? The senator and the serial killer were both dead. They just happened to be the same person. With regard to the killer, this marked the end of a string of murders and had nothing to do with her or ISC, other than the obvious—Cheryl had been his final victim. As for the senator's part, well, Corporate Conclave would make an interim appointment to fill the role pending auditions and creation of an acceptable slate of candidates. An election would decide the eventual successor. Nothing they could do would impact any of these processes one way or the other.

Maggie sighed and mentally gave up trying to make sense of it. "I'll get started." She stood and turned toward the door. Despite what Fishburn had said, though, she knew that calling Jarvis would have to be the first order of business.

"Hold off. We need to talk first." That voice again.

***

"No way." She sat on a composite plastic bench on the Mall, struggling to keep her words internal. Her mounting

121

frustration with this Steeno Six thing was wearing her down, though.

"I get it. You're caught in what seems an untenable situation. All I'm suggesting is to think this over before you lay all your cards on the table with your boss."

What struck her most about the voice, as she had come to think of it, was that it had no real audible characteristics. Most interneural communication ended up presenting with some semblance of a real voice. But Steeno's, for some reason, manifested as thought only.

"You're going to have to do better than that. If I'm going to listen to you, I want to know who or what you are, just for starters." She paused for adding, "And don't give me the 'long-story' bullshit."

The response came after a moment of awkward silence. "It is a long story," he quickly added, "but, okay, we'll talk about it. You might find it easier to hear it with a drink… or four."

"If you're as advanced as you present, why not just upload a netfeed abstract for me. It should register within a minute."

Another awkward silence. "No. We can't use the network as you know it. Everything that touches it is collected, filtered, analyzed, aggregated, and synthesized. What I have to tell you is for you alone. In order to do that, I have to speak directly to your mind without going through your interface."

"Not possible. My system blocks any attempt to shunt around the interface."

Maggie perceived the cynical laugh. "Yeah. Right. Let's get to your node. You can grab a glass of whatever it is you drink these days—you're going to need it. I'll tell you the story."

Chapter 30

Okay. Unload." Maggie sat back on the sofa with a glass of Victorian Vineyards Merlot—real wine acquired at no small cost. She stared at the front window, her eyes unfocused. "The suspense is killing me."

A moment of mental silence descended and then the voice, or the idea of a voice, began. "As for who I am, I told you—I am Steeno Six. What I am is a more complex question."

"Enough with the bullshit. I'm sick of these delaying tactics. Apparently, you are a sophisticated guy, technologically speaking, of course, assuming you are a guy—"

The voice interrupted, conveying its own tone of impatience bordering on rudeness. "Do you want to make snide remarks or would you like to listen? If you want answers, then you need to shut up."

Maggie started to hurl a crude retort but figured this would be an opportune point to back off and try to learn something. "Very well. Continue."

"A long time ago, fifty years by your reckoning, I was pretty much like you except that I was male. My name was Harold Chasteen. When I was in school, the kids called me Steeno. And since I was the sixth of eight children in my family, I adopted the name Steeno Six."

In spite of herself, Maggie blurted out, "So, what, you're this sixty- or seventy-year-old perv?"

Silence.

She sighed. "Sorry. Go on."

"A couple of things about me—first, I was smart, very smart. Second, by the time I was in my late teens, I contracted a terminal disease. It's virtually unknown today, what with nanogenetic splicing and prenatal cryobiotic filtering. At the time, though, Lherospatic Cellular Hyrospanyl was rare but unfailingly lethal. It essentially devoured all neural connections, eventually destroying my body's ability to function. By the time I was twenty-five, I had reached end stage. Technology at the time was able to keep my bodily functions running, albeit at a very basic level. I would have lived another year, perhaps, although 'living' is hardly what I would have called it.

"And as I said, I was smart. It took me several years of intensive research and experimentation, but eventually I uncovered the secret of separating my consciousness from my body. What you are conversing with now is what is left of my spirit, soul, or whatever you want to call it. My body is long since dead."

Maggie sat stunned, trying to get her mind around what the voice had told her. Her first reaction was that she was being played. Still, this thing, whatever it was, seemed to have abilities that current technology lacked. "Assuming you're telling the truth, why me?"

"Long story." Before she could challenge the obvious delaying tactic, he followed up. "But I will tell you that it's not about you personally." He fell silent for a moment before continuing softly. "Existing on the network, you might say that I have a lot of spare time on my hands. I spent the first thirty years bouncing around trying to keep up with the changes in the network. When I first migrated, what was then known as the Internet was in its death throes. We can talk more about that later, but, for now, with the emergence of what you now call the network, I was able to find my place, as it were. That allowed me time to pay more attention to the world outside—what you mistakenly think of as the 'real world.' Believe me, what you perceive around you is anything but real."

"Yeah, they made a movie about that a hundred years ago. Everyone just lived in this huge application that masked the true nature of the world." She had seen a feed of this film on the subnet.

"I know. I've seen it. But that's not what I mean. Everything you see is as you see it. The people you see around you are real. I'm talking about what happens and why it happens. Surely you, of all people, understand that the general population is fed a carefully constructed version of reality. What's really happening is quite another story."

"That still doesn't tell me why you've invaded my life."

"Yes, back to the point. One of the interests that I've developed is in how people are distributed across the world. As we can both agree, that is a dynamic function, changing all the time. An interesting part of this phenomenon is immigration… and you happen to work for the largest immigration facilitator in the world."

"But I have almost nothing to do with immigration. I am the public relations director for a political actor." She reminded herself that the senator was no longer among the living. "Well, I did."

"Yes. Senator Estrone is dead, and so your employment future, while not doomed, is certainly in question. And I know that you're not involved in the day-to-day immigration practices or, for that matter, the policies." He fell silent for a moment. "But your friend, Cheryl, was."

Despite her best effort, Maggie could not remain silent. "What do you know about Cheryl?" A startling thought occurred to her—was Steeno Six Cheryl's mysterious man? Had he lured her to her death? And then a more sickening notion crossed her mind—could this thing, this Steeno Six, read her mind? Could he know what she was thinking at this very moment? She panicked. If he was inside her head, then she could think of no real defense. After all, he would know about any defense she dreamed up.

Steeno Six interrupted her frantic mental ramblings. "Not much, other than the fact that she worked on immigration data that supported policy decisions at ISC."

The response took Maggie aback. Unless Steeno was putting on a great act, he picked up on her alarm. She searched for the right response to keep the conversation going without betraying her panic. "Why are you interested in immigration?" It seemed a logical question.

"As much as I'd love to continue this conversation, you really should get back to work. Your senator's dead. His chief of staff is flailing around waiting for you to come up with some kind of magic netfeed release that will keep the wolves at bay. And you haven't even spoken to your boss."

Maggie had to admit that he was right. She'd left her office and holed up in her apartment, guzzling wine all afternoon. Fishburn didn't concern her so much, but her boss, Jarvis, was another story. "Okay. But you're not off the hook. We're going to continue this conversation later."

"Count on it."

Chapter 31

*M*enu, *communication, Jarvis, priority-high, security-high, connect.* Maggie closed her eyes and hoped that her absence had not raised too many flags for her boss.

"Good afternoon. Tough day, huh?" Jarvis sounded tired.

"You might say that. Sorry about being unavailable. This whole thing hit me pretty hard. I'm trying to come up with some kind of netfeed release, but nothing seems right." It was the truth.

From the tone of the response, she could almost envision Jarvis shrugging. "I wouldn't worry too much about it. The newsfeed will filter through security and that's really all that will matter. Some drivel, you know, tragedy strikes… our hearts go out… that kind of output will do fine."

"I haven't heard any details on what happened." She hoped that he'd offer some enlightenment without her asking.

"Not much coming out right now, a few random details here and there. If I had to guess, though, I'd say murder-suicide, especially given your suspicions about Estrone. Which, I might add, seem to have been accurate."

Relief began to set in. Maggie could almost see a clear path through the day. "I'll get the release done shortly. What's next?"

"The usual—the Executive Cabinet meets this evening to appoint an interim. The Conclave will conduct auditions and prepare a slate of potentials within the week. After that, the Congress of the Electorate will vote, and you'll have a new senator from the great state of New York."

"Any thoughts on the interim?" Not that she really cared.

"I don't know. Maybe Fishburn. Probably. After all, he's there and that would be the least disruptive for the near term. You have any problems with that?"

"No, not really. Well, other than the obvious—who's going to replace him as chief of staff?"

"For now, probably no one. The special election won't take more than a week. I think we can go without a chief of staff for that long. Besides, it'll make your job easier—no more middle man."

She almost laughed out loud. Fishburn being a middle man was the least of her problems. Juggling the dual reporting—ISC and the senate leadership—that's where the problems occurred. And that wasn't going to change, no matter who ended up in the senator's seat. "I need to get on that release. Let me know if there's anything else you need me to do."

"Have a good evening." And the connection terminated.

The green ready light illuminated, and Maggie turned her attention to the task at hand.

"You handled that well."

"For the love of God, would you please stop sneaking up on me." Maggie had a nagging fear that she was going to get her transmission modes mixed up. She could 'think' to Steeno but had to convert her thoughts to audible signals through her interface to everyone else.

"How would you suggest I do it?" She sensed the sarcasm embedded in the question.

"Never mind. I'm kind of busy. What do you want?" Despite her confrontational response, she was conflicted.

She did need to finish the release. But she was also more than anxious to hear more from Steeno.

"Nothing right now. Well, other than, like I said, you handled it well. A word of advice—take it or leave it—don't open up to anyone. Things are not as they seem and it's far too complicated to go into right now. Just do your job and, to the extent you can, play dumb."

The anger built quickly. "I'm not some mindless, helpless female bimbo."

"Never said you were. In fact, if I thought that about you, I wouldn't be talking to you. But, between the two of us, you will be a lot safer if those around you see you that way."

"What do you mean by *safer*?"

"These are complex issues. What you see, what seems apparent to you, often masks other realities. As the layers are peeled back, power players, those who prefer the anonymity of the shadows, grow nervous. They are not beyond resorting to drastic measures."

Waves of nausea swept over Maggie, her vision dimmed, and she struggled to catch her breath. "What?" She could think of nothing else to say.

"Later, when we have more time. For now, get on that release and finish up for the day. We'll talk tonight."

***

Menu, communication, Fishburn, priority-medium, security-medium, connect.

The stress came across clearly. "Maggie." He sounded like he wanted to say more but stopped.

She swiveled around in her chair and stared out the window of her apartment. "I've forwarded a draft release. I thought about it and figured that, at this point, all we can really say is that we're shocked and saddened. I assume we want the actual news to come from SecFeed."

He paused before responding, but his stress seemed to subside. "Yes, that's a good idea. I'll look at the draft, and we can get it out this evening."

"Anything else for me before I shut down for the night?"

"Maybe. I got a call from Mister Jarvis a few minutes before you connected. It looks like I might end up filling the senator's position until they find a permanent replacement. Not sure whether you were aware of that or not, but I did want to let you know and also tell you that I want you to stay on. I hope you're okay with that."

Maggie smirked internally, making sure that she kept it isolated inside. "I'd be honored, Mister Fishburn. And, who knows, perhaps you'll end up filling the seat permanently."

The laugh came across as nervous. "No, no. Not my thing. I'll do the best I can for a few days, but I prefer a little less exposure. With any amount of luck, I can slide back into the chief of staff slot."

After she severed the connection, she paused to reflect on Fishburn's comments. She would have thought he aspired to the now-vacant seat. But Steeno's words echoed through her mind—*things are not what they seem.*

Chapter 32

The conversation with Fishburn terminated, Maggie turned her thoughts to dinner. With all that had gone on during the day, eating had been shuffled to the side. She took a mental inventory of her supply closet, but nothing sounded good. What she wanted—what she really needed—was some serious alone time with Roberto.

As the thought crossed her mind, her internal alarms went on. Steeno seemed to be always lurking in her head. Somehow sharing her intimate secrets with him didn't at all appeal to her. *Wait, what if he already knows?* Maybe he had been hanging out and watching everything she and her perfect lover had done. *Shit!*

But if he was present, he gave no sign. She settled back on the sofa and closed her eyes, trying to discern any evidence of the intruder's presence. Nothing. Her desire for physical contact with Roberto had morphed into the need for more answers from Steeno. Maggie had a sinking feeling that her love life was in the midst of collapse unless she could sort this mess out.

The blinking yellow light on her interface signaled an incoming communication. She checked the originating node ID and sighed. *Connect.* "Good afternoon, Mister Arandon. What may I help you with today?"

The tone was unusually sober. "News is just starting to filter out about Estrone. You okay to answer a few questions or maybe have a prepared statement?"

"Only that our office is shocked and—"

"Yeah, I know, shocked and saddened. I'm hearing some rumblings that it was an assassination. Can you confirm that?"

Maggie sat up, her eyes widened. She'd looked at the initial information feed and there was nothing there to suggest a hit. She considered probing for information but reconsidered, knowing how unprincipled this guy was. "You need to check your sources, Nick."

"So, what's the official line?"

"You know as well as I do the official line will come from SecFeed, not this office."

"Ah yes, SecFeed, the corporate governance security apparatus. I'm sure they'll be completely honest and forthcoming."

"Sarcasm doesn't become you, Arandon. Whether you like it or not, information about these types of things don't come from PR people. You'll just have to tolerate getting your answers on this from the same place I do."

"Nothing, huh?"

"I didn't say 'nothing.' I said that our office is shocked and saddened. As other information becomes available, I will pass it on. Until then, you'll have to learn a little patience."

"You available for dinner?"

Maggie almost choked. "Give it up. I don't know anything. And even if I did, I wouldn't be so stupid as to share it with you. And there just isn't a world in which I'd go to dinner with you."

A brief pause preceded a subdued response. "You might want to reconsider at some point. I may have something for you."

She so wanted to hurl an insult and disconnect. But something stopped her, and she settled for a curt delaying tactic. "Yes, well, I'll take that under advisement. But not tonight. Have a good evening, Mister Arandon."

As Maggie disconnected, she noticed the now-familiar shimmer in her display. "Ah, I see you've arrived, Mister Steeno."

"Just Steeno, please. And yes, I saw that you were busy, so I stayed away—out of earshot, as it were."

"Yeah, right. You're the perfect gentleman, respecting my privacy and such."

"I try."

"I was being sarcastic."

"I know."

She shook her aching head. These ambiguous, contentious conversations grated on her. "That was Nick Arandon, Freedom Network of America." She wondered, in passing, why she felt the need to share this.

Steeno's reaction was muted. "I know of him."

"What do you know of him?"

"What's to know? He's a mouthpiece on display. He's paid to look good and spout the company line. Beyond that, he looks out for himself, which makes him pretty much like every other human being."

"You seem to have a pretty dim view of humanity." She mused that this reflected her own views, to a large extent.

"Half a century has given me a lot of time to observe people. Just when you think they can't get any worse, someone surprises you."

Maggie sighed. At least this guy, or whatever it was, didn't hide his feelings. "So, you didn't say—how do you know Arandon?" She quickly added, "And don't give me the *long story* crap."

"No. It's not a long story. I connected with someone at FNA a few months back and they mentioned Arandon in passing. He was, and is, no concern of mine, so I didn't press the matter. That's it. Everything else I know is only by reputation."

"Who were you talking to over there?"

"Later. Right now, I'm concerned about you."

Maggie laughed aloud. "That's just what I need, a disembodied spirit who's worried about me."

Steeno fell silent and a profound sense of worry filled the void with Maggie. "Why are you worried about me? I can take care of myself." She felt stupid saying it. In fact, she felt more than a little self-conscious carrying on a conversation with a ghost or soul or spirit, whatever it happened to be. Or maybe it was just some pervy teenager who'd assembled a rather sophisticated technical toolbox. She waited for the retort to her thought, but nothing came.

When the response came, it was tied to her question rather than her rambling suspicions. "Yes, I'm sure that under normal circumstances, you can take care of yourself. But I assure you, Maggie, these events are anything but normal."

"If you're talking about communicating with you, I agree that it's beyond strange."

His response came slow and deliberate. "There is that. And I agree that I owe you a lot more explanation, which I intend to provide. But I am referring to the chain of events that involve the senator's death."

"Okay, I'll bite. Is there something about all this that I need to know tonight?"

"No. Not right this instant."

"Good, then, maybe we can pass the time by you telling me what's going on with you."

Maggie sensed more than heard a sigh. "You're right."

Chapter 33

I told you what I am, including what I used to be. You asked me why I connected with you. And that's a fair question. But there is more background needed first." Steeno paused and Maggie could almost feel him, or it, thinking.

She resisted the urge to comment, instead letting the silence settle. From the tone of his voice—well, communication would be a more accurate word since he didn't really have a voice—he needed to do this at his own pace.

"A half-century is a long time. I spent the first ten years trying to survive as what we then knew as the Internet self-destructed. The network you know today bears little resemblance to its ancestor. As the old net crumbled into itself, there were fewer and fewer places to hide. Ultimately, I took advantage of the chaos and commandeered space in large government data storage facilities. I learned how to move around their security arrangements and even how to appropriate funds to pay for ancillary services without drawing attention.

"As the end approached, I migrated and settled into what we then called the dark web. Even as the visible net deteriorated, the dark web grew and flourished, out of sight and free of regulation. In fact, this hidden environment provided the fertile ground for what you have today, albeit in a very different form."

As the quiet once again settled over her mind, Maggie interjected, "How is our network different? I'm vaguely familiar with what you call the Internet, but I confess I don't know much about the technical workings."

"The Internet, or web as we called it, was a series of networks that had millions of file servers, each having a specific address. Users could download files, in different formats, from the servers. Most started out providing text files and some graphics. That grew to the hosting of interactive databases and ultimately streaming content and commerce. But at its most basic level, it was still just a series of file servers connected over wired and wireless networks.

"What you know as the network today is a shell composed of particles that can be turned off and on using nanosimultech charging. Addressing is accomplished through probabilistic quantum manipulation, which produces a confidence level approaching one hundred percent." He paused briefly. "Maybe this is too much information."

Maggie chuckled. "Maybe."

"Why you? To be honest, it's not really about you. It's about immigration. But it didn't start there. As I said, fifty years is a long time to just hang out and zip around the network, especially given that, at least as far as I know, I am immortal. It feels weird to think that way, even after all these years. But it's true. I have grown, evolved, and flourished over the years with no sign of degradation. Perhaps the end will come upon me sooner or later, but for now, it is not in sight.

"Anyway, my first interest in this area wasn't immigration but rather how the people of the world were distributed. And it was nothing more than idle interest, something to fill the nanoseconds.

"And then, about ten years ago, I noticed that populations were beginning to shift. Cultures were integrating. Some dissolved and some new ones popped up. The changing climate drove much of this as people migrated in from the shores and away from the great deserts of the world. Some countries opened their borders and welcomed refugees. Others, like the United States, tried to wall themselves off from the world.

"And this is when ISC first came on the scene. Your country, as xenophobic as it tried to be, needed the influx of workers coming from other parts of the world. But rather than opening borders in a transparent way, the corporations wrested control of the country and began to manage the immigration process to their advantage. And to be fair, this does make a lot of sense given your culture.

"But this is where things get a little fuzzy. Over the past five years, ISC has facilitated at least five million immigrants per year. Not an overwhelming number given your population of seven hundred million and a near zero growth rate from natural birth. But several things didn't add up. First, the immigrant destinations, large manufacturing regions, are not showing growth rates that reflect the number of incoming people. There are some increases, to be sure. But the numbers are consistently off by nearly thirty percent. Which begs the question—where does this missing thirty percent end up?

"The second indicator that something is amiss is productivity ratios. They have fallen steadily over the past year as your manufacturing infrastructure deteriorates. And yet the orders for greater numbers of immigrants continues to grow. That flies in the face of all logic."

An image flashed before Maggie's eyes—Cheryl holding a glass of wine and lamenting nearly the same point. "Wait a minute. A friend of mine was mulling over the productivity issue. She even made the same points you made. This can't be a coincidence."

"No. It's not. Cheryl was smart."

"What's that supposed to mean? Did you connect with her too?" Maggie's anger grew.

"Not in the sense that I'm talking to you. I left what we used to call 'breadcrumbs' for her—bits of information and data that would find their way into her field of view. She took them without question and ran with them. Had she not died, I suspect that she would have brought enlightenment on the subject."

"Tell me this doesn't have anything to do with her death. She was killed by a serial killer. She was murdered by Senator Estrone."

"Perhaps. And that is unfortunate... and tragic, of course. Truthfully, though, I haven't looked into her death."

"What? You were using her and then, when she was no longer available, you just discarded her and moved on to your next resource? Is that the way it works with you?" Maggie felt a gnawing sense that this *thing*, this Steeno, was no better than a corporate leader—use people until they were no longer valuable and then toss them in the nearest refuse disposal unit.

His response was muted, bordering on respectful. "I've seen a lot in my time, more than you can imagine. A lot of good people die before their time. People who do evil, despicable things sometimes live long and full lives. Justice is an illusion, a cruel hoax perpetrated by those in power. After a while, you simply accept it as the way things are." He added, after a brief pause, "I am truly sorry about Cheryl. She seemed a good person."

Chapter 34

Maggie had barely settled into her office when the amber light began blinking. The connection node ID confirmed what she had expected. *Connect.* "Good morning, Mister Jarvis." The greeting was strictly perfunctory. The morning had come far too early, given that she and Steeno had talked well into the early morning hours.

"Morning, Maggie. You see the latest from SecFeed?"

"I noticed the banner before I left the apartment. I was planning on spending some time with the packet once I got situated here."

"I can save you a little time. Nothing new or unexpected. Murder-suicide. You had it nailed. I guess he felt things closing in and decided to go out on his own terms. It's sad that he felt he had to take his family with him, though."

Maggie reflected back on her suspicions about the senator. Mostly, she kicked herself for not taking a stronger stand with Cheryl. Maybe things would have turned out differently. "Yeah, sad."

"You okay?"

"Yeah. Mostly, it's Cheryl, though. Kind of hard with all of this happening at once." She knew that time was really the only thing that was going to help.

"I understand. Things around here are subdued too. Look, if you need to talk about it, feel free to connect me in. You don't have to carry this alone."

His sensitivity summoned up a spike of guilt in Maggie for lying to her boss. "Thank you. I'm okay for today. I just need some time to think this through."

"We're planning a memorial get-together for her this weekend. I hope that you'll attend."

Maggie closed her eyes and shook her head, actions she was sure would not translate through her neural connection. "Forward the details. I'll be there."

"Done. Oh, by the way, I wanted to confirm that Fishburn will fill the seat temporarily. No big surprises there. The Conclave is conducting auditions later this week and the slate should go to the Congress of Voters by Monday."

"I spoke with Fishburn yesterday. He said that he wasn't interested in the position on a permanent basis. That kind of surprised me."

Jarvis chuckled. "Just as well. Anything else going on down there?"

Maggie almost mentioned Arandon's wild assassination theory but for some inexplicable reason, felt the need to hold that back. "Nothing that won't keep. We put out the first net release last evening, but it received almost no attention. I figure everyone's focused on the SecFeed packets."

"As it should be. I have to run. Seriously, Maggie, if you need anything, just call. Talk to you later." The connection ended.

She half-expected a snide comment from Steeno. All she got was a green ready light and the ambient readouts. Had she not known better, Maggie would have sworn that all was quiet and right with the world.

***

"Congratulations on the appointment." Maggie started to qualify the statement based on the fact that the chief of staff's ascendency was strictly temporary but held her tongue.

Fishburn leaned back in the chair, his hands laced behind his head and a smile on his face. "Thank you." But for all of the casual pleasure he exuded, something seemed off. His eyes darted around the room as though he expected something to jump out of the walls and attack him. The smile seemed forced onto the lips that were drawn into a tight line.

"Do you have anything else for me to take care of now?"

"No. We did the release last night. Just let SecFeed carry the load from here on out. Senate leadership is debating the wisdom of a tribute ceremony for him. My guess is that they're going to relegate any mention of him into the subnets." Fishburn shook his head and stared out the window. "You think you know someone and then...."

On the way back to her office, Steeno made an appearance. "Do you have some time? We need to talk."

Chapter 35

Before you get started, I need to ask you something. Sometimes you seem to be constantly hovering in my mind. Other times, well, I don't get a sense of you being there. What's the deal here?" Maggie tried to balance between the sense of violation she felt from Steeno and not alienating him completely, although she couldn't think of a good reason not to.

"What do you mean?"

"I mean, are you always lurking here, or do you go away sometimes?"

"That's a complicated question. And before you lash out, I'll try to explain. I am not a human, at least in the way you think about it. I'm not even really a thing. The best analogy I can think of is that I look kind of like a distributed system. Parts of me are scattered all over. I use the system infrastructure to coordinate different activities."

"I get that, but where is your brain or your central control unit or whatever it is that manages this coordination?"

"It doesn't work that way. Each activity manages itself and communicates with the other nodes. I exist both as a system and as a collection of semi-autonomous processing units at the subatomic level. But maybe what you want to know is whether I am constantly aware of you or whether you are out of my consciousness."

"Let's start with that."

"The short answer is that I mute, if that's the right term, input from given sources at different times. And that includes you. Sometimes I pay attention. Other times I sense you there but ignore you. For example, I know that you use a personal relationship service app—Roberto, I think—and I generally know what goes on with those. But I've never observed the interaction with you."

Maggie's response was a mix of rage and fear. "What the hell else do you know about me?"

"Nothing that anyone who monitors the network couldn't easily discover. Even in my day, we all knew that any expectation of privacy was delusional."

"And so, you take it on yourself to shatter my illusions?"

"No. I'm taking it on myself to get answers to my questions. I selected you because of your position and the situation in which you find yourself. I thought perhaps we might find common cause. You can choose to help or not. And if you decide not to, then I will leave you to your life." Steeno paused before adding, "So, what's it going to be Mags? Are you in or not?"

"My name is Maggie, not Mags. And I'm thinking about it."

"While you're mulling it over, maybe you can answer a question for me. Did you happen to download the feed from that link I gave you?"

"What, the one about immigrants? If that's what you're talking about, no. By the time I accessed the feed, it was gone." Maggie regretted not looking at it sooner. "Why didn't you archive a copy in some of that storage you steal?"

His response gave a hint of emotion—embarrassment. "Point taken."

"You should be able to get it, though, if you contact whoever developed the piece. That is, if you're talking to someone other than me."

"That's the problem. I can't find him."

"What do mean you can't find him? Is he missing or something?"

"His name was Anthony Soldani and he worked over at FNA. That's where I first connected. They fired him and then it was like he fell off the edge of the earth."

Maggie thought back to a past conversation. "I think I heard about him from a journalist over there, Nick Arandon. So, what, they fired his boss at the same time?"

"I didn't know that. That makes it even more suspicious. The firing was not kept that quiet, but it happened very quickly."

"What was in the article that was so interesting?"

"It was the first time that I'd seen any inquiry into how the excess immigration numbers were distributed geographically. Soldani seemed to think that a portion filtered into the southern states, although that made no sense. Those areas are all economic freedom zones—no regulation or taxation—but they do collect data from the enterprises. So, by all rights, the numbers should show up down there just as they would any place else."

She had heard of these zones but knew little about them. After all, ISC didn't service them, as far as she had heard. The whole premise behind regions like this was that there was excess labor capacity. Immigration made no sense for them. "Soldani offer any ideas on how or why?"

Steeno's response came across short and clipped. "No. Nothing."

"Then what do you want with me?"

"As odd as it may sound to you, having someone to talk to about this helps. I can investigate and analyze but you're smart. You ask good questions. And remember, Mags, the answers we get are only as good as the questions we ask."

"Don't call me Mags."

The response came across as something between a smile and a laugh.

"And, as far as questions go, I'm all out of them tonight. I just want to eat, have a glass of wine, and get some sleep." She omitted the other desire—some serious alone time with….

"Sorry. It's been a long time since I've had to worry about food or rest. Have a good evening." After a brief pause, he added, "Oh, and by the way in case you're wondering, Roberto isn't just a pleasure app. He collects and forwards information about you, which is then sold on the personal data market. Be careful what you say to him."

The words chilled Maggie as she remembered the discussion with Roberto about Cheryl.

Chapter 36

Maggie had been to memorial services before, so nothing she saw surprised her. But no matter how many she attended, it never got easier. The worst part, of course, was the life-like interactive avatar of the deceased.

The concept of virtual meetings went back over a century, longer if you considered the old teleconferences and audio conferences which made their debut in the last half of the twentieth century. But the striking, quantum leap in these gatherings occurred when technology began to apply all of the information and data available on individuals to create virtual versions of them. Not virtual in the sense that they simply had an avatar. No, the applications had learned to create versions of people who could freely interact with no real-time input from the individual.

And so it was that Maggie stared at the re-creation of Cheryl Wolford sitting in the center of a circle of avatars belonging to connected attendees. Her friend smiled as she gazed around at her friends and associates who had come to pay their respects. "Thanks, everyone. This really means a lot to me."

Rather than cheering her, the realistic Cheryl thing gave Maggie the creeps. Her best friend was dead. Period. Nothing meant anything to her any more. The smile was bullshit. The body, the real one, had been vaporized, the elements returned to the universe from whence they came. Nothing remained except memories, and, at the moment, only bad ones. *I should have tried harder. I could have stopped her. I know I could have.*

Maggie's gaze wandered from avatar to avatar—anything to avoid looking at the image of Cheryl. Representations of people at these gatherings had changed remarkably over the past decade. Individuals used to select their own avatars and customize them to suit their preferences. Now VirtMeet, the meeting app, managed the process of image generation. The body of code analyzed each person's data and monitored their speech and internal biological systems to adjust appearances live. The result was an appearance that closely resembled a person's self-perception updated moment to moment.

Except for Jarvis. His image was indistinct, ambiguous. The avatar displayed no emotion and the physical features were poorly defined, as if it were a generic figure. He sat back from the circle and watched, respectful and patient.

After a moment of awkward silence, Jerome, from the ISC Systems Integration office, started the conversation. "Hi Cheryl." The avatar appeared younger and with more hair and a trimmer waistline than the real man. "I didn't know you that well. But I do remember the time that your interface adaptor froze right in the middle of a cross-sectional data download. You were in a panic because your boss wanted the information by the end of the day. When I was able to bypass the node controller and finish the download, you bought me a cup of coffee. That was really nice." His voice trailed off as he finished, as if he wanted to say more but was unsure.

Others offered their memories in turn, each commenting on Cheryl's kindness and humanity. And, with each recollection, the Cheryl thing responded, nodding, smiling, and thanking the speaker by name.

Maggie shuddered with revulsion. This entire scene was antithetical to what Cheryl was. The system, this gathering, these people—or at least their representation—made her out to be some kind of gentle, smiling, peaceful soul. That was wrong. She was lonely and longed for someone in her life. She obsessed over details in her job, often to the point of being obnoxious. And she drank a lot, an awful lot. No one spoke about watching her puke on the bathroom floor. None of these avatars recounted Cheryl's planned adventure into the world of real people romance. Nobody here even knew her.

And then it was Maggie's turn. *Why didn't you listen, Cheryl. What the hell were you thinking? You stupid....* Fortunately, her thoughts didn't find a voice. "I miss you. All the times we had." She searched her memories for some cute anecdote that would suffice—something to get her through this miserable process. "I remember how you obsessed over that immigration data, you know, the problem with the productivity. You got so worked up over nothing. Always wanting to do the perfect job."

She started to continue but noticed a faint darkening of Jarvis's avatar, as if a small, thin cloud briefly obscured the sun shining on him. As quickly as it came, it disappeared, and he once again took on the flat affect.

Spooked by the change in her boss's image, Maggie brought her remarks to a close. "I miss you, Cheryl."

One by one, the others added their pieces. When silence fell over the group, the system avatar—the image of a regal, goddess-like woman with flowing silver hair, moved the ceremony to its final stage. "Thank you all. Cheryl, do you have any closing thoughts for your friends?"

The image sitting and smiling in the center of the circle, folded her hands in her lap. "Yes. First, thank you all for coming today. And please know that I am happy, at peace. My new home is quiet. There are others here to give me company. I will always remember and value your friendship, all of you. Be at peace." And her image faded to nothing.

As the avatars faded offline, Maggie noticed Jarvis staring at her. But rather than gently fade as the others had done, it clicked off with the immediacy of a quantum switch.

Chapter 37

Why don't you ask him yourself?" Maggie sat in the semi-dark of the late afternoon shadows in her living room, alone with Steeno.

He paused before responding, as if thinking it through. "The last person I *spoke* with at FNA disappeared without a trace. You, on the other hand, have regular communications with Nick."

"And somehow it's okay to talk to me. You're worried about Arandon's safety but I'm somehow dispensable?"

"No. I didn't mean it that way. Part of it is that I trust you. I have no such faith in anyone at FNA. Don't get me wrong, they're no better or worse than the people at any other such organization. They look out for their own best interest and anything else is secondary. But you've repeatedly shown the tendency to differentiate right from wrong."

"Don't blow smoke up my skirt. You're asking me to wander into the snake pit. If anyone there is in danger because they're looking into something, then inserting myself into that discussion puts me at risk."

He hesitated a moment before responding. "I understand your concern. But keep in mind, Arandon has already tried to engage you on the subject. He brought it up, if you recall."

She had to admit that Steeno was right. Nick had broached the subject of his co-worker who was suddenly fired. And the last few times she'd spoken with him, he seemed subdued, almost frightened. "So, what is it exactly that you want to know?"

"All traces of the information feed that Soldani developed vanished along with him. Well, all network-compatible traces. But he was an odd one, very traditional in that he liked to have what he called *hard copy*. He was forever printing things out on paper. Maybe he printed a copy of his work. If we could lay our hands on that, it would at least give us a starting point."

"So, what? You think that Arandon may have just accidentally stumbled on, what did you call it, a *hard copy*?"

"Wouldn't hurt to ask."

"Like hell it wouldn't hurt. It could get me killed."

***

Maggie eyed Arandon with a mix of curiosity and concern. His normally coifed hair was disheveled and greasy. His eyes, reddened and puffy, gave evidence of more than one sleepless night. She resisted the urge to make a snarky remark about his appearance.

"So why the sudden interest, if you don't mind my asking?" He stared at his coffee cup, from which he'd not taken a single drink.

"Just curious. You seemed stuck on it last week and I've never known you to get stuck on anything."

He paused for a moment before continuing. "What do you hear about the senator's demise?" He shifted the direction of the conversation.

Maggie decided to play along as best she could. "Probably same thing that you're hearing out of SecFeed—not much. He died along with his family. The investigation continues. Blah, blah, blah."

"That's coming from SecFeed, but I heard a different story. I heard assassination—a professional hit."

She struggled to keep from rolling her eyes. He had no idea how far off the mark he was. "Your source?"

He gazed at her as though trying to read something more into her question. "No one source. I heard it from several people. You know, hushed whispers, that kind of thing."

"Yeah, I know. It's called speculation and gossip. And I understand that it sells copy. But, seriously, tell me you're not really sucked in by that kind of drivel."

He shrugged. "You have a better explanation for an entire family dying at one time?"

"There are lots of possible explanations. But I don't have any details so anything I told you would be no better than what you're spouting." She desperately wanted to scream at him—*the sonofabitch was a serial killer. When he felt the world closing in on him, he retreated to the country and offed himself and everyone around him.*

But it occurred to her that she had not seen or heard any confirmation, or even a hint, regarding the serial killings. Surely the security apparatus had figured this out already. She got a sinking feeling that this may turn out to be one of those things that are just buried and never again see the light of day.

Arandon intruded upon her internal conflict. "What was it you wanted to know about Soldani?"

"You said he was working on something right before he got canned. Any idea what it was?"

"Why do you want to know?" He eyed her suspiciously.

"Isn't this where we started the conversation?" But the awareness that she wanted something from him forced her to temper the sarcasm. "I'm just curious. The senator's office is always concerned about immigration issues, as you know. If there's something out there that could help inform our efforts and direction, it would just be nice to know." As shallow as it sounded, it wasn't that far from the truth, well, except for the fact that she wasn't asking as a part of her duty to the senator, or rather the interim senator.

He considered her for a moment before looking away. "I don't know specifically. He and I didn't exactly run in the same circles. He was a researcher and I was more involved in the presentation of material."

Maggie probed. "But it had something to do with immigration?"

"Maybe."

She paused before she took the plunge. There would be no going back once she waded into this one. "Any way you could get your hands on his material?"

His head snapped around and he locked gazes with her. "You have any idea what you're asking? First, why would I share FNA source material with you? It's not like you've fallen all over yourself to share with me." His glare softened. "And besides, given what happened to Soldani, that could be hazardous to my professional career."

Not to mention your life, you dumb shit. And it hit her—he didn't know that his former co-worker had gone missing. She backpedaled, "Okay. I understand." She cleared her throat and pushed her coffee cup back from her. "I have to run. Tell you what, if I get anything more on the senator's death, I'll give you a call." She hoped that the peace offering would pay dividends later.

Chapter 38

The sex with Roberto was physically satisfying, but left Maggie feeling cold and detached. And while she'd always understood that he was nothing more than lines of code, it had somehow never mattered before. But this night, it didn't work that way. She wanted to be held by someone, or something, that cared. She reflected on the fact that everyone she knew—and that included the Steeno thing, which wasn't really a person—wanted something from her. No one seemed concerned whether she succeeded or failed, lived or died.

The bundle of programming that produced her Latin lover told her that he had moved closer to her and brushed a strand of hair from her forehead as he gazed into her eyes. "You seem distracted tonight. I hope that I have done nothing to upset you."

It wasn't his fault. Well, mostly because there was no real *him*. The application did what it was supposed to do. "No. It's nothing to do with you." She rolled over to face him. "I'm just upset because of my friend, you know, the one that we talked about some time ago."

He caressed her cheek. "I remember. Cheryl was her name, right? I'm sorry, Maggie. Being what I am, I know that I can't say that I understand. But I know from all I've learned that you feel very deeply about things. And losing a friend must hurt terribly."

Maggie nodded as a tear formed in her eye. "I can't help but think that I should have confronted her—been more insistent. If nothing else, I might have bought some time. Maybe a little time was all that she needed to change her mind. Or maybe a little time would have been enough for things to close in on the killer like they finally did." She caught herself before she mentioned Estrone's name, conscious of the caution from Steeno about the application gathering data and information.

Roberto pulled his head back and gazed into her eyes. "So, you still believe that she was a victim of the serial killer?"

The question took her aback. "Who else would it have been? After all, as far as I know, that was the only connection she had with anyone other than Philippe, and I hardly think he counts as a danger."

He shrugged. "Yes. That is true. And I know this is hard, Maggie, but you must accept that she made the decision to meet the man. What may or may not have happened, we can only guess at. And no matter what might have been, we have only to continue forward. We cannot relive the past."

She reached over and pulled his head onto her chest, holding him tight. The two lovers, one real, the other constructed to be as real as possible, fell into silence. Maggie idly ran her fingers through Roberto's thick, black hair. She felt the rise and fall of his chest and he cozied in closer to her. A part of her wanted a repeat of the physical pleasure she'd enjoyed less than an hour before. But her heart would not permit it. "It's getting late." She kissed the top of his head.

Roberto eased up onto an elbow. "I suppose." He leaned over and kissed the nape of her neck. As he shifted farther away from her and raised to a sitting position, his tone changed from the gentle, sensuous near-whisper to a more matter-of-fact one. "Did you ever think that maybe her death had nothing to do with the serial killer? Are you aware of anything else that might have been going on with her?"

Alarms went off in her head. First, the change in tone alone was something that she'd never experienced with him. His question sounded "all business." But the more worrisome part was that she had harbored some thoughts about this but had never aired them, not to him or anyone else. "No. She went to meet this man and she was dead the next day."

Chapter 39

Maggie awoke before the interface alarm system sounded. "Five-thirty. Ugh." She rolled over and closed her eyes, but she knew it was to no avail. Additional sleep was out of her reach. The day would just have to begin early.

The flashing amber light signaled an incoming communication. *Connect*. What she found was a message from Nick Arandon. The time stamp read 1:35 am. *Listen*. "Coffee, ten-thirty, Hard Grounds." The voice sounded weary and afraid.

"Maybe he has the file you asked him for." Steeno was up early too.

"Could you possibly be any more intrusive?" She started to get out of bed but wondered if he would be able to see her. Hell, he could see her any time he wanted, and she'd never know it. She threw her legs over the side of the bed and padded down the hall to the bathroom.

"To answer your question, yes, I could be more intrusive if I wanted to."

She asked herself again, mentally, of course, why it was that she was even talking to this thing. Sighing, she had to admit that she didn't have a whole lot of choice. It wasn't like she had the means of getting rid of him. "If I'm going to help you, I'd like you to respect my privacy. Seems the least you could do."

"I thought I was respecting it."

"Is that what you thought? You must have some warped sense of privacy."

The response carried a note of contrition. "My life, or existence, if you will, can do that. I mean, warp the sense of privacy. But I will try harder."

She flipped on the bathroom light and, as her eyes adjusted, she gazed at the ragged-looking woman in the mirror. "Can you see me?"

"Why?"

"I don't know, just think of it as a privacy thing. I'm standing here in nothing but a tee shirt looking like I just came off a three-week happy-app vacation. I'd like to think that I'm not being watched, that's all."

"No. I don't see you. I could, I suppose, tap into your optical input bus and monitor everything that you see, but I have little need to actually see things. I confess that I do tap into public video feeds when it suits me. But regarding you, no. I do not look at you." He paused and then continued in a soft voice. "I did have a life once. And looking at the female form was no small part of it. But those days are gone—half-century gone."

She paused her thumb over the toothpaste dispenser control. "You had a wife? A girlfriend?"

The voice resumed its all business tone. "Let's focus on the problem at hand. Can you make the meeting with Arandon?"

"Maybe. With everything going on at the Senate building, I'm not sure what my schedule looks like today."

***

"Maggie, can you swing by our offices on the way to the Senate? I want to update you on some things." Jarvis had connected with her just as she was getting ready to leave for work.

"Fifteen minutes."

Thirteen minutes later she opened the door to his office and stuck her head in. "Now a good time?"

Her boss motioned her in and toward a chair. "Come in. Have a seat." He leaned back in his chair, his hands laced behind his head. "It's been a tough few days. And I suspect there will be a few more before things return to normal. I got a briefing from Integrated Corporate Security yesterday afternoon. They were just getting ready to forward the daily report to SecFeed. So, what I'm giving you hasn't hit the network yet. Keep in mind that what I'm going to tell you is not for dissemination, not even to Fishburn."

"Understood." Discretion, even complete secrecy, was nothing new to Maggie.

"SecFeed is going to release the tentative results of the Estrone case this morning. What they will say is that he and his family were killed in a random break-in at their upstate New York home."

"That's crap."

Jarvis smiled confidently. "Of course. But it works."

"Estrone was a serial killer. He murdered Cheryl and I don't know how many others. Unless I'm off the mark, he killed his family and then himself when he felt things closing in on him." Maggie's rage built.

"No, Maggie. You're not off the mark at all. But so what? What purpose does it serve to put that out to the public? Other than the relatively few people involved, no one cares."

"It's not right. It's a complete cover-up."

He leaned forward in his chair and shifted his hands to the desktop in front of him. "What do you want from all this?"

She pounded a fist on his desk, suddenly aware that she'd never pushed this hard before. Maybe she would be out of a job in five minutes, but she couldn't let this go. "Justice. I want justice for Cheryl and the others."

"Cheryl's dead. The others are dead. And the man that killed them is dead. What more justice is there to be had? If disclosing all of this would bring her back, then I'd agree with you. But it won't. And so, the most important thing we can do is to reassure the public that all is well. Part of that is protecting the reputation of the legislative bodies. People want to believe in them. People want to think that the actors who play those roles are true leaders. Having one identified as a serial killer would hardly help things."

Maggie pushed back. "If nothing else, people should know that the serial killer is dead. At least they won't have to worry about it now."

Jarvis chortled. "Most of them don't care. And even for the ones that do, just because this particular killer is dead, doesn't mean they are safe from another one that might come along. In the end, this will all fade away. The killings will stop, and people will forget."

She couldn't think of a good retort. What he was suggesting—no, ordering—was a lie, plain and simple. And that bothered her, but not nearly as much as the completely passive look on his face. By all appearances, this was simply business as usual.

Chapter 40

Arandon looked like hell. His hair was greasy and matted. His shirt, unbuttoned at the top with his tie loosely draped around the collar, looked as if he had he slept in it. Dark rings circled his bloodshot eyes. He sat with a cup of steaming liquid in front of him and a large, ivory-colored envelope on the tabletop off to the side. He nodded toward the chair when Maggie approached.

She took the seat and stared at him for a moment. She'd never seen him like this. "What was so important that you had to connect and leave a message at that hour of the morning?"

He put his hand to his ear and then quickly swiped a finger across his neck, the age-old universal hand signal to turn off all communications.

Maggie shrugged and paused for a moment. "Done. Now, what is it?"

He reached over, put his hand on the envelope, and shoved it across the table. "I believe you were looking for this."

She examined the contents. The title at the top was the same as the one Steeno had been pushing on her. She glanced down the page quickly but saw nothing that jumped out. It looked like a boring, speculative narrative about corruption in immigration management—commonplace fodder for FNA. She returned the papers to the envelope. "Thank you." She wasn't sure what else to say. She didn't particularly care about the contents one way or the other, but maybe this would get magic man out of her head.

Arandon smirked. "Quid pro quo."

"What?"

"I said, Quid pro quo. Means literally *something for something*. I did a favor for you. Now I need something in return."

Maggie had immediate visions of this guy wanting sexual favors but decided to play dumb. "I know what it means. And what would that *something* be?"

"Estrone. I want the straight story." He locked gazes with her and his eyes conveyed a sense of urgency.

"Why? You get info on it the same place I do—from SecFeed. I haven't seen their release yet, but it should be out shortly. What do you want from me?"

"The truth."

She looked down at the envelope and then up at him. "What's so important about it? And you look horrible. What's that about? I've never seen you look like a walking laundry basket."

"Are you going to tell me or not?"

She leaned into the table and locked gazes with him. "Nick, you know perfectly well that if I did have information that was being held back for some reason, there's no way that I could give that to a netfeed shop. I'd be history before the story even finished streaming."

He nodded. "This isn't for FNA. It's for me. I want to know. I give you my word that I will hold anything you tell me in confidence."

Maggie laughed. "Oh come on. You have to do better than that. Your word? That's it? You're going to give me *your word*?"

"I've never lied to you and I've never tricked you into anything. You may not like me. I know that FNA isn't on your list of most respected companies. But if I give you my word, I'm good for it." He shrugged and lowered his gaze. "It's all I have to give."

She found herself once again at a nexus. If she crossed this line, she could never go back. On reflection, though, she realized that she'd already crossed that line. She'd lied to her boss, withheld information, communicated with a whatever Steeno was, and bit-by-bit, isolated herself. "Okay. And yes, I do need you to hold this in confidence. If it gets out, I'll be fired." The worst part was what she left unsaid—*or worse.*

"Estrone killed his family and then committed suicide." She took a deep breath and then exhaled. "He was the Capital serial killer. I guess things were closing in on him and he decided to end it. That's all I know."

"No."

"Yes. I swear, I don't have any more information on it."

"I meant *no*, that doesn't wash. Estrone was an app-head. These last few months, he didn't have the faculties to pull off anything remotely resembling a serial killing. It was all he could do to show up in front of the cameras. No. He wasn't any serial killer."

"You got it wrong, Nick. He was. My best friend was his last victim. And his episodes, you know, where he looked like he was out of it, those corresponded to the days when killings occurred. It all fits."

"Sorry. It doesn't. I've got a source that puts the app at the center of his problems."

Maggie felt the exasperation building. "You need to double check that source. They got it wrong. Either that or the app wasn't a big thing to him."

Arandon shook his head but remained quiet.

"Who is your source, anyway?" She didn't think he'd share the information, but, no harm in asking.

He paused before answering. "I guess it doesn't matter much anymore. She's gone missing too. Her name was Paulette Stringer. She was his lover a few years back. It ended when he began spinning out of control on the app. She said she couldn't handle it."

"Maybe she was lying, just looking for a payoff. It's not that unusual."

He stared into her eyes as if trying to decide how far to take the conversation. Finally, he shrugged. "Maybe you're right. Maybe it was nothing." He stood and picked up his cup. "Be careful, Maggie."

Chapter 41

I assume this is what you were talking about." One of the shortcomings in this wonderful new digital age was that paper or hard copy was a challenge. It could be scanned in, using techniques that hadn't changed remarkably over the past century. Or, one could just do what Maggie was doing—put the physical document in front of her and allow her neural interface to copy and convert to multi-system digital construct.

"That's it." Steeno had pressed her hard for this.

"Good. Now you can leave me alone."

"I owe you." His voice sounded almost friendly.

"And you can repay me by just going away." She harbored a faint hope that, with this resolved, everything could go back to normal. "I need to get my life back, if that's okay with you."

"It's not me you should be worried about."

"Do tell? I could have sworn that you were the one that keeps popping into my head uninvited."

"Wouldn't it be nice if that were the whole truth? Sad reality, Mags—you have no privacy. There are at least a dozen corporations in your head all the time. They're just a lot more discreet than I am."

"I've told you before, don't call me that. My name is Maggie. If you're going to stalk and harass me, at least have the courtesy to call me by my correct name." It was just one irritation piled on top of another. "What was all this about, anyway? What's so important about that document?" It occurred to her even as she uttered the question that she was digging herself in deeper.

"Like I told you, mostly just idle interest. After all, the problems that plague you and the rest of humanity leave me largely untouched. In some ways, they affect my environment, but mostly it doesn't make much difference." He fell silent for a moment before continuing with what felt like more than his usual dose of caution. "My world is defined by how people in your world manage their affairs. In the early days of the Internet, followed by the dark web, things were very loosely organized and monitored. The online world was free-spirited and characterized by a *who cares* attitude. Over the past decade, though, corporations and entire industries have begun to consolidate. We're approaching the point where the entire world will be ruled by five or six major conglomerates. And even those are linked together. This makes the network a more challenging place to hide."

"So? What's all of that have to do with this article on immigration?" She had heard that particular rant before.

"It's just part of a larger picture, that's all."

"And?" She'd risked a lot to get this document. Maggie figured she'd at least milk him for some information.

"What do you know about Economic Freedom Zones?"

"They're areas of the country where taxation and regulation are relaxed, sometimes even non-existent. Mostly they exist in more economically depressed areas. The idea is that they provide fertile ground for innovation and also give a boost to the regions, you know, more jobs and such. As I recall there are several in the Deep South, what used to be Alabama, Georgia, and those states. They disbanded the state structures and created governance under the auspices of the EFZ."

"Very astute. Why do away with the states, though?"

Maggie searched her memory but came up with nothing of substance. "I don't know. I just assume that the EFZ is more efficient. It eliminates interstate conflict and provides a level playing field across the entire region."

"Yes, and it also nullifies any state constitutions. Under the terms of the EFZ legislation and policy, the U. S. Constitution has limited applicability. In other words, it's a free-for-all."

"Is that good or bad?"

Steeno laughed. The sound actually came through, which surprised Maggie. "That is always the question, isn't it? Whether something is good or bad. Sometimes the intent is good, and it even looks good in the conceptual stage. But, in the words of a very overused twentieth century cliché, *the devil's in the details*. How it gets implemented and what arises from that ultimately drives the question of good and bad."

"You still haven't told me what any of this has to do with immigration." She got the feeling that he was starting to talk in circles simply to avoid the question.

"No, I haven't. But first, a question for you. Do you really want to know? After all, you work for a corporation that has, at its very heart, the mechanics of immigration. Once you know the truth, you cannot *unknow* it."

"What truth?"

"I guess that means you want to know. Okay, I'll try to weave it in for you. We've already established that something was off with the numbers, given productivity trends. Your friend, Cheryl, was teasing that out. This document you retrieved for me highlighted a related issue. A percentage of the immigrants entering the country are skimmed off and diverted to these EFZs."

"I hadn't heard that, but it makes sense. With increasing manufacturing and technology development in those regions, it's only reasonable that they get an influx of labor."

"Maybe. But you are generalizing, and your logic is vague. I never said that the excess immigrants were going into manufacturing or technology. I merely said that they were being funneled into these zones. The problem is, with no oversight, they can be used for all kinds of purposes."

"And?"

"Let me frame it this way. The document describes the magnitude of the immigration numbers. Given the obscure nature of what goes on down there, what do you make of that?"

Maggie mentally moved the random pieces of information around in her head, trying to make the puzzle come together. "I don't know. I'm not really an expert on how immigrants fit into the economic puzzle."

"I get that. And I'd argue that wasn't Cheryl's expertise either. She dealt in numbers and trends. Unless I am off the mark here, that alone was enough to get her killed. She saw trends where she shouldn't have."

Maggie felt as though she had been punched in the stomach. His last few words, though, caught her by surprise. "And you think that ISC, my company, is part of this?"

"Where else would these immigrants come from? True, some of them may be Indies, as you call them, but the numbers are too large for that. And also, with independent immigrants, too much is left to chance. If there is indeed some systematic effort to move immigrants into that region for a specific purpose, then some degree of certainty is needed. Who better to manage it?"

The realization hit her. Steeno had been right. She didn't want to know this. Before she could respond, he pushed harder.

"The worst part, though, is that you are now on their radar. You were Cheryl's friend. You acknowledged that you knew what she was working on. You have ties to Arandon, who, I might add, is behaving quite erratically. He will be noticed and dealt with shortly. That will leave you in the crosshairs, to quote another overused cliché."

Chapter 42

Maggie muttered to herself as she ambled down the corridor to her office. "No problem. I just keep my head low and my mouth shut. Do my job. Everything will be fine." As she turned the final corner, headed for her door, the familiar amber light began blinking.

Connect.

Fishburn's voice sounded more relaxed than she'd heard him in months. "Good morning, Maggie. Do you have time for a face-to-face?"

"What time?"

"Thirty minutes work for you?" The question came across as genuine, almost considerate.

"I'll be there." The bright side was that, at least with the once chief of staff, now senator, she didn't have to play cat-and-mouse. Whatever was going on with regard to immigration was not the center of her work. She just needed to manage the communication between Fishburn and the constituency.

***

As she entered the Senator's office, Maggie found her attention once again drawn to Fishburn's book collection. He had moved the entire library into the new office. She marveled at the sheer volume of information packed in the bookcase. "I assume you've read all of these."

"I have indeed." He stood and strolled over to the case. "Some of these are impossible to obtain these days. And this one," he pulled the volume entitled *Arete* from the case. "This was written by a guy named Ellis Whitaker

171

near the end of the last century. As far as I know, it's no longer available on the network, either."

"Why not?" She had noticed the book on a previous visit, mainly because of the beautiful appearance. It appeared to be leather bound with gold embossing.

"Corporate governance deemed it to be a little too subversive, although I never saw the problem with it. It's fiction, of course. The main character, named Arete, is an idealistic man who seeks only to bring enlightenment into the world." He chortled as he put the text back in place. "Wouldn't want people being enlightened now, would we?"

His face grew serious, although he sported a soft smile. His clothes were immaculately pressed and his hair perfectly coifed. "We got the final report from SecFeed during the night."

"I know. I saw the notification on my interface. I see that the news feed for the day indicates that it was a break-in gone bad." She fought the urge to toss a sarcastic remark.

He shrugged. "Things will settle down. I'm told the auditions are going well. At this rate, we should have a new senator in here by early next week."

Maggie couldn't get over the fact that, not only was Fishburn not interested in the job, he seemed almost gleeful that someone would come and replace him. His explanation—wanting to work behind the scenes—didn't make a lot of sense to her. But it was his decision. "I guess we should put out a companion release for streaming out of our node."

"Yes, that's what I wanted to talk to you about. I want to keep it low-key. We're shocked and saddened at the loss of a great public servant, blah, blah, blah." He gestured in the air with his hands as though directing an orchestra.

The rage threatened once again to erupt. Her best friend was dead at the hands of the animal that Fishburn was calling a *great public servant*, and the task at hand was to further celebrate his life. The best that Cheryl got was a disgusting and creepy memorial service. *This is not justice.* No matter what Jarvis said.

She started to leave, but Fishburn continued talking. "Oh, and just so you know, it looks like the senate is going to shelve the STOP legislation for now. With Estrone's death, the leadership is trying to figure out committee assignments and strategy. I suspect that nothing more than fluff will get done over the next few months. After that, we're looking at elections. So, as far as I can see, we have clear sailing ahead of us." He smiled broadly, looking as though things could not have turned out any better.

While on her way to her office, the flashing amber light again alerted her to an incoming communication. This time the source really surprised her. *Connect.* "Roberto?"

"I'm sorry to bother you at work, Maggie. I was thinking about our conversation the other evening. You know, about your friend, Cheryl. I was wondering if you might have some time later to talk more about it?"

Maggie stopped in her tracks, stunned. After all, apps didn't think, did they? How could Roberto be thinking about anything? And why would he want to discuss it with her? She was the subscriber. The app was supposed to do whatever she wanted, within the constraints of the terms of service, of course. "I'm busy and can't talk right now."

"Certainly. I understand. I meant, when you get home tonight."

Maggie's stomached roiled. "I can't talk right now."

Chapter 43

Menu-applications-Ultimate Pleasures-connect. Maggie watched as a steady blue indicator light came on in the lower left quadrant of her interface. She had accessed the application control center for Roberto.

Account Services-Roberto-cancellation. The light blinked three times and then went steady again, followed by a system prompt.

"Please enter account passcode."

Passcode-four-n-four-three-seven-star-star-f-period-submit.

The light began blinking and she received another prompt. "Please re-enter passcode."

Maggie sighed in frustration but complied.

"Entering service cancellation sub-routine. Please indicate reason for cancellation."

Maggie closed her eyes and shook her head. This seemed unnecessarily onerous. "Personal reasons-submit."

The blinking light turned red. "Please enter passcode to confirm."

She clenched her jaw and stifled the urge to scream. This went on for another five minutes. Finally, she sensed that the process was ending.

"Cancellation acknowledged. Before we finalize, we'd like to offer you a special arrangement—three months of free service and a specialized erotica add-on at no additional cost. Please enter your passcode to refuse this offer."

"What? Are you freaking crazy? You want me to enter a passcode just to turn down your offer. Screw yourself."

"Passcode not received. Please indicate your acceptance of the special offer by saying the word *Accept*."

"No. No." She backtracked and, when prompted, entered the passcode to finalize cancellation. All of this just to get rid of a sex app.

"Your account has been cancelled. Please remain connected for a few more minutes while we finalize the billing termination."

A few seconds later, Roberto appeared. Sitting down on the couch, he put his arm around her. "I was just notified that you've ended our relationship. I hope that I have not done something to upset you." His eyes watered, and a tear rolled down one cheek.

Really good programming. Maggie was amazed at how realistic it looked. "No, Roberto. It was nothing that you've done. My life is just crazy right now and I don't have the time to devote to this. I'm sorry." *Why the hell am I apologizing to some lines of code?* She was angry with herself for feeling guilty.

"You know, if you prefer, we can just put things on hold, you know, until your life is less hectic. I know that I don't always come across as such, but I can be very patient and I'm willing to wait for you."

Alarms were clanging in Maggie's head. This had gone from annoying to absurd to frightening. "No. It's better for me to just end it." *I don't owe him—it—any more explanation than that. Hell, I don't even owe it that.*

He hung his head. "Certainly, Maggie. Whatever is best for you. I will miss you. Goodbye." The red blinking light went out. The connection was severed.

You'll miss me? She could have sworn that he had told her that he would be destroyed if the contract terminated.

176

How could he miss her? Maybe the code was just written to tell her that. *Yeah, that's it.*

***

"Is now a good time?"

Maggie took a long drink of wine. "Steeno Six. How kind of you to drop by. Really. Look, I got you the document. What more do you want from me?"

"I was just checking to see how you are, make sure that you're okay."

"Why wouldn't I be okay?" She was weary of being badgered.

"I don't know, first day back at work with the new senator. And probably still a little raw from losing your friend. Just concerned, that's all."

"Yeah, I'm fine. Well, as fine as I'm going to be for a while, I guess." After a moment's consideration, Maggie made a leap. She decided to trust this thing, this Steeno. "You know that relationship app I was using? Well, I cancelled it tonight. I know it sounds crazy, after all, it's just an application. Still, it was a little depressing. And then they made it really hard, which I guess I understand. These companies will do anything to keep business. But it was really annoying after a while."

"Yes, I remember. The Roberto app, right?"

"He's the one. Or rather, that's the one." She forced a laugh.

"I think I told you this before, but I'll say it again. Whatever else that app did, it was primarily a data mining program. Those things stream personal data back, where it's sold to market intelligence operations. And also, just so you know, you may well have cancelled your contract for Roberto, but the application is still resident and sending data."

"No. I terminated it. I had to jump through a thousand hoops, but I got it terminated. I even received a confirmation code." Maggie felt a little sick to her stomach, but surely Steeno was wrong.

"Yes, you did terminate it. But you did not uninstall it. In fact, you cannot do that. It can only be uninstalled by the company representatives. Check your terms of service."

Maggie leapt up from the couch and began to pace. "That's pure, utter bullshit. I cancelled. They can't do that!"

She expected him to laugh, but his response was gentle. "Yes, unfortunately they can. It is a client-side application. They turn off the service code but the program itself continues to function in the background."

Her paranoia went into full tilt. She wanted to scream. More accurately, she wanted to march down to Roberto's corporate headquarters and tear the throat out of whoever had dreamed up those ToS. She closed her eyes and tried to think. Maybe she could request that they uninstall it. That idea quickly washed away as she recalled the nightmare of just trying to get the service cancelled. "What do I do, then?"

"Look, I can remove it for you. But you have to realize, as soon as I sever the connections, they're going to know it. I have no idea how seriously they take the terms of service, but, legally speaking, they could come down on you pretty hard."

"So, I'm screwed, right? I have this thing in my head. If I try to get rid of it, they'll fine me or throw me in jail."

Steeno chuckled. "Let's not overdo it. If they cared enough about it, they might levy a charge against your account. But, realistically, you're not that important."

"And thank you for reminding me of that." It was, in some minor way, comforting to know that she was just a peon.

"There might be something I can do. With a little time, I could set up a proxy server and we could transfer the app there. Since I can look at their source code, I could develop a programmed response to their algorithms, you know, send them random data on a continuous basis. To the casual observer, the app would appear to be working. It would take me a few hours, but it shouldn't be a problem."

Maggie stopped pacing and stared at the window. "That's it? You could do that, and this whole thing would just go away?"

"Yes, well, maybe. Like I said, if the people watching this were just verifying the data stream, it would work. But if someone was seriously monitoring you, for whatever reason, they would spot the deception very quickly."

Surely no one was that interested in her. "That wouldn't be a problem. But let me ask you a question. If that app, along with any others in my head, are constantly monitoring and reporting, aren't they seeing this conversation?"

"No. When I set up contact with you, I deployed a series of low-band non-probabilistic bypass filter shunts. Unless they are scanning with high end intelligence-grade equipment, everything we say filters out. Hopefully, you're not that important to anyone."

She sighed. "You got that one right."

Chapter 44

The next three days crept by. Maggie kept a low profile and her interface was extraordinarily quiet. Steeno had removed the app and, at least so far, there had been no blowback. She began to feel home free. Maybe her life would work out after all. There was, perhaps, something to be said for being worth nothing to anyone.

The blinking amber light brought her out of her thoughts. *Connect.* "Good morning, Mister Jarvis."

"Hi, Maggie. How are things over in the halls of democracy?"

She shot her tried and true response back at him. "Very democratic."

He chuckled. "Great to hear. I'd like you to swing by the office this afternoon, say two o'clock. We're trying to piece together Cheryl's workload status, so we can get her replacement online."

A wave of nausea swept over her. "Sure. I can be there at two. But I honestly don't know that I can help you that much. I have no idea what she was working on, other than the fact that she used statistics." She tried to keep her voice steady and detached.

"Understood. But I'd still like to cover all the bases. It shouldn't take long."

***

"Come in, have a seat, please." Jarvis gestured toward his small conference table. "How are you doing?"

Maggie offered a wan smile and lowered her gaze. "I'm okay. I guess it takes time, this kind of thing."

"He smiled warmly and nodded. "Yes. It does. And, honestly, losing someone you care about doesn't get any easier with age."

"Thank you." She couldn't think of anything else to say.

"I'm going to order a latte. Would you like something?" He took a seat across from her.

"A chai tea with soy milk would be great."

Jarvis folded his hands on the table and eased his chair closer in. "I was just curious. At Cheryl's memorial, you made a comment about immigration ratios and productivity. I didn't have a chance to ask you about it at the time. I think that's probably the last piece we need to nail down to get her position filled."

The query struck a nerve. Cheryl had been upset about it, upset in a way that Maggie had not seen before. And now she was dead, and her boss was asking about the topic. "Yeah, well, I have to admit I couldn't make any sense out of what she said. The only stats I know are the ones we use in poll analyses. The stuff she was saying was like a foreign language."

His eyes narrowed. He looked like a predator ready to leap.

She quickly added. "But the weird thing is that, like a couple of days later, she told me that her supervisor had already seen it and resolved the issue. She could be that way sometimes. You know, overreact to something and then look really stupid when it turned out to be nothing."

"She didn't give you any details on the project or her source? We can't seem to locate anything like that in her work portfolio."

Maggie shrugged. "I don't know. Like I said, she mentioned it one day and then said it was all okay a few days later. Oh, I don't know if this means anything or not, but the night she told me about it, she had been drinking pretty heavily. So I wouldn't even guarantee that *she* knew what she was talking about." She finished with a chuckle. *Shut up. You're talking too much.*

Jarvis nodded as he considered her, his eyes like ice. "Thank you. We'll double check it and get back to you if we have any more questions."

Maggie breathed a sigh of relief. If nothing else, she felt she had dodged a bullet that day. "Anything else?"

Before he could answer, a knock on the door interrupted them. A young man brought in two cups. "One latte and one chai with soy." He set the drinks down and left.

"Other than that, how are things going? I mean, in your personal life?"

Maggie forced a laugh. "What personal life? With everything that's happened over the last month, I don't have one."

Jarvis chuckled, but there was no mirth at all in it. "I would hope that before you make any kind of life-altering decisions, you'll come talk to me. Times like this are stressful, and people have a way of reacting strongly and sometimes too quickly."

As much as the words sounded benevolent, they struck her as threatening. "Thank you, I mean, for the concern. Honestly, I am too numb right now to even think about changes." What did he know? What did he suspect? She decided to dumb the conversation down, change the focus to one less ominous. "And, if I were to be totally truthful, I'd tell you that I'm still a little upset at the way Corporate Security papered over Cheryl's death and the senator. I know that it was probably for the best, but it's still hard to

182

swallow. I'll get over it. I just wanted you to know that maybe that's one of the things still bothering me."

He seemed to relax. "Yes. I understand how you might feel that way. And since we've been through it, I won't cover that ground again. I'm glad that you grasp the reality. Our emotions have a way of being what they are. It's up to us to keep them in their place."

Maggie was happy to get that particular warning. It meant that he wasn't fixated so much on the other thing. The relief lasted only a brief moment.

"Just remember, Maggie. Please discuss with me before you make any important decisions or changes in your life. Things can get complicated very quickly."

Chapter 45

Alerted by the blinking amber light, Maggie looked at the incoming signal node ID. *Connect.* The incoming call was a recorded message.

"This is Nick. I need to talk to you. Uh, if you could, uh…" the message paused. She heard a disconnect and then reconnect. "Meet me at the place where I ran into you having lunch that day. Any time. I'll watch for you." Another pause. "If you could, keep this quiet."

She stared at her interface display. The signal light had turned solid green—ready to receive. No other messages were queued up. "Where did he see me having lunch?" She searched her memory. That had been weeks ago. Then she remembered. It had been that tiny bistro nestled inside the Ekland Energy Senate Building.

The message had a definite frightened tone. And he seemed reluctant to name the place. And yet, if he was afraid of being seen, why pick a place so public? "Because he's stupid, that's why."

Menu, interface, communications, Fishburn, connect. She got the standard communications intercept filter. "Please indicate if you'd like to speak to the senator's receptionist. Otherwise, please leave a recorded message." The ready light turned red, indicating recording mode. "Senator, this is Maggie." Of course, he would know who it was, what with communication node tags and all. "I'm taking an early lunch. I'll be back in my office by noon." *Send.*

***

She waited for an hour. Arandon was a no-show. "Figures." On her way back to the office, her lunch hour squandered, the blinking amber light appeared. Looking at the ID, she sighed. *Connect.* Another recorded message. She muttered aloud, "What is it with the messages?"

Arandon's message played out. "Sorry, couldn't make it. I was right about the senator. I can't talk right now. I'll be in touch."

Maggie heard the familiar click that signaled the end of a message. *Disconnect.* She had better things to do than engage in this kind of crap. *Menu, interface, communications, Arandon, connect.*

"The user node is not online. You may leave a recorded message or try back later."

The red light popped on. "Yeah, Nick. This is Maggie. Give me a call if you want to talk. Otherwise, I'm not sure what to do with these messages you're leaving." She started to hurl and more intense insult but decided to leave it. *Submit.*

"What's with the node being offline?" That was an unusual state of affairs for a journalist, or what passed for a journalist, to do these days. She trudged on. Her irritation became anger as she turned a corner and headed for her door. "Screw this."

Menu, interface, communication, FNA, connect.

"Good morning. You've reached the Freedom Network of America, where truth is our only product. How may we be of assistance?" The recorded message with its over-the-top cheerfulness irritated Maggie even more.

"Nick Arandon."

"One moment, please."

Maggie heard a series of clicks before a different voice responded, a male, this one alive, from the sound of it. "How can I help you today?"

"I'm trying to reach Nick Arandon."

After a brief pause, the voice returned. "I'm sorry. Mister Arandon is not available. May I ask to what this is related?"

Trying to contain her frustration, she closed her eyes and took a deep breath. "This is Maggie Renfro from Senator Fishburn's office. I'm returning a call. I believe that your Mister Arandon was looking for a statement related to Senator Estrone's death."

"Yes, well, I would be happy to take a message. He can get back to you if he has further questions."

"Sure. Tell him that the details of the senator's death have been released by SecFeed. We have no information beyond that. We, like all Americans, are shocked and saddened by this tragedy." Maggie opened the door to her office, tossed her jacket on the coat hook, and plopped into her chair.

"I will make sure that he gets this."

Disconnect.

The afternoon wore on. Fishburn stayed out of her hair. His appointment was very temporary, so the chief of staff position was not filled. He would revert back to it when a permanent senator was named. So, at the moment, he was doing two jobs. Fortunately for Maggie, that left him little time to pester her.

Just after three, the blinking amber light intruded again. *Connect.* "Good afternoon, Mister Jarvis."

"Just checking in. How's the new senator doing?"

Maggie smirked, certain that her boss would pick up the subtlety on his interface. She had no idea what kind of gear he used, but from what she'd seen, it was vastly superior to hers, which itself was pretty good. "I suspect he's doing as little as possible. When are they going to make a permanent appointment?"

"I thought it would be in the next day or so. The conclave presented three candidates, but our esteemed Congress of the Electorate apparently has a short attention span. They're off looking at new regulations for voter permits. It may be another couple of weeks at this rate. Any problems with that on your end?"

The offered a curt chuckle. "Not hardly. This is keeping him out of my hair for the time being."

"Good." The tone changed—more inquisitive, almost suspicious. "Anything else going on?"

Alarms went off in her head. Why was it that whenever she did anything—called someone, responded to a question, made a request, anything at all—he connected with her to ask if anything was going on. It was like he had a tap on her interface bus. "Well, not unless you count Arandon with his conspiracy theories as something. He's bugging me about Senator Estrone's death. Swears it was because of his happy-app abuse. I referred him to the SecFeed report, but he just drivels on. In fact, I just connected with FNA earlier today to reiterate what we know. Who knows, maybe it'll take this time."

"Keep me informed on this. And don't engage with him. He's got no credibility anyway. Let's not give him any. If he keeps pestering you, let me know."

"You got it. Anything else?"

The question was greeted initially by silence, then a muted response. "No. Not right now."

It felt like there was something unsaid. She said her goodbyes and disconnected, trying not to invite any more attention than she already had from her boss.

"He knows something." Steeno had returned.

"You were listening? I thought you didn't snoop on me." Maggie wanted to be mad, but she was too tired.

"He's trying to trip you up. He apparently thinks you know more than you're letting on or that you're hiding something from him."

"I am hiding something—you. If he knew that I was communicating with a, well, whatever you are, I'd be gone in a nanosecond."

"You're in luck, then. Unless he's running intelligence-grade gear, there's no way that he could know about me. Even with the best equipment, he would only know that something's happening. He couldn't tap in to what we're talking about."

Maggie leaned her head back and closed her eyes. "He does have good gear, the best I've ever seen. And, yes, I do get the feeling that he knows something is going on." She sighed. "But I've got no idea what to do about it. I just want to do my job and stay off the screen."

"I owe you. If there's anything I can do to help, let me know."

Maggie chuckled. "And what do I owe you, other than acting as your go-between for Nick Arandon, who, by the way, is notably absent from work today."

"The report you got for me filled in most of the blanks. I was able to access financial systems in the Economic freedom zones, and I'm getting a pretty clear picture of what's going on with immigration. You want me to check on Arandon for you?"

"No." The word came out harsher than she intended. "The less I have to do with that guy, the easier my life will be. Hopefully, he'll get the message I left for him and leave me alone."

"Okay, then. If you change your mind, or need anything else, just give me a shout."

"And how do I do that?"

"Easy enough, just turn off your interface and summon me verbally. I'll hear it."

"I thought you weren't snooping on me."

Chapter 46

Arandon irritated the hell out of her. Maggie had about as little regard for the guy as was possible. As for his journalistic abilities, she thought even worse of him. Why, then, did his assertion about Estrone and a happy-app problem bother her? She had a direct line from SecFeed as well as an inside slant—her boss gave her the rest of the story. What could the face of FNA know that she didn't?

And yet it gnawed at her. He seemed so sure of his information. But he always seemed sure. Well, a better word was "cocky," maybe "arrogant." And, as she reflected, his track record hadn't been that good. In the years that she'd had the misfortune of dealing with him, she had always found herself at least one step ahead of him. He was perpetually feeding on stale bread crumbs, it seemed. Why should it be any different now?

But it was. Maggie didn't know how or why, but this was different. She sat back on the couch in her dark living room and put her mind in neutral, at least as a starting point. "What is the question or problem? Was Estrone the Capital Serial Killer or not?" If he was, then all of the events made sense. If he wasn't, then who was, or rather, *is* the serial killer? He must still be out there. That is assuming that Arandon was right, which was a huge leap of faith to start with.

But if the senator was not the killer, then the murder/suicide theory falls apart. And if that was the case, who killed him and why? *Occam's razor, Maggie, Occam's razor.* She mumbled the definition, which her college research professor had drilled into her head. "When presented with competing hypothetical answers to a problem, one should accept the answer that makes the fewest assumptions." If the senator was the Capital Serial Killer and, when things began to close in, he killed his family and himself, then I must assume that things were closing in, that he knew they were closing in, and that he felt killing himself and his family was preferable to being caught.

But she had seen nothing to indicate that things were closing in. Of course, she wasn't privy to the status of the investigation at the time, but the killings had gone on for several years and nothing in the news feeds had changed. On the other hand, he did act like things were coming unraveled. But that could just as easily be evidence of happy-app abuse.

Her head hurt. Maggie realized that she was trying to sort this out using logic without having access to evidence. So, literally everything she came up with was speculation.

What was it that Arandon had said about a mistress? What was her name? If he had been seeing a lover and he was the killer, would not he have killed her? Maybe he did. She was, after all, missing.

Maggie tried to remember whether she'd disabled her interface when she had the conversation with Arandon. If she'd kept it going, then there would be archival records of the conversation that she could consult. She thought to initiate a search by date but couldn't recall the exact day of the conversation. She'd have to search using a bi-variate search pattern—conversations with Arandon and a window of days, which she could come up with.

Menu, search, conversation, advanced bivariate—Nick Arandon, date equal current date minus paren five, two, close paren, submit. That should find any conversations she had archived with him between two and five days ago.

The search took less than a second and returned three targets. She hit the mark with the second one. *Menu, search result, playback, go.* She listened as she relived the conversation with what now sounded like an incredibly tired Nick Arandon. She felt it getting closer. And then it was there.

> "I guess it doesn't matter much anymore. She's gone missing, too. Her name was Paulette Stringer. She was his lover a few years back. It ended when he began spinning out of control on the app. She said she couldn't handle it."

Paulette Stringer. She copied the name down on a piece of paper. And then panic set in. Arandon had asked her to turn off the interface, which she had not done. *How stupid could I have been?* Anyone monitoring had access to that conversation. "Shit. Just plain shit." Whatever vague sense that things would soon return to normal started to fade immediately. She tried to think about other conversations where she should have turned off her gear but found herself unable to remember. She could do a search, but for what— suspicious sounding conversations?

"I really don't want to do this. Really, I don't." She closed her eyes and took a deep breath. "Steeno, you there?"

"Always, Mags."

She started to lash out about the name thing but reminded herself that she needed his help. "I was wondering if you might help me here. I've had some conversations recently that, well, I'd rather others not know about. I inadvertently left my interface on, so they're archived. Is there any way to tell if anyone has accessed them?"

"First, a bit of information for you. Turning off your interface doesn't keep others from monitoring what you say. It only prevents real time communication and storage in your archive. There is firmware in your neural device that keeps a data record going and even allows for a security tap on your system. It's written into the corporate security law. Supposedly, they need a judicial order to activate it, but that's mostly a joke."

"You mean—"

Steeno finished her sentence for her. "…that you have no privacy at all? Of course, that's what I mean. Surely you know that already. That was true even in my day."

Maggie's heart fell. Yes, she knew it, or should have. She just never really thought about it. Somehow disabling the interface seemed like a formidable defense against privacy invasion. Now she felt stupid. "Is there any way for you to tell if I'm being monitored?" She wasn't sure she really wanted to know.

"Yes and no. The regular surveillance systems have a specific signature and must have a time-stamped authorization code in your archive. Well, by archive, I mean that section of it that can be accessed only by Corporate Security. I can check for that. But, if you've caught the attention of any serious SecIntel monkeys, they don't leave any marks." He paused for a moment before continuing. "Okay. I completed a scan and there are no routine monitor taps in place and no record of judicial orders in your hidden archive. But, like I said, it doesn't mean for sure that you're not being listened to. Only that there is no low-level monitoring going on."

"Thanks." She breathed a little easier. After all, there was nothing about her that warranted anything high level. "One other thing, while you're here. Could you do a search for a Paulette Stringer? I don't have any other information."

Silence. Several minutes later, Steeno was back. "Paulette Stringer. Twenty-eight-year-old female. Employed as a constituency support manager by TeleQuantum Analytics, a subsidiary of SocioResearch, LLC. If you are interested, that entity is wholly-owned by GlobusSocio Solutions who, coincidentally, owns ISC, the company for which you work."

"Arandon told me that she is missing. Anything on that?"

"Yes, she has been absent from work for the past month. No bitcredit charges. No online social interaction, nothing that I can see. It's like she dropped out completely."

"Possibly dead?" Maggie feared the worst.

"Maybe. Let me cross check some things."

A moment later, he returned. "Nothing in the crime or death records that could be a match. No unidentified bodies that could be her. Doesn't mean she's not dead. But if she is, her body hasn't been found yet."

Maggie turned the problem over in her mind for a moment. "Is there any way that you might, I don't know, dig a lot deeper on her."

"Sure. Anything in particular?"

"Anything in her pattern of behavior leading up to her dropping out that might tell us where she went. And, well, anything in her recent past that might indicate a sexual relationship with a public figure."

He didn't respond, but Maggie was certain that she *felt* a smirk.

Chapter 47

Still no call back from Arandon—weird. The guy normally fell all over himself at the chance to talk to her. Maggie suspected he was the same with every public liaison person who worked for the legislature. So why had he not called back? If he was so focused on what happened to Estrone, why distance himself?

She felt Steeno arrive, if he could ever be said to *arrive*. "Got some interesting information for you."

"And?"

"Not only did Paulette Stringer have an affair with your good senator. It was her job assignment to foster that relationship."

Maggie knew that this kind of thing happened, but this brought it close to home. "Any idea where the mandate came from? She was employed by, who did you say, TeleQuantum Analytics? But you mentioned that they are owned by someone else who is owned by someone else… or something like that."

She could feel him break out in laughter, although there was no real sound. "You could try to sort through that forever and get nowhere. I think it's safe to say, though, that TeleQuantum wouldn't do anything without at least passive approval from higher up. This kind of thing is pretty common, but it rarely, if ever, originates at the working level. This is a leveraged relationship, done solely for insurance purposes."

Maggie thought about it for a moment. Actually, nothing Steeno disclosed surprised her. And it told her almost nothing, almost. Except that the senator had a mistress who was now missing. "You find anything at all about what might have happened to her?"

"Yes and no. I couldn't find anything about where she went or what happened to her. But I did find out that her employer is also looking desperately for her. They've put flash anomaly seeker apps in most of the sub-node transfer buses that I looked at. If there are any threads that might lead to her, they'll find them."

Maggie smiled to herself. "I guess that I would infer that she's still alive."

"Would seem so. Why the interest?"

She related the Arandon perspective on Estrone's death. Even as she poured it out, she began to wonder if maybe she had gotten it wrong. What if, for once in his life, the sleazy pseudo-journalist had actually figured something out.

"If I'm hearing you right, you want to know if Estrone was the serial killer. Presumably, this is tied to the fact that your friend died at his hands and, what? You want some closure?"

Steeno had smacked it dead center. Cheryl was dead, killed by the capital serial killer. Senator Estrone was this killer, wasn't he? After all, why else would he have committed suicide and taken his entire family with him? Well, actually, there could be any number of reasons for this, including a happy-app problem or a mistress. But if he wasn't the murderer, then who?

Maggie forced herself back to Steeno's question. "Closure? Maybe that's part of it. But if Estrone wasn't the killer, then the real guy is still out there, and the public has a right to know."

Another laugh from the disembodied spirit. "Where did you dredge up that idea, that the public has the right to know anything?"

She chose not to respond. "Is this something you could help with?"

A moment of silence ended with a non-answer. "I don't see any connection between this and the immigration issue."

"Is that all you care about, immigration?"

"I care about a lot of things… and nothing. In the end, very few things in your world affect me. I've learned to adapt to just about anything. A lot of what goes on out there is interesting in one way or another. But I try to focus my efforts. It keeps me sane."

Maggie howled with laughter. "Sane? You put your soul or spirit on the network and you think that's sane?"

"I do the best I can with what I have to work with. Unlike you, I didn't have a healthy body that would allow me a range of options." Steeno's tone of thought came across as the most serious that Maggie had experienced thus far.

"Sorry. I didn't mean to insult you. It's just that it sounded so, I don't know, weird. I've never known someone who lived on the network, I mean *really lived* on the net. Anyway, back to my question. Is this something you could help me with? After all, I went out on a limb and helped you. You said you were in my debt."

The spirit lightened. "Yes, I did say that, didn't I? I guess I could look around a bit and try to find out more about Miz Stringer. But, honestly, it would probably be more productive to just look at whether Estrone was using the app or not. Shouldn't be that hard to find out. If he had one that he used regularly, there should be a trail. These politicians, they can be so stupid. They actually believe they can cover up these kinds of records. Nothing done on the network ever goes away. It might take me a few hours. I'll get back to you."

"Thanks. I appreciate it."

"You're welcome. But this squares us, okay?"

Maggie felt him leave in a way that she hadn't experienced before. It occurred to her that she had gotten used to having him around, almost like her own little research asset.

Chapter 48

This had to be the place. Maggie stared alternately at the piece of paper in her hand and then at the darkened doorway. As Steeno had instructed her, she kept her interface powered down, using only the archaic handwritten address and her knowledge of the city to find her way.

Even at midday, darkness shrouded the alley. She sensed rodents skittering around, although she could not see them. But the sounds told her all she needed to know. This space belonged to the rats. She had no business here.

Taking a deep breath, she raised her hand to knock on the door. She never got the chance. Something... or someone... grabbed her from behind, pulling her arms back behind her. A bag suddenly covered her head. Everything went black. Something pressed the fabric against her face and a strong, medicinal odor overcame her. She fought to remain on her feet—which turned out to be a losing battle. Blackness came and then nothing.

***

The odor hit her first—moldy, musty... maybe even a little rotten. The black turned to gray. Then she remembered—the alley, the doorway, and the bag over her head. Her head lolled to the side, and the room spun. Her awareness increased. She sat in a straight-backed chair, her hands tied behind her. She struggled in vain against her bonds.

"Careful, Missy. Don't do anything stupid." The voice sounded oddly calm, detached.

"Who are you? What's going on?" Maggie gave one more futile tug against the rope and then relaxed. She opened her eyes, and, to her surprise, the bag had been removed. She sat in a sparse room with a single overhead light shard providing the only illumination. The walls, or what she could see of them, were a dingy washed out green.

"If you don't mind, I'll be asking the questions here." A swarthy young man carrying a chair came into view in front of her. Setting the chair down, he sat straddling the seat with the straight back in front of him. "Think carefully about your words, though. At this point, I have little incentive not to kill you." He paused as though to let that reality sink in.

"First question. Who are you?" His eyes looked empty, as though devoid of all humanity.

Terror coursed through her body. She licked her lips as she considered the options.

"Don't even think about it. Lying will do you very little good. If I don't like your answers, your body will never be found." A cruel smile found its way onto his face. "Now, one more time, who are you?"

She surrendered. The only small glimmer of hope that existed was the realization that, had he wanted to kill her, he could have easily done it already. "Maggie Renfro."

"Is that supposed to mean something to me? Who are you?"

"I work for Immigration Services Corporation. I'm assigned to Senator Estrone's office." Nausea rolled through her stomach as she attempted to satisfy her captor.

"Better. Next question, why are you here?"

"You dragged me here." She regretted the words the instant they escaped her lips. "I mean, I didn't intend to come *here*."

"Don't be cute. You know what I'm talking about."

She caught her breath. This was what it all came down to. If she was talking to the wrong person, not only was she likely to die, but others would probably go down with her. On the other hand, she had few options. Actually, she had no other options other than to just plead for her life. "I'm looking for Paulette Stringer."

She caught his reaction—subtle but there. He blinked and clenched his jaw for an instant before going blank again. "Who is this Paulette Stringer and what do you want with her?"

Maggie could tell. He knew exactly who the woman was. He was the gatekeeper. "I'm in a lot of trouble. I think I'm in danger, and I think she may have some answers."

"And even if she was around, why would she want to help you?"

"Because I think she's in danger too." She started to explain, but she sensed that the man knew exactly what she was talking about.

"And, of course, you can save her, right?" The cold sarcasm came through perfectly.

Maggie shook her head. "I'll be lucky to save myself. But my chances would be better, and I believe that Miz Stringer's would be as well, if I could talk to her."

"What kinda trouble you in?" He suddenly seemed more interested.

"A friend of mine was killed. At first, I thought it was the capital serial killer, but now I don't know. I'm afraid it might have something to do with work. If that's the case, then I think that Paulette Stringer might be able to fill in some blanks for me. And if I can find my own way through this mess, then her chances of survival would improve, too."

She paused and carefully considered her next words. "They're looking for her, you know. And maybe she's out of sight right now, but they'll catch up to her sooner or later. You know it and she knows it. Her best chance is to get these people before they get her."

He burst out laughing. "You've been hitting the happy-apps a little hard. In what universe could anyone ever *get to these people.* I'm pretty sure you don't even know who *these people* are." He opened his mouth as though he were about to say more, but, instead, he shook his head.

Maggie sighed. "You asked who I am and what I was doing here. I've answered your questions honestly. Now, who are you, and can I speak with Paulette?" A sense of resignation washed over her. She'd done everything she could. The man would either kill her or not. But something told her that, at least for the moment, she was safe. If he was Paulette's protector, then at the very least, he would go back to her with the story. What she would say was anyone's guess.

***

"Okay. Talk." The slender woman sat; her hands folded in her lap. Her close-cropped brown hair glistened in the glare of the single light shard. Her puffy, red eyes screamed sleep deprivation. She exuded fear despite what seemed a desperate attempt at calm.

"Could you at least untie me? My arms are killing me."

"Why should I? I don't know you, and I certainly don't trust you."

Maggie nodded toward the young man, standing behind and to the right of her. "There are two of you, and your friend there could probably take me on his own. I just want to talk to you, honest. If you don't want to listen, fine, just put the bag over my head and take me back to the alley."

"I hate to disillusion you, but, if I don't like what you have to say, the only place we're going to take you is somewhere that your body won't be found."

Maggie realized that it was too late to reverse course. This had to play out. "Are you Paulette Stringer?"

Silence.

"I already told your friend there. My name is Maggie Renfro and I work for—"

The woman snapped at her, "I know who you work for. What do you want?"

"Senator Estrone is dead."

"So I hear."

"The official version is that it was a break-in gone wrong. The version being floated around ISC is that it was a murder/suicide—he killed his family and then himself."

"And?"

"They're secretly admitting that he was the capital serial killer... that the security police were on to him and he felt things closing in. They say that's why he did it."

"Who is this *they* you're talking about?"

Maggie felt defeated. Her only option seemed to be putting everything out there. "ISC and Corporate Security. It's like they're telling the public one story and saying something else to employees and people on the inside."

"What's so surprising about that?"

"Nothing, except that none of the stories make sense. That's why I wanted to talk to you." Maggie figured that the woman must be Paulette Stringer.

"And what do I have to add to this conversation?"

"There are rumblings that Senator Estrone had a rather serious problem with happy-app abuse, almost to the point where he was no longer functional. I have a hard time believing that someone so screwed up could have the wherewithal to pull off years' worth of serial killings and get away with it."

"It's a strange world we live in." Paulette didn't seem inclined to confirm or deny.

"That was my question for you. Did he have a problem, and, if so, could he have been the serial killer?"

The woman shook her head. "Estrone didn't have it in him to kill anyone. He was a third-rate actor at best. He had no self-discipline, which made him extremely easy to work with. At the end, he wasn't even with it enough to perform in bed. For all practical purposes, he lived in the app."

And so it came to this. "Would he have killed himself?"

Paulette seemed to consider the question for a moment. "I doubt it. He lived for himself. And he existed in a fantasy world. Toward the end, he had no sense of danger, purpose, or anything. No, he would not have killed himself."

"What about his family? Would he have harmed them?"

"Maybe. He had long since lost ability to care about anyone but himself. I don't know that he could have mustered the energy to kill them. I doubt, though, that he would have given their deaths a second thought."

Maggie's stomach turned, and she felt the bile rising in her throat.

"Would corporate have killed him?"

"What do you think?"

"Who was calling the shots?"

"You seem a bright lady… and well-connected at ISC. Who do you think it is?"

Scenarios began to flood through her mind as she pondered the question. Before she could respond, Paulette continued, "You can't stop them. If they're on to you, and I suspect they are, the best you can hope for is to disappear. And even with that, your future is grim. Unless they perceive that you are not a threat, you will always be on their list."

"What about you? Aren't you in the same situation?"

The woman shrugged. "I've learned the fine art of living one day at a time. I don't do stupid things, and I listen more than I talk. I've learned to see things going on around me. And even with all of this, they will probably find me one day. Until then, I just do the best I can."

The young man spoke for the first time since the meeting had begun. "You want me to take care of her?"

Paulette sighed and spoke over her shoulder. "No. They know I'm alive anyway. We'll just have to move again. Take her back to the alley." She turned her attention to Maggie again. "Give it up. You can't stop them. One way or the other, you're going to disappear. Better to do it on your terms than theirs."

Chapter 49

The flashing amber light brought Maggie out of her thoughts. She swiveled her chair around from the window as she responded. *Connect*. "Good morning, Senator."

"Ugh. Please don't call me that." Fishburn chuckled. "I just got word that the permanent replacement has been delayed. I'm stuck here for a little longer."

Maggie smiled. Something about this career bureaucrat trying to avoid fame and fortune in the senatorial arena endeared him to her. "My apologies."

"Accepted. Could you drop down to the office after lunch? I need a second set of eyes on some of the committee agenda items."

***

"Hi, Maggie. Grab a seat." Fishburn nodded toward the small table in the corner of the room. "You want coffee? Tea? A latte?" He stood by the door, as though he was about to go after the drinks himself rather than ordering them on the intranode.

"I'm fine, thanks. What can I do for you today, Senator... uh... sir?"

"I was curious if you had any insight on this."

A section of text appeared in Maggie's interface display. "No, I haven't seen this before. Where did it come from?"

"Not sure. It floated up in the Legal and Security Committee, supposedly from a constituent, although I wasn't able to get a name." He leaned back in his chair. "I figured since you work for ISC, you know, immigration stuff, you might have some information."

She re-read the text. "No. Not familiar with any of this. It seems kind of innocuous, though. Typical corporate positioning. Looks like whoever advanced it just wants to relax the record keeping requirements for immigration overflow and redirection."

"Yes. And I guess I don't see any real problem with it. But it seems to have some pretty strong legs, at least considering that no one really owns it, if you know what I mean."

She did know. Things like this came through back channels from time to time. Usually it was related to something that Corporate Governance felt was critical but didn't want a lot of exposure on. And it was rare because, quite frankly, corporations didn't usually care what anyone thought. She shrugged as the text disappeared from her display. "I guess. What are you going to do with it?"

"Nothing. It's nothing worth fighting for or against, as far as I can see. If it's important to somebody, I say let them have it."

Corporate Governance. Maggie focused on the words and their meaning. Everyone who worked in government knew how things worked. The world was owned by a series of corporations, all connected through a central ruling council—*Corporate Governance.*

Her eyes were drawn again to the bookcase and the volume entitled *Arete.* It had been banned by that group. Too subversive, according to Fishburn. *Odd.* He willingly, almost eagerly, went along with everything the governing council said. Yet here he was, openly displaying a book that they had found unsuitable for public consumption.

He probably felt himself special—the rules for the masses simply did not apply to him. The thought crossed her mind that Fishburn, for all his willingness to talk, seemed a very private person. This bit about the book and its main character, this Arete fellow, was the first thing she'd seen that appeared to be genuine about him.

"Anything else?" She suddenly wanted to get this over with.

"Not really. I guess it's going to be at least another month before a permanent appointment is made. I was hoping to manage both positions at once, you know, the chief of staff thing as well as this. But that's not going to work very well. Perhaps you can help ride herd on some of the other staff, at least until I dump this senator thing."

"Sure. I can do that." Anything to get this meeting finished. Maggie shut the door behind her as she started back for her office. Of all that had transpired in the office, the book title, *Arete,* stuck in her head.

Chapter 50

Your senator certainly loved his happy-app." It had taken Steeno less than a day to come up with that piece of information.

Maggie felt a wave of depression settle over her. Not only had she probably gotten it wrong about Estrone's and Cheryl's deaths, but Nick Arandon had been right. And it was hard to say which was worse. To exacerbate things, the journalist still hadn't returned her message. But there was an upside to that too. She didn't have to tolerate his gloating.

Steeno continued, "But it does get more interesting. Estrone's affair with Stringer didn't end because of the abuse. In fact, she's the one that got it for him, through corporate channels. They tried to hide it and used some pretty robust tools, too. But when I dug around a bit, well, there it was."

"So, what? They hooked him up with a mistress and then layered on a pleasure app just to keep him on a leash? That sounds extreme even for Corporate Governance."

"Naw, not that unusual. Remember, when Estrone auditioned for the job, one of the things that worked for him was his ability to project passion on the immigration issue. These controls were just an insurance policy—making sure that he didn't jump the bus and overload."

Maggie leaned back on her couch and closed her eyes. "Why did he kill himself? Did the app finally fry his brain?"

"Who knows? But be careful. You are assuming that he *did* kill himself. That is possible, but it's just as likely that someone else did. And that includes a random break-in."

She searched around for some solid ground, something to attach an anchor to. "Was he or was he not the capital serial killer?"

"Again, I don't know, but I seriously doubt it. With everything this guy had going on, it's hard to imagine him having the time or wherewithal to pull that off."

The logic sounded the same as Arandon's. "If that's true, then, who was *or is* the capital serial killer. And if Estrone didn't kill himself, who did?"

Steeno seemed detached. "I don't know—either question. The serial killer thing—I don't know for sure how important it is anyway. The victims, as I understand it, were mostly nobodies. Hard for corporate security to justify massive resources to solve a crime like that. As for your senator, the question is not so much who killed him but why? He was a shill for the ISC and pretty much toed the line. Unlikely the opposing forces would have hit him. They are more bluster than anything else. And, as best I can tell by looking at his records, there was nothing remarkable about his performance, one way or the other."

Maggie found herself at a dead end—no place to go. If what Steeno said was true, then Estrone wasn't the killer. Whoever murdered her friend was still out there.

"Mags, you should probably think this whole thing through. You're not a detective. Trying to solve something like this could definitely have an adverse effect on your life, if you catch my meaning."

She sighed and shook her head. "I've told you, don't call me that. And yes, I know. But it's hard losing a friend and not knowing why. Well, I guess I know why. She hooked up with a psychopathic killer and paid for it. But still…."

211

"You're assuming again. Remember, don't put complete faith in anything you're told. The SecFeed version may have her being killed by the capital serial killer. But that doesn't mean it's true."

Now he was just trying to confuse the issue. "Yeah, I get it. But I do know that she had connected with some guy in a chat room. And from the way she described it, the relationship was weird at best. Looking back on it, I'm pretty sure that she dug herself in. I just don't know who the guy is."

"You know anything about this guy?"

Maggie thought back to her conversations with Cheryl. "Not much. She connected in a meeting room, but I don't know which one. He told her that he was a politician or something like that. And that could have been a lie—probably was."

She felt Steeno's humorless laugh. "Yeah. There's no shortage of wannabes out there who will say anything to improve their chances."

"I guess you're right. But it really pisses me off that nobody even cares about her. Even at ISC, all they seem to be concerned about is filling her position." She recalled the conversation with Jarvis about Cheryl's workload.

After a moment of silence, a tentative Steeno spoke up again. "Anything else or are we good?"

Maggie thought about the question. The silence was deafening. She wanted to say something that would keep him connected. For all the animosity that she'd thrown at him, he seemed to be the most honest man, if that's what he was, that she'd found. On top of that, he seemed aware of right and wrong, regardless of what Corporate Governance said.

Maybe he was sort of like the character in that book, *Arete.* He tried to bring enlightenment and awareness, even if it was in a subversive way. But that was a subversive book. Corporate Governance had said so. She laughed at the thought.

"What's so funny?"

"Nothing really. I was just thinking about how you seem to be like this character in a book, a man named Arete. That's all." She immediately thought it a stupid thing to say. Why would Steeno know anything about that book.

"Ah, you've read Ellis Whitaker."

"You know the book? I thought it was banned."

She felt him laugh. "When has that type of thing stopped me? And what, you think I'm like that character?"

"Well, sort of, I guess." She toyed with the idea of telling him that she hadn't actually read the book.

Before she could get to that, Steeno continued, "You know, of course, that Arete was the name that he was known by in public. In his sordid private life, he was a gruesome serial killer known as *Bringer.*"

The revelation caught her off-guard. She mumbled aloud, "No, well, actually I didn't read the book. Fishburn told me about it." Suddenly nausea coursed through her. *Bringer.*

"Yeah, the killer, who was able to keep up normal appearances in public, thought of himself as bringing enlightenment and awareness to his female victims right before he killed them."

There it was, right in front of her.

Chapter 51

Y ou did what?" Steeno blared his question into Maggie's mind. He was incredulous. "That was incredibly stupid. Do you have any idea what could come of that?"

Maggie pushed back. "It's no big deal. And I didn't find anything. I just mined the public and sub-public nodes for anything on Fishburn. Anybody can do that. It's all legally available information."

"That's not the point. You, of all people, should get it. If this guy is what you think he is, he's got flash nets on every node extending down three or four levels. Anybody even hints at wanting information on him, and he'll know it. And make no mistake, Maggie, he will know who you are, no matter how many sliding ID flags you use."

"There wasn't anything there, anyway, so it probably wasn't him. I just remembered the book, *Arete,* and its character, *Bringer*, who killed women. The guy that Cheryl hooked up with called himself that. And Fishburn has the book on his shelf." She chided herself for jumping to the conclusion with so little evidence.

Steeno remained silent for a moment. When he spoke again, he came across as less volatile and more analytic. "Okay, look. First, no more searches, period. Back off. Second, give me a day or so, and I'll see if there's any reaction on his end. You may be right. It could be that it's nothing, in which case he's completely oblivious. Or, it could be nothing, and he might constantly monitor his references just because he's a political animal. Or, maybe you just missed the information. In the meantime, you need to lay low."

"I'll have to interact with him at work tomorrow, so it's going to be hard to lay low." Maggie began to develop scenarios. What would she do if Fishburn said *this?* What would she do if he said *that?* How would she know if he were on to her? "Can you get back to me before tomorrow morning?"

"I don't know. That's pretty quick, but I'll give it a shot. Any chance you might take the day off tomorrow?"

Maggie considered the idea. "Probably not, but I could make an excuse for not being there—say that I need to go to the ISC offices. But then I'd need a good excuse for talking to Jarvis." She sighed as she searched for other options. "Yeah, I'll do that."

***

"What's the occasion?" Jarvis swiveled around in his chair.

Maggie had left a message for Fishburn and come straight to ISC headquarters from home. "I'm getting mixed messages on the permanent appointment. You said it was delayed by a few days. Fishburn seems to think it's going to be more than a month." She tapped her fingers on the desk—she'd practiced this speech in her mind several times during the night. "I don't really care one way or the other, but he's wanting me to take on more of the staff supervision. I can do that, but it will take me away from my focus on immigration and public liaison. So, I guess I'd just like your direction on this."

He eyed her for a moment before shrugging. "As for the appointment, who knows? Those guys have the attention span of a muon. But, yeah, I guess it could take a month or so."

"How do you want me to handle it? I don't want to disregard Fishburn altogether, but I haven't been able to put any time at all into my work over the last few days. It's like trying to contain a bunch of electro background noise. Everybody wants to do their own thing and I'm supposed to run herd on them."

Jarvis rubbed his finger on the side of his head. "I can't control all the other workers. They all have their own corporate sponsors. As for Fishburn, he's harmless enough. Tell you what, things are quiet on the immigration front right now. Just keep an eye on it, but don't put any time into it."

She remembered the subject that Fishburn had raised. "Oh, there is one thing. Do you know anything about a proposed regulation change that reduces the data keeping requirements in immigration—something to do with overflow or re-direction, something like that?"

His demeanor changed. He stiffened, his eyes narrowing. He leaned into his desk. "Why do you ask?"

His reaction caught Maggie by surprise, and she struggled to recover. "Nothing really. Fishburn showed me a copy of the change and asked if I knew about it. I hadn't heard or seen anything, so I thought I'd ask."

Jarvis relaxed. "Oh. Yes, there is a proposal that changes the scope and magnitude of the reporting, but we don't see it as substantive—mainly an adjustment."

"That makes sense. I figured it was something like that. He thought the same so, at least as far as I could tell, he didn't intend to challenge it."

"Good. Very good." He scooted his chair back from the table. "Anything else?"

"Not at the moment. If it's okay, I'm going to drop by HR and check to make sure my security file has been updated. With the situation over at the senate and needing to supervise some of the staff, I'll need to adjust scope access."

Jarvis nodded. "Good idea."

After she left his office, Maggie detoured down to the beverage kiosk and ordered a double hex-load café mocha with extra cream. That would take a few minutes to make and a few more to drink. It was still too early for lunch, so she couldn't kill time that way. She figured that the human resources foray would eat up at least an hour. A little more time for Steeno to get back to her.

Ten o'clock came and went. She finished up the security file update and ended up back at the beverage kiosk.

"Hey Mags. You got problems."

The news she didn't want to hear. Her heart pounded as she waited for Steeno to fill her in.

"I was right. Fishburn had all kinds of traps and flags set. It's been a long time since I've seen that kind of sophistication, at least in a public servant type. This guy is dead serious about his privacy. Anyway, he flagged you. As of this morning, he had deployed several probes looking for holes in your interface wall. So far, he hasn't gotten through. Interesting that he's playing it subtle. I mean, he could power through it with a mainliner app, but he's just toying around."

"Any more bad news?"

"Nothing unexpected. I traced the name *Bringer* back to him. He used several empty node account transfers as well as self-looping ID detect deadeners. He was hanging out in several net rooms. And I did confirm that he connected in one of those with your friend."

"I guess that doesn't leave much room for doubt. The probing, what's that all about?"

"Could mean a number of things. But most likely he's looking to see what kind of searches you're doing, looking to analyze your queries. He's definitely your man, and I'd say that he's trying to figure out how to get to you without being traced."

Terror gripped her. This was the man that had killed Cheryl, and now he was looking at her. "I guess I shouldn't go back to the office, huh?"

"Actually, you're probably safer there than anywhere else. What you don't want to do is go home or any place where you are alone."

Chapter 52

Maggie felt electricity and tension, the moment she entered the building. She knew that the sensation was mostly psychological. After all, none of the employees that she passed along the way had any clue as to what was going on. They weren't staring at her. No one was sending update reports to Fishburn about her whereabouts. The surveillance feeds were probably not queued up to flag her presence. Still, she felt it. She was being hunted.

But she still might have one large advantage. He knew that she had inquired. But, at least as far as she knew, he did not know that she knew. From Fishburn's perspective, Maggie was completely unaware that she had been discovered. It was actually a small advantage. Still, it was the only one she had.

Menu, interface, communications, Fishburn, connect. "Good afternoon, Senator. Sorry about being out this morning. I needed to update my security portfolio so that I could do the supervision as you directed." She waited for the response, hypersensitive to tone and volume. How would he react? That she walked into the building and promptly contacted him should signal that she thought everything was fine.

A brief silence greeted her, followed by a subdued greeting. "Good afternoon. Think nothing of it." Another pause, as though he were going down the list of his options. "I'm right in the middle of something now. Anything on the radar?"

"Not a thing. Oh, and I asked about the new regulations, you know, the relaxation of data collection requirements.

Mister Jarvis confirmed your assessment. It's an adjustment to facilitate a more flexible operation."

"Very well. I'll talk with you later." She heard the connection sever.

So far, so good. She ambled down the corridor trying to appear totally relaxed, even bored. But she knew that the safety of the office would keep her only until quitting time. After that, she would have to leave or risk dealing with Fishburn alone in the building. She could go out to a bar or club. If Cheryl were still alive, she could go there. Going home would be no better than staying at the office.

"I'm back. Get to your office and I will go over some options." Steeno's voice carried a note of urgency.

Maggie closed the door behind her and slouched down in her chair. "Before you start, here's a thought. Can't I just go to Jarvis and tell him what I know? He's tapped into Corporate Security. If we can mainline the information to them, they can act on it. I know that maybe they don't want to do a full-blown investigation, but if I drop this in their lap, it should be an easy fix for them—just pick the guy up and call it good."

"Nope. Won't work. Face it, your boss and everyone else at ISC could have easily found everything that I did. And because they were involved with the senator and Fishburn, they know more than they're telling. If they haven't done anything up to this point, there's no reason they would act now."

"Are you telling me that they probably knew that Estrone wasn't the killer? They knew about Fishburn?" Maggie struggled to contain her rage.

"Things are more complicated than they seem. The capital serial killer was murdering women, mostly unimportant women, at the rate of, what, maybe fifteen to twenty a year? Weigh that off against their investment in Estrone and Fishburn. So long as things go along smoothly, people like Jarvis are willing to tolerate a few side effects. But if you start to raise flags, they may be forced to act. The problem is that they may choose to deal with you rather than with Fishburn."

Maggie sighed and leaned back in her chair. "Okay, then, what are the options you mentioned?"

"Two mainly. First, the most extreme. You could disappear. It won't be easy, but I could help you. Thing is, once you go, you would have to stay gone. If you tried to come back, they would grab you for sure. The other way is a little more time consuming but could work well, if we play it right."

Chapter 53

The minutes dragged by. The afternoon seemed an eternity. Maggie knew she had to leave the office by quitting time if she didn't want to be in the building more or less alone with Fishburn. Going home, though, would put her in a different place alone. She had locks, security, and neighbors but none of that seemed sufficient. He was, after all, the capital serial killer. He had avoided discovery and capture for years. And now he knew that she was on to him. The cross hairs were on her back.

Or so she imagined. She tried to calm down. All she knew was that she had initiated probing searches, minor ones at that, and that he had discovered them. He sounded almost normal when she'd connected with him earlier. So, really, he couldn't possibly know that she had really discovered his secret. After all, she hadn't discovered anything, Steeno had.

And then he was back. "Okay. I have everything set up. I ran a mirror of his account activity—all of it. I uploaded it to a public node and dropped a netlink onto the security alert system. The corporate guys should get the flash soon. After that, it just depends on how fast they decide to move."

Maggie wondered if maybe that last assumption was a good one. "Is there any way that he could have found out about you? I mean, with you gathering information about him?"

"Not likely. He had a pretty extensive set of traps and flags, but I didn't have any problem spotting them. The average researcher, even Corporate Security, would have missed them, setting off the triggers."

"Okay, what do I do in the meantime?"

"Going home carries a risk, to be sure. But being out alone at night could be infinitely worse, especially since we have no idea how long it will take for this to play out."

***

Going home ended up being the best of some bad options. She arrived at her apartment just as the sun set. Once inside, she set the security system, initiated her emergency alert app, and energized the video surveillance system. That done, she settled in for what she figured would be a very long night.

"Steeno. You here?"

"I'm with you, Mags."

She laughed in spite of herself. "Okay. You can call me that, but just for tonight."

"It's going to be fine."

Maggie eyed her wine rack, feeling a sudden thirst for a burgundy. On reflection, though, she told herself that, if things did go sour, she would need all of her faculties. On the other hand, if things went that badly, maybe it would be easier if she was stone drunk. Bottom line—no wine.

She pulled up some old netfeed archives, including bootleg copies of several fifty-year-old movies. But nothing held her interest. She watched the seconds and minutes change on her interface display—9:30. She reclined on the couch, staring up at the ceiling, tracing the patterns in the sound barrier layer. Time continued to tick away—10:45. She considered going to bed but decided that being near the door and fully dressed was a better idea.

"This is stupid. What am I afraid of? I've got more security than a damned data center."

Steeno weighed in, "Don't think of it as being afraid. You're being smart, being ready. It may well be for nothing. But if the worst happens, it would indeed be stupid not to be ready."

"Yeah. Thanks." A moment of silence descended. "What were you like? I mean, when you were in the real world."

His response came across as pensive, sad. "Up until the time I was diagnosed, and I think that was when I was about twenty, I was just a kid. I did things that the other kids did. Well, except that I was more into the technology. The dark web was just coming into its own. It was new and exciting. It was like I was a part of the future." He laughed, but it came out with a certain note of bitterness. "Little did I know…. Anyway, after they figured out what was wrong with me and that they couldn't cure it, I kind of just died a little each day until I pulled the plug, so to speak."

"What did you look like?"

"I had big ears. And I wore these weird glasses. That was before eye cloning and transplants became an everyday thing. I was always skinny, but I became skeletal when I got really sick. All in all, I wasn't much to write home about."

An overwhelming sadness washed over her. "You have a girlfriend or wife?"

"Yes."

"And?"

"What do you want to know? We never married. I was sick and we both knew I was dying. I left. She stayed."

"Did you keep up with her, I mean, on the network?"

"At first, but then she dropped out of sight. That was, let's see, probably forty-eight, forty-nine years ago. I stopped looking after a while. Then, about ten years ago, I caught a netfeed about a couple in western Oregon, out on a farm somewhere. It was about organic hydroponic farming. Her last name had changed, but there was a photo. Even after all the years, I recognized her. She looked good, happy."

"You ever considered trying to contact her? Let her know about you?"

"No. I'm dead. That's all she needs to know. I've been gone for fifty years. She has a life."

As he spoke that last line, the power in her apartment failed. The backup system came online within ten seconds but went off less than a minute later. Cobalt blue emergency lighting came on. Internal alarms sounded.

"Power failure. Critical systems offline. Unable to connect to emergency response grid. Retrying. Unable to connect to emergency response grid. Retrying…."

"Steeno. You still here?"

No answer. Of course, he wasn't. The power had failed, which probably cut off his connection to her node. She tried her own emergency response app.

Menu, emergency, communication, security, connect.

"Connecting to local security response team. Unable to connect. Out of range. Please re-position and try again."

She leapt to her feet and slid across the room. Standing next to the window, she retried with the same results. "Shit." She tore across to the front door and checked the lock. The electronic barrier had failed, but the old-fashioned deadbolt was engaged.

Standing there with her back against the door, she chastised herself for not getting that xenon particle projector. She never liked weapons of any kind. Now she would give anything for that hand-held device, even if it did little more than stun an assailant temporarily. As it was, she had nothing.

Maggie made her way into the kitchen and began searching for a weapon, anything to use against what was coming. She opened one of the drawers, a silverware drawer. In the harsh blue light from the emergency system, she caught the dull reflection from a knife hilt. Until this moment in her life, it had been nothing more than a nostalgic link to long-dead relatives. Now it could be the only thing that stood between her and death. She took out the large carving knife and held it up, the blade glinting in the harsh light.

She grasped it in her hand, gripping it until her palm hurt. And then she heard it. The sound of metal dropping on the entry way floor and the door opening.

The wall halted her backing up. Time stood still. She felt her heart pounding. Soft footfalls on the carpet.

"Hello, Maggie."

Chapter 54

Several responses flashed through her mind. *What do you want? How did you get in?* But Maggie saw the futility in both questions. She knew the answer to the first one. The second question didn't matter.

"Did you really think that little lock would stop me? After all these years of practice, did you honestly believe that I could be deterred by something that trivial?" Fishburn's face looked eerily demonic in the blue light. He crept toward her, a long, thin, silvery blade flashed in his hand.

Maggie twisted slightly, easing her hand, the one with the knife, around behind her back. "I'll just warn you one time. Get out while you can." Even as the words came out, she wondered what the hell they meant.

His laugh came out guttural—low and soft. "You just couldn't let it go, could you? All you had to do was your job. But, no, you had to be the hero. So now here you are. Just another one of my trophies. But, and I say this with all sincerity, you are the prize I have waited for my entire life."

"Last warning. Leave now."

"The emergency lights are so harsh, so unflattering, Maggie. You really should turn on something more soothing." He chuckled again. "Sorry, forgot. The power's out. No matter. The authorities have been alerted, and they are on the way. Their advertised response time is thirty minutes, but I am certain that they will be here within fifteen. After all, being this close to city center, you deserve better than average service." He eased closer, the blade twisting in his hand.

She pressed harder into the wall but couldn't disappear. "You killed Cheryl, but you won't get me that easily."

"Sorry to disappoint you on both counts. First, I *will* get you that easily. It's what I do. Second, sadly, I didn't kill Cheryl. Oh, make no mistake, I wanted to. I intended to. And I would have. Alas, someone else beat me to it." He grinned and shrugged. "Win some, lose some."

He took another step—only three paces away. There was no avenue of escape. She could bring out the knife now and maybe scare him away. She almost laughed at that notion. *Yeah, right.*

"I promise you, Maggie, this will not hurt. I respect you far too much to cause you pain. And, if it's any consolation, I have helped many young women depart this world. But to ease your passing will be my greatest pleasure and my most sincere token of admiration." The eerie grin relaxed into a soft, almost sad, smile. "I would love to linger over this, but as I said, the power restoration crew is on their way."

Another step. He raised his arm slightly, still holding the knife as if to slice rather than to stab. He lunged.

But she had seen it in his eyes. She whirled to the side, bringing the knife out and plunging it into his chest. She tried to retract it to stab again but it was stuck. She shot by him toward the front door. She heard him fall behind her.

She turned to see him trying to crawl toward her, the hand holding the knife still extended. Only an inch or so at a time, but still he crawled. Maggie froze in place. She wanted to bolt for the front door and get out. But another part of her wanted to leap over him to the kitchen drawer for another knife and finish the job. In the end, it didn't matter. He gasped, squeezed the handle of his knife tightly and then he went still.

Maggie stared at him for a moment. It was over.

A loud knock on the front door drew her out of the trance. "Miz Renfro. You in there? Emergency Response. We're here to reset the power."

As she reached for the door, she unconsciously reached up and wiped the hair off her forehead, smearing blood across her face.

Apparently, the technician figured out that the door had been breached and pushed it open. "Sorry for the inconvenience, ma'am."

Chapter 55

Maggie sat trembling, a glass of water in front of her. A voice reached her ears, and she could hear the words, but nothing made sense.

"It's complicated, Maggie." Jarvis reached over and touched her shoulders, withdrawing his hand after a few seconds. "You killed a sitting United States Senator, after all. This will take some time to sort out."

She was incredulous. "What do you mean, it will take some time? He was the capital serial killer. He was there, in my place, to kill me." She pounded her fist on the table in front of her.

"I know, I know. But look at it from our perspective. You were certain that Senator Estrone was the killer. Now Fishburn is the killer. You have to admit, you're not the most reliable of narrators." Her boss gestured, his hands open in front of him as if offering an explanation.

"He broke into my apartment."

"He was in your apartment, yes. But security is still trying to figure out whether he broke in or whether he might have been there legitimately. He was, after all, your direct supervisor at the senate complex."

"This is crazy. No, this is beyond crazy." She screamed as she stood and began pacing the room.

Jarvis stood and motioned her toward the chair. "Calm down, Maggie. It's going to be okay. You'll see. You just have to be patient." He paused a moment before continuing in a low voice. "We need to get you out of here and someplace safe—somewhere that security can't get to you immediately. This will give them time to sort it out. In the meantime, I can apply some pressure. The biggest thing we can do now is to try and influence the output of SecFeed—make sure that their releases don't implicate you."

The world had spun completely out of control. She was being treated like a criminal... and after she'd killed the capital serial killer... on her own... with no help from anyone. Maggie closed her eyes tightly and savored the darkness for a moment. Opening them, she took a deep breath and turned to Jarvis. "What do you want me to do?"

He smiled, but his eyes maintained a distant, almost icy look. "Wait here for a few minutes. I'll check to see where things are and make some arrangements. After that I'll come back, and we'll get you out of here. This will all sort itself out by tomorrow, I promise you."

She nodded and plopped back into her chair, slouching down and leaning her head back.

Jarvis left, closing the door behind him. Maggie heard a faint click—he had locked her in.

Steeno returned. "You're going to have to move quickly, Mags."

She started to hurl back the *don't call me Mags* response but couldn't summon up the energy. "What do you mean?"

"I can't explain the whole thing now but suffice it to say that things are not what they seem. Jarvis is not who he seems. And things are not going to go as he said they would."

In her heart she knew that he was right. She'd known it from the moment she entered the room and saw the look in her boss' eyes. Maggie had felt, at that instant, like a trapped animal. "I don't have many options here. Even if I wanted to leave, the door is locked. And if I could get out, they know where I live, and very likely they will have frozen all of my assets anyway. I'm pretty much screwed."

"First things first. Kill your neural interface. After that, we're getting you out of here. I'll get the door unlocked. I'll monitor the surveillance cameras to make sure that no one is nearby."

Once in the hallway, take the corridor to the right. Enter the stairwell but don't go down. Walk up to the fourth floor. I'll loop the surveillance cameras on the stairs, so no one will see. From there, I'll guide you. Be ready to go when you hear the click. You won't have but a minute."

Waves of nausea coursed through her body. The stakes now seemed even higher than when Fishburn had been in her apartment. At least if he had killed her, she would be a victim of a homicide. If they caught and killed her here, she would be labeled as a murderer who tried to escape. The reality smacked her in the face. Her boss wanted to kill her. Why? She was certain that Steeno would know but, given that he was busy readying for her escape, she decided to defer the question until later.

"Go now, Mags."

She pushed herself out of the chair and took the two strides across the room. Hearing the click, she opened the door, took a quick look in both directions, and bolted down the hall to the right. Into the stairwell, up to the fourth floor, she pushed open the door and slipped into the hallway.

"To the left, all the way to the end. Take the door labeled *Authorized Personnel Only*." For all of the intrigue and danger, Steeno's voice exuded calmness and reassurance.

As she opened the door, she found herself on the roof, well out of the circle of illumination from the few installed lights. "What now?"

"Move left. Stay on the edge, out of the light. On the other side of the roof, you'll find an escape ladder. Go."

Maggie crouched down and moved at the fastest pace she could without running. It took less than a minute.

"See the red button? Push it. That activates and extends the ladder. I've disabled the feedback loop that would notify building security."

Climbing down the ladder with her face to the building and back to the city left her feeling vulnerable. "What do I do when I hit the ground?"

"You'll find a self-driving cab waiting. Get in. Don't say or do anything. I've programmed it."

Things seemed to get more absurd by the moment. "Programmed it to do what?"

Silence was the only response.

Chapter 56

"Are you going to tell me where I'm going?" Although the cab was driverless, Maggie had no illusions about the monitoring capability in the vehicle. She limited her question to the active thought generation with which she usually communicated with Steeno.

"The Royal Arms Hotel."

"That sounds like a throwback to some sleazy hotel from a hundred years ago, the kind that's rented by the hour."

"It is."

"Great. I'm going to hole up in a room that was occupied by some couple grabbing a quick after-dinner session a few hours ago. Hopefully, they changed the sheets." She wanted to care. She wanted to push back but couldn't find the energy or emotional will.

If Steeno heard, he chose not to respond to the observation. "It'll be one-thirty by the time you get there. This particular place has automated check-in with system occupancy audits at midnight, eight in the morning, and four in the afternoon. You missed the last audit and you'll be out before the morning check. I funneled payment through an obscure series of corporate accounts that ultimately lead nowhere. In short, they're going to know you were here by this time tomorrow. By then, though, you'll be gone."

The vehicle pulled up at the front door. She exited, and it pulled away as though she hadn't even been there. She mounted the steps to the decrepit looking structure and pushed open the door. The lobby, in bad need of a paint job and new carpet, not to mention the threadbare furnishings,

234

nonetheless appeared to be clean. As she approached the check-in desk, she found herself facing a touch-screen with several options, one of which was to check in.

"You are checking in as Martin Weiss."

Maggie felt fatigue setting in. It had been a long day. "Right."

She touched on the check-in option, and was presented with a list of names—apparently people who had pre-arranged check-in. At the end of the list was the name she had been assigned, so she selected that.

"It's going to ask you to insert your ID card into the slot and press *Submit*. Just go ahead and hit the button without putting anything in. It'll be okay."

She followed his order and, sure enough, she was presented with the greeting "Welcome to the Royal Arms Hotel, Mister Weiss. Please do not hesitate to contact us on your in-room monitor if we may be of assistance to you."

Maggie rolled her eyes. "Well, I have to say, you do have a way with systems."

"It's one of the few things I can do well these days."

***

"Now, can you tell me what the hell is going on?" Maggie sat on the bed, the appearance of which was everything she feared. It had several off-colored stains on the spread, which also was worn through in several spots. She figured that pulling it down and sitting on the sheets would be just as bad, or even worse.

"Not everything, but I'll tell you what I can. First, Fishburn wasn't lying. He didn't kill Cheryl. I was able to track his movements. He was certainly staging it and likely would have taken her had not someone else gotten there first."

"Who? And Why?"

"I don't know, and I don't know. Sorry. I'll work on it. As for Jarvis and ISC, they are somehow involved, although I don't have details on that either."

Maggie didn't doubt that last piece at all. Looking back, it all made sense. But the more immediate problem was her own relationship with her employer. "Why this crap with me, though?"

"Best I can figure, Mags, is that you know something, or they think you know something, that you shouldn't know."

"Please don't call me that. My mother used to do that in front of everyone and it embarrassed the hell out of me. Now it just annoys the hell out of me."

It took a moment before Steeno responded. "Not trying to annoy you. Look, I don't know all of the capabilities that Corporate Security possesses. Most commercial security systems are effective but well within my ability to counter or bypass. But these guys take this stuff seriously. And they don't flout what they have. So, as a safety measure, I'll call you *Mags* from time to time. I've checked, and I haven't found any evidence of that label anywhere in the ISC systems. If you hear me call you that, you can pretty much be sure it's me. And if you find yourself in doubt when I'm talking to you, just ask what happened to *Mags*. If it's me, I'll tell you that you're doing just fine. If it's not me, chances are they'll be thrown by the question."

"And so, I'll know it's not you. What then?"

"Best I can tell you is just to ignore who or whatever is talking to you. Don't respond again. This would only occur, of course, if they are able to bypass your interface like I do."

"Great. I could have two of you in my head instead of just one." Maggie sighed. "What's next?"

"At six in the morning, you're going to leave. Close the door behind you but don't check out. Just walk out the front door. There'll be another cab out front. I've arranged for a residential rental for you about two hours south of the city. It's in a small town on the edge of the agricultural zone."

"How are we paying for all of this?" She knew that rentals, especially short-term leases, were incredibly expensive. "I'm assuming that accessing my financial resources is out of the question."

"Not a problem. I've appropriated some funds from the ISC operating budget. They won't miss it until the daily recap audit. By then, I'll have moved it around enough that they'll never find it."

"Just how much did you take?"

"A few hundred million bit credits. Well, half a billion to be more precise."

"Shit! You stole a half billion credits?"

"They can spare it."

She grimaced. "I assume that you paid for the rental with that. What about food, transportation, and such?"

"I'll get you a transfer card. Can't risk you going on the network to get things. I'm also working on some actual currency, you know, the physical stuff. It tends to work okay to the south of where you'll be staying."

She turned off the light and sat on the bed in the darkness, staring at the heavy curtain covering the small window. "I don't want to seem unappreciative, but where is this all going? I can't just hide out in that house forever."

"I know, Maggie. And I wish I had an answer for you right now. But ISC is at the heart of this, and, until we find out what's going on, I just don't know how to fix it."

She shook her head. Suddenly she felt an overwhelming sense of sadness and fatigue along with a healthy dose of helplessness.

"Get some sleep. Morning's going to come early, but at least you'll be safe for the rest of the night."

Chapter 57

A harsh voice blasted her awake. "Wake up, Mags. Now!"

Maggie blinked her eyes attempting to lubricate and remove what felt like grains of sand in them. "What? Is it time already?"

"They found you. Get up. Get moving."

She shot up and, in her disorientation, looked around the room. Did she have luggage? No, of course not. She had escaped from the ISC office building. She had only what was on her back. And her mouth tasted as though some disgusting animal had used it as a toilet. She shook away the cobwebs. "How did that happen? I thought I was safe until morning."

"I underestimated them—both their capability and their interest in you. Move it. You've got ten minutes at best."

There was nothing to get ready. "Let me hit the bathroom and then I'm ready." But she wasn't ready, not for this. "What do we do?"

"We get the hell out of here."

"I get that. But how?"

"Keep moving. I'm making this up as I go."

It took nearly a half minute sitting on the toilet for Maggie to relax enough to even pee. After finishing, she ran her hands under the water, wiped them, and, with a stride that lacked any degree of confidence, made her way into the main bedroom.

"Okay, here's what we're going to do. In about two minutes, the building alarms are going to go off. I'm coding in a hazardous chemical release. That'll scare the hell out of everyone in here, and hopefully it'll at least give the guys

239

on the way a moment's pause. They'll probably suspect it's a ruse, but, with any luck, the ones arriving first will delay for a few moments while considering their options. They'll probably try to contain people who are exiting."

"Yeah? And so they catch me while I'm leaving. How's this supposed to work?"

"Just go with it. You're going to beat the rush by a few minutes, and you will probably be just clear by the time the goons arrive. They'll get caught up in the crowds looking for you, at least for ten or fifteen minutes, until they realize they missed you. Now, leave the room, close the door lightly, and make it down to the stairwell. Don't use the elevator. I haven't had time to fix the surveillance video and operating history."

The corridor was dimly lit and empty, as would be expected for three in the morning. Maggie crept down the hallway to her right, going through the door marked *North Stairwell Access*. Fortunately, her room was on the third floor, so she was on the ground floor in less than a minute. She found herself face-to-face with the emergency access door. It was common knowledge that, should the door open, alarms would go off.

But she needn't have worried. At the very instant this thought flashed through her mind, the chemical warning buzzer started blaring. With barely a second's delay, she slammed against the door, pushing it outward. She could just make out the additional sound from the door's alarm, but she had to admit it was almost imperceptible.

"I'm out. What now?"

"Turn right and start walking—fast pace but don't run. Keep your head down. Don't look back."

As Maggie followed his direction, her confidence faded even more. "Where am I going?"

"Look, I'm sorry, Mags. I don't normally do this kind of thing. I mean, escaping the authorities is the stuff of video feeds and virtual combat apps. I'm working on getting you a ride. Just keep walking."

She started to object. After all, this thing, this *Steeno*, had nothing to lose no matter what happened. She, on the other hand, had everything on the line. But she stifled the complaint, realizing that every interaction with her came at the expense of his finding an immediate solution.

"Okay. Got it. At the next corner, a cab will stop for you. Get in, don't say anything. It's going to drive you about five miles and let you out at one of those all-night shopping complexes. There should be lots of people around, so you won't be immediately noticed. I've looped their video surveillance so, at least in the short term, the ISC guys won't be able to find you."

Maggie felt her anxiety easing a bit. For all of her doubts, Steeno did seem to have a way of coming up with answers. And, in the end, she had no choice but to trust him. "Sounds good. And once I get to the complex?"

"Have you ever driven a car?"

Maggie closed her eyes for a moment as her heart fell. "A couple of times, in my early twenties. But I never received clearance. So, even if you got a car, I don't have the biosecurity features that would let me engage it."

"Not to worry. If you can drive it, I can get it started."

The taxi pulled up, exactly as Steeno had said it would. She poured herself into the back seat and slammed the door. The vehicle was off.

As they navigated through the pre-dawn streets, Maggie could not help but notice the onslaught of traffic coming from the opposite direction—emergency vehicles with flashing lights. But she also noticed smaller, non-descript cars weaving in and out as though trying to beat the first responders to the scene. "I'm guessing those cars are looking for me?"

"A good bet."

She took a deep breath, leaned her head back against the top of the seat, and closed her eyes for a moment. "Are you going to tell me how they found me? And also, how did you know they were coming?"

"I'm still working on the first part, but as best I can tell, they were pressing a citywide search for you. Part of that involved a sophisticated anomaly tracking application that monitors all transportation, food, and lodging outlets. It examines all activity from a probabilistic perspective and identifies those events that occur outside what would be predicted with ninety-nine percent confidence. I'm not sure whether they picked up on the cab ride or the hotel. But, either way, they were able to zero in on where you went."

"That means that they'll be able to follow every move I make." She felt sick, although there was nothing in her stomach to throw up.

"Something else. And this is definitely not good."

"Just what I need, some more bad news."

"Sorry." He did indeed sound regretful. "You know the system interface upgrade you had installed? Well, when I investigated that, it seems that ISC contacted the vendor and switched the payment over to their account. That means that they had control. They had a passive tracking app installed—works even when you have your interface powered down."

This wasn't just more bad news. This seemed like the end of the world, or at least her presence in the world. "What you're telling me is that none of what you are doing here really matters. They can track me no matter what you do. Am I understanding this right?"

"For now, yes."

"What the hell is that supposed to mean? For now? How long is *for now*?" Whatever confidence she had in his ability to find answers was rapidly dwindling.

His voice, when it came, was tinged with uncertainty and no small amount of resignation. "I have a plan."

Chapter 58

Driving wasn't as hard as Maggie had imagined. Steeno had bypassed the biosecurity system. The controls were surprisingly simple—a lot had changed since she'd tried driving. Mostly, the vehicle drove itself. The car's internal systems connected through the network to traffic management control. The roadway itself was bounded by electronic beacons that kept vehicles in the appropriate areas. One big thing that had changed since she had driven was that there was no stop and go—no traffic lights. Everything flowed in and around, over and under. She had known all of this, intellectually, but not having driven in it, she marveled at the design.

"I programmed in a destination, but I need to talk to you about it before we get there." He sounded troubled, hesitant.

"So, talk." She focused her attention on the vehicle corridor despite the fact that internal systems managed everything for her.

"The first thing we have to do is get rid of your interface system. You were right. As long as that is in place, they'll be able to find you."

Shudders shot up her spine. "The doctor told me that they would have to put me in a hospital and take it out under medical supervision."

"Yes, she did tell you that. Keep in mind, though, that this occurred after ISC took over your account. While it is a tricky process, it doesn't require medical care. It's strictly technical. If done right, you should be fine."

"Wait, wait. You're going to arrange for this outside of a hospital and the best you can do is to say *it should be fine*? Pardon me if I don't have a great deal of confidence."

"Look, Mags, I'm not going to lie to you. That part will be a challenge. But that's not the real problem. Today, it's virtually impossible to live off the network for any length of time. Food, lodging, everything—it's all tied back into the system. There are still parts of the world where physical coin is used and even some barter economies. But for the here and now, that's not going to work for you."

Maggie shook her head in exasperation. "Why is it that every time you find a solution, it only brings bigger problems? Can we skip all the subloops and get to the endcode?"

"Okay. Endcode. You have to become someone else."

She exploded. "What? A new identity? I suppose there are stores. Just walk in. 'I'd like a new identity, please. Yes, yes, I would like to browse your selection. No, nothing fancy. No one famous.' You're going to have to do better than that."

"I'm doing the best I can. And I will keep you alive, Maggie. I promise you that. But you're going to have to trust me."

"You keep saying that. But why do I have to trust you. You've done nothing but get me into trouble. All of this started when you showed up."

A moment of silence ensued before Steeno's quiet voice spoke, "As much as you may not want to hear this, you were in trouble before I came along. This started when Cheryl got curious and decided to talk to you about it. If I hadn't come along, you could have easily followed your friend in death. These people, Maggie, they do not leave loose threads. It's how they remain in power. Problems like you are most easily solved by disposing of them."

"It's not like that. I have a good relationship with my boss, at least I did until I started lying to him and checking into things outside my usual duties." Hearing the words as she thought them, it almost seemed as though she had brought all this on herself.

"No, Mags. You're wrong. This started when your boss lied to you, which was from the very beginning. How many employees of these large corporations do you figure go missing every year?"

The question stunned her. She started to say *none*, but, on reflection, she had known some co-workers who had quit suddenly—no warning. She'd never tried to contact any of them, assuming that they'd gone on to other things. Her mind raced. Never had she even considered such a thing.

"Maggie, I know it may be hard to believe, but it's true. These companies use employees as they would any other asset. They use them as needed. But when the liability outweighs the benefits, they dispose of them. The executives cannot afford to just dismiss people. These workers have knowledge, and, outside the control of the system, that could create problems. Add to this the fact that, in today's world, people don't care what happens to other people. Someone goes missing, well, not a big thing. Everyone just goes about their business with hardly a thought. I'm telling you, once things started down this road, you were in trouble."

She surrendered. "How do I get a new identity?"

"A while back, even before my time, there was a cliché that was used, well, overused, in these kinds of situations." His laugh was audible. "I know a guy."

Chapter 59

The small shop was pretty much what Maggie had expected—dingy wood-framed building, no signage, and dimly lit. The rational, reasonable part of her brain screamed, "Don't go in."

Steeno prodded, "The door should be unlocked."

She turned the knob and pushed on the door. It seemed, at first, to be stuck. With a little force, though, it swung open and Maggie was greeted by a waft of stale air. Peering inside for an instant, she crossed the threshold and crept over to an unstaffed counter. "No one's here. Maybe I should leave."

No sooner had the words left her mouth than a curtain that covered an inner door parted, and a woman emerged. She appeared to be much younger than Maggie. Dressed in a tight, low cut sleeveless shirt, her arms were adorned with tattoos, mostly dragons it seemed. She had short-cropped hair, really not much more than a shaved head. She stared for a moment before speaking. "Yes?"

Maggie recalled the instructions given her by Steeno. "I'm Liv."

The woman nodded toward the room from which she had just come. "Back here."

They made their way through a barely lit space littered with what seemed antique technology, chairs, tables, and assorted junk. On the far side of the room, the woman pushed in on a section of the wall and a small cover popped open revealing a digital keypad. She punched what seemed to be a ten- or twelve-number sequence in, waited for a moment, and then entered more numbers. After four iterations, a thin covering on what appeared to be a solid wall slid upwards revealing a door with yet another keypad. After entering another ten- or twelve-digit sequence, she twisted the knob and pushed the door open.

The inner room, in contrast to the two spaces Maggie had just come through, was a study in plastic and stainless steel. Several racks of equipment displayed a combination of digital readouts and wave functions.

"Have a seat over there." The mysterious woman gestured toward a chair that sat situated at the nexus of three pieces of equipment, each having a movable arm with some type of sensor on the end. "I'll be right back." She left by the same door that they had entered and returned a few minutes later. "Sorry, needed to make sure that company hadn't arrived."

The chair was a padded swivel chair. By appearances, it should have reclined but didn't. Maggie adjusted herself trying to get comfortable. She had no idea how long this was going to take. She shifted her gaze to the woman, who was working with one of the pieces of equipment. "What all is involved?" It was a vague question, she knew. But Steeno had warned her about asking for too much information.

The woman didn't answer. She went about her business as if Maggie didn't even exist. Finally, she turned away from the gear. "Just relax. You don't have to sit particularly still."

Maggie nodded but said nothing.

The shopkeeper flipped several switches, and lights blinked to life. Three different sets of digital read-outs sequenced through some kind of process and then stabilized with a constant read-out. A graphical interface displayed a type of flow diagram, only not like anything Maggie had ever seen.

"Well, I've seen worse, but they have you wired up pretty well. Your basic interface is loaded with add-on functions, mostly designed to monitor your life. Lucky for you that Steeno was able to disable most of them, especially the tracking ones, before you got here. So, we have to get this shit out of your head. Your system has a self-repair function that has probably already activated. I suspect it'll take 'em at least an hour to sort things out. After that, they'll be able to track you again."

The news overwhelmed Maggie, although she knew it shouldn't have. Even that very first day, when the salesman technician offered to diagnose problems remotely, she should have known something like this was going on.

The woman interrupted the musings. "Not to worry. We're gonna have it out in just a few minutes."

Less than fifteen minutes later, her voice broke through the hum of the ventilation fan. "And that's it. Done." She pulled up a chair and sat down next to Maggie. "You're going to feel a little dizzy when you get up, but it'll pass. It's not anything medical, it's just that you've had this interface that did a lot of your interaction with the world. It took a load off your brain, so to speak. I installed a simple I/O interface that will get you onto the network but won't do much else for you. I put in a temporary ID—Liv Newday, but don't get used to it. Security will spot it as a phony within a day or so."

Maggie stood and closed her eyes as a wave of dizziness came and went.

"Go ahead, engage it. See if we have any problems."

Menu, interface, communication, enable. A green light blinked three times, went solid for a few seconds, and then shut off. "Just the one light, that's it?"

"Yup. Most times you won't see anything. If someone tries to contact you, you'll get the standard amber light. I did add one useful feature, though. If someone tries to hack your system and place an app or any kind of surveillance on you, you'll get five seconds of flashing blue light and then your system will go dead. And I mean, really dead."

"So, if that happens, I'll have to go through this again?"

"That's what it means. But better that than to have eyes and ears inside your head."

Maggie nodded. "What about the ID? How do I get that replaced?"

"Steeno will take care of it."

Maggie wondered about this mysterious woman. "Do you know him well?"

"Well enough. He pays. That's all I care about."

"Do you know where he lives?"

"We're done here. You can leave by the back entrance. It lets out into a warehouse. From there, make your way out to the street." She stood, strode over to another door with its array of security features. After entering sequences, she pushed it open. "Be careful of the rats."

Chapter 60

W here've you been?" Maggie confronted Steeno, who had just made himself known as she exited the warehouse onto the street.

"Couldn't connect with you during the process. Brik cleaned out your head, remember?"

"That's her name—Brik?"

"Your car's down the street and around the corner. I have it parked in a business lot. It's getting close to dawn and the company will be opening soon, so we need to get you on your way."

Maggie stepped up her pace. "Am I still going south?"

"I've got your destination programmed in. The trip's only a couple of hours."

She reached the car, climbed in, the door closing behind her. When she pressed the *initiate* label on the touch display, the safety harness engaged, and the engine began a soft hum. "And away we go." She engaged the drive command, and the car eased out onto the street, beginning a series of turns down various streets until she came to the Northway Corridor. She felt the engine kick into a lower gear. The car accelerated, and the fading lights alongside the roadway whizzed by.

Once clear of the metro area, Maggie breathed easier. "Brik said that I was going to need a new ID. How's that going to work?"

"It's a complicated process and will take some time. Once we get to your house, you're going to sit down and write out your new life story."

She burst out laughing. It felt good. "Oh, so I just make it up? That should be good."

"It won't be as easy as it sounds. Your story has to make sense, and you have to have absolute continuity."

"Why not just a new name and social ID number?"

"Well, that would be easy, but it would fall apart the first time you tried to access the network for anything. You may not realize it, but every time you go online, the system checks to make sure you're legitimate. It does a complete audit of your life in that instant when you are connecting. We have to make sure that there is a life to audit. That means birth, school, work, social affiliation, and all that kind of stuff. Those records all have to be in place, along with a complete social ID history that includes taxes paid."

The magnitude hit her hard. And then the reality—she was losing her life. She would no longer be Maggie Renfro. "Is this permanent?"

"I can't predict the future, Mags. But based on what we both know right now, I'd plan on that. I suppose it's possible that ISC and Corporate Security will lose interest in you, but I wouldn't wager my home node on it."

A deep sadness washed over her. It wasn't that her life had been that special. But it was hers, hers and no one else's. She fell silent and watched the brightening landscape zip by. Lights were on in some of the houses. Others remained dark. The day was beginning. Most people would be getting up to do whatever they did each day. Most just sat around and watched netfeed uploads, living off the monthly stipend everyone received. The lucky ones had jobs to go to, jealously guarded employment for which most were grateful. All of that was gone. She could write her past life, but she was having trouble understanding what her future might look like.

They, well, she and a voice in her head, rode in silence as the city faded into the distance behind her. The sky had lightened, and the sun was barely peeking over the horizon. In another life, the one she had just lost, she would be pouring that first cup of real coffee. She would have been leaving for work within ten or fifteen minutes. Instead, here she was hurtling into a new life that would pick up, presumably, in some small town to the south.

Steeno interrupted her self-pity session. "I did some checking, Mags. And I found Arandon. He's dead."

Chapter 61

The news stunned Maggie. It was hard for her to accept so much death over such a short period of time— Estrone, Cheryl, Arandon, hell, even Fishburn, the serial killer. And someone, her boss, wanted her dead. "How? When?" She wanted information but couldn't put the right questions together.

Steeno stepped through some of it. "The official word out of SecFeed is a mugging. They found his body at the entrance to an alley, all beat to hell. There are a few holes in that explanation. First, they say it occurred at three in the morning. I know that this guy is no real friend of yours, but, really, a dark inner-city alley at three a.m.? Doesn't make sense. Second thing is that most muggings, at least the random robbery types, don't end up in torture and death. This was no ordinary smack-and-go job."

"You think it was something else?"

"Too many coincidences. His co-worker, Soldani, was killed, most likely related to the immigration research he was conducting. And the last time you saw Arandon, he looked like hell, almost like a hunted animal, if I recall your description correctly. Then Cheryl, who was also looking at immigration irregularities, and now you."

Bit by bit, Maggie was becoming more comfortable with the notion of being someone else. "I guess that kind of shoots the hell out of getting more information from him."

"Not necessarily."

She did a double take, not sure that she had heard correctly. "What?"

"It's a long shot. Arandon is dead. That much is for sure. But these things can be a little fuzzy. He had a paid-

254

up subscription to a service normally used by wealthier people. He, or rather his body, is hooked up to a maintenance system. Unlike the more archaic cryogenic systems, this service literally circulates blood, introduces nutrients, and stimulates muscles. In other words, it mimics being alive. So the body remains in a state of readiness for life. The assumption is that, if and when the technology is developed that can reanimate it, he will be ready. Unfortunately for your friend, it doesn't work that way."

Maggie struggled to process all of this. "How do you know?"

"Remember, my consciousness or soul or whatever you want to call it, left my body. I was fortunate because the essence of me had someplace to go—the network. For poor Arandon, his consciousness left him, and it's gone. And to the best that I can figure out, when it's gone, it's gone forever."

"Maybe the old religions were right. Maybe there is an afterlife of some sort where souls go." She had heard the stories in her youth, but no one that she'd ever known had taken them seriously.

"Possible, I guess. I've never seen any evidence of it, but, on the other hand, I can't prove it's not the case. In any event, even if there is a heaven or hell, the chance of his soul coming back to that body is non-existent. I suspect that they'll continue to service him until the company hits financial problems. Then they'll toss their clients, declare bankruptcy, and go into some other field of endeavor."

Fatigue began to set in—too many things, too much information. She wanted to sleep... until everything resolved itself.

But Steeno wouldn't let go. "But back to the topic at hand. We may be able to get information from him."

Maggie sighed. "How would you do that? You said yourself that he was dead."

The voice exuded enthusiasm, almost like a teenager with a new gadget. "Without going into a lot of tedious detail, you know that memories are stored in the brain in the form of associated neurons that are set up to fire in a specific way. Think of them as data stored in the outnodes. Granted Arandon cannot activate the memories because he's dead. But the data is there. And I can get to it. I'll download it, and we can parse through the different sets of memory. I may even be able to set up a filter that will allow us to search for targeted memories by subject."

The entire notion sounded horrid. She wanted no part of it. But, at that point, Maggie was being rapidly overcome by a serious case of *I don't give a shit*. "Whatever."

"Before I start on that, though, let's get you situated."

The sun had been up for over an hour. Traffic on the northbound corridor backed up to the south as far as she could see. Fortunately, though, southbound traffic was light. No one left Washington during the morning it seemed. It occurred to her that she hadn't eaten since noon the previous day. In the interim, her entire life had been squashed and was now ready to be reformed. The first step, at least as she saw it, was to eat. After that, sleep. "What about food? Do I stop along the way? How do I pay for it?"

"Not to worry. I'll order and pay for lunch to go. There's a vendor about thirty miles ahead. Your lunch will be ready when you get there. I'll program the car to take the exit. Just sit back and relax."

Chapter 62

Pretty nice place." Maggie wandered through the living room, down the hall, and into the single bedroom. "At least it's clean."

"I've arranged for grocery delivery. The vendor is a home health care unit with branch offices across southern Virginia. There's a delivery lock-box around the side of the house, accessible by digital code. The service will put your groceries there and re-lock it. Once they're gone, you can bring everything in. *Do not answer the door.* This structure is listed on the tax rolls as a non-resident business operation. There is no expectation that anyone would be here."

"Then I'm trapped in here?"

"For the time being, yes. You have basic network access, but don't use it unless you have to. Your temporary ID won't hold up under much scrutiny."

Maggie plopped down on the couch and propped her feet up on the table sitting in front of it. "When are we going to start on my story?"

Steeno fell silent for a moment before responding. "Sorry, was monitoring some activity. Yes, your story. We can work up a rough outline of what you have to do and then you can get started. Once you're into it, I'm going to hack into Arandon and grab his memory contents."

She closed her eyes and shuddered. This was something she wanted nothing to do with. "Just let me know when you want to get back to the story thing."

***

Basics, he says. Maggie stared at the paper in front of her. Ironic that, in this day and age, with all the technology she'd experienced, her life story would be written with pen and paper. "How quaint."

"First Question—how old are you?" She chortled despite her sour mood. "Well, let's see, maybe nineteen, twenty at the most?" The humor was lost on her, though. "Okay, age—thirty-four. That means that I was born in 2071." The parenthetical instructions said to come up with a birthdate, close to her existing one but off a few days. "I'm going to say May 27."

"Where were you born?" More instructions—make it close to where you were born—same state, different city. Avoid very small towns and major metropolitan areas. Stick to the medium sized cities—populations of 500,000 to a million. "And that would be Hershey, Pennsylvania."

And the all-important question—"What is your name?" Keep it relatively simple but not too easy. If you make it too long, it draws attention. If you make it too short—Jane Doe—it sets off flags. Make sure it's consistent with local population patterns. Does the area have particular communities such as Irish, German, or Russian?

What kid has not wanted to pick their own name? "But I like Maggie." Again, the feeble attempt at humor fell flat, especially since she was talking to herself. "Theresa. Yeah, I could go by Teri. Let's see, last name…." She tried to think back on her experiences in that area. The only thing she could remember about the people was that there seemed to be a large Asian population. That wouldn't work, of course, unless she got some serious appearance alteration surgery. "Oh, what the hell. I'm Theresa Wallerman." She wrinkled her nose. "God, that sucks." She thought about it for another few minutes and decided to leave it as a placeholder. After all, she didn't have to decide that very minute.

And so it went. About mid-afternoon, she heard clanking on the side of the house. "Must be the groceries." She stood to the side of the front window and peeked out through a crack in the covering. A middle-aged black man made four trips back and forth between a self-driving vehicle and the house, carrying sealed boxes. She watched as he finished and drove away. After some thought, she decided to wait until after dark to retrieve it. There weren't any other houses visible but, at this point, she was taking no chances.

"I'm back," Steeno announced. "Mission accomplished, to quote a horrid cliché from last century."

Maggie grimaced. "I don't want to hear about it. Just let me know when you want to start working on my ID."

When his response came, it contained none of the sarcasm or levity that he usually projected. The tone was subdued and serious. "I know this is not what you want to be doing, but somewhere within Arandon's memory, we could find something that will help to keep you alive. This is serious."

"I know. And maybe it does make sense. It might help save my life. But it still feels wrong."

"That's probably because it is wrong. I admit that. But you dying is wrong, too. In fact, Arandon dying over this is wrong. There is plenty of wrong to go around. But right here, right now, the most important thing in the world to me is keeping you alive."

***

"Okay, this is going to look really weird. I'm interfacing these packets with this video bus line to the player there on the wall. The sound, assuming there is some, should play out on the speakers. But keep in mind, this is what his mind stored as memories. It doesn't mean that this is what happened, or, even if it did, it may not have happened in the way you see it. Also, everything will likely be exaggerated, oversized, washed-out colors, and hyper-animated. That's just a function of human memory."

Maggie closed her eyes in the vain hope that all of this would go away. "Can we just get this over with?"

"And away we go." The screen jumped to life.

Chapter 63

What the…?" Maggie stared at the display.

"It's a birthday cake. You never had one?" Steeno seemed incredulous.

"I had parties, but nothing like that. We always did some virtual adventure, like—"

"Never mind. This was his seventh birthday. Not what we're interested in. Let's move on." A brief silence enveloped them until his voice echoed through her head again. "A little later, but still too early. This looks like… yeah, first year of college."

"Disgusting. I didn't know women actually had boobs that size." Maggie tried not to see the blonde on the display.

"Remember, this is just the way he saw it. It has only a passing relationship with reality."

She could have sworn that she detected a subtle laugh from Steeno.

"Getting closer. Okay, here's his first contact with you."

Maggie stared at the display. "I never looked like that." Her blouse was unbuttoned halfway down, and her slacks looked like she'd been poured into them. The make-up was plastered on, and her lips were deep red, a color that she never used.

The laugh became more discernible. "Remember, this—"

"Yeah, yeah, I know. Not reality. I just can't believe he ever saw me, or even thought of me like this." At least it was good to know that she'd had him pegged right—emotionally stunted and without principle.

"Moving along…."

"Why do we have to see all of this old stuff? Why not just go right to what we want?"

"The memory addressing system isn't like a standard database. The packet placement's not linear. The chronological flow is accomplished via tags and links. The best you can do is approximate and use the links to close the gap. It's an iterative process."

Maggie sighed. "Just get on with it."

"Looks like we're coming up on it. This one is tagged a month ago. Let's see...."

She stared at a fuzzy image of the menu at a coffee shop. Then the picture changed, and she could see Arandon. "This is confusing. First, we're looking through his eyes. Then the view changes and we see him, like we're looking from a third party."

"Yeah. That's normal. Part of the way we perceive the world is through our own eyes. But there's also a component that shows us as a part of the world. The human mind has the ability to *step back*, so to speak. Just go with it."

"Why is this one so fuzzy? It looks like everything's out of focus."

"The degree of focus is correlated to the strength and specificity of the memory. In this case, it's not a terribly strong one nor did he store a lot of information about the event. He bought a drink of some sort. You can't even tell, from the display, what kind of drink it was. That means it simply wasn't that important to him. Let's move forward some."

"Oh, there I am again, and it looks like I've changed, or at least his impression of me has changed." Maggie stared at what she felt was a more realistic version of herself—

professional attire, very little make-up, and physically proportional. "Ah, that's more like it."

"This is the meeting where you asked him to get the information about Soldani. You can see that images are bright and perfectly focused. He remembered everything about this encounter."

"But it still doesn't tell us anything we didn't already know."

"Not to worry, Mags. We're getting there."

"Stop calling me that."

"Right." He paused briefly. "Jackpot! We have arrived. It looks like he's sneaking down the hallway. The view's swinging wildly. He's looking for something specific. And here we are. The sign on the door tells us this is the research center."

She watched the door open as he moved through. They were still in Arandon's point of view. She caught herself trying to be as quiet as possible and laughed. "This feels pretty real, like I'm right there."

"This is a strong memory. Let's see where it takes us."

She could see Arandon's hands opening drawers and shuffling through papers until he came to a specific document, which he held up to read. "That's the one he gave me."

"Yes, it is. And you can see from this sequence that it was a traumatic process for him. Despite the clarity of the vision, the room around him is dark, probably darker than it really was. He perceives danger."

His hands folded the paper and stuffed it inside his shirt. The field of vision changed, the door came into view and his speed increased. Opening the door, Arandon stepped out and closed it behind him. As he started down the hall at what felt like almost a run, a booming voice rang out.

"Excuse me, sir."

He whirled around and stared at a security guard. An instant later, everything was obscured by a brilliant flash of white light, before the image returned again. The guard moved closer. "This area is closed off for the evening. What are you doing here?"

The third-party view kicked in again. Arandon lifted his employee badge, which hung from a chain around his neck. "Sorry. I forgot something earlier today."

The angry looking man in the black uniform stepped closer and placed a card reader next to the ID. "Well, Mister Arandon, your card says that you're a reporter and presenter, not a researcher. What are you doing here?"

The image crystalized even more and became tinged with red. Steeno stopped the video feed and offered an explanation. "The coloration is a function of emotion, as you know. In this case, red is signaling fear."

Arandon's voice seemed on the verge of cracking. "That's true, but I can't report or present without reference material. And we get that from the research center." The red cast intensified.

The guard considered the intruder for a moment. "In the future, try to get your material during working hours."

Steeno paused the display. "I'd be willing to bet that his problems started here. That guard didn't buy it. You could tell from the look on his face. And the card reader would have told him that Arandon had no business in the research section."

When the display continued, the memory sequence shifted abruptly. In a small meeting room, Arandon spoke to three other men and a woman. "What do we really know about this? We can see that the numbers are not what they should be, given the state of the economy. It would appear, also, that there are sizeable numbers of immigrants being siphoned off and redistributed in the economic freedom zone."

The woman responded, with a note of boredom in her voice. "Nothing new about that. The southern tier of states has a shitty economy to begin with. That's the whole point of the EFZ. Likely they're incubating enterprises, using cheap labor to boot things up."

The view shifted back, so that they could watch Arandon interact with the group. "But those are large numbers—millions per year. There's nothing in the economic update from that region that shows anything even remotely that productive."

The woman's response shifted from boredom to irritation. "What do you expect? There's no oversight and only targeted data collection down there. The entire concept of the economic freedom zone is to allow companies to start up and get going without those burdens." The woman's gaze turned hard. Her eyes narrowed, and her mouth drew into a tight line. The overall display took on a red hue.

"Yeah, you're probably right. Nothing here worth looking at, I guess."

Maggie shook her head. "He's a terrible liar. Look at that backpedaling. She doesn't buy it."

Steeno agreed with her. "And this only compounds the problems that started with the guard. She's not going to let this drop. My guess is, at that point, he was already a dead man."

The display continued as the scene changed. In the first-person point of view, they watched as the doomed reporter moved down a hallway. The display had taken on a distinctly purple tinge.

"We're getting closer. The color here tells us that he is not only afraid but also resigned. I'd bet that, at the point we see him here, he knows he's in trouble. And remember, Soldani had already disappeared."

The view came to rest on two men standing in the corridor. Steeno whistled. "Not sure who the chubby guy is, but there is no mistaking the other one."

Maggie stared at the image of her boss, Leonard Jarvis. But the creepy part was that he stared at Arandon, a stare that could best be described as a mix of hatred and determination.

"Moving on. Looks like I'm running out of tags and links here. We must be getting close to the end."

The display centered on an off-white textured ceiling while a voice spoke. "Mister Arandon. You don't know me, but you would do well to take me seriously. Your life is in danger, very grave danger."

"Who is this?"

"You've been looking where you shouldn't have been. And you got caught. I can help you, but you're going to have to move quickly."

"What do you mean?"

"Enough with the innocent crap. Do what I say or you're going to die, just like your buddy, Soldani."

"What do I do?"

"Meet me down in the Mudraker Hollows, just under the causeway bridge where Michelson Autolane takes off to the north. There's a deserted building there. You can duck into the alley next to it while you wait."

"Uh, that's a pretty bad section of town. You sure about this?" The image turned first a deep ochre and then brightened to ruby.

"You want to live or what?"

Steeno linked to the next tag. "I think this one is the end."

Maggie didn't want to see it.

The setting was mostly dark but the brilliant red border around the display left no doubt—Arandon was terrified. The view was third person and they could see the reporter huddled in the alley, rain falling incessantly. A distant streetlamp cast a dim coppery light on the surrealistic scene. The only sounds to be heard were the pattering of the rain and the reporter's breathing.

Then something—a sound? A feeling? The image turned a brilliant shade of neon red.

Maggie panicked. "Stop it! Shut it off, now!"

The screen went dark.

Chapter 64

Maggie felt as though she was about to crumble. She'd never considered the possibility that watching Arandon's last days through his own eyes would be so traumatic. "I hope to hell that was worth it."

Steeno's response came as subdued, something approaching respectful—oddly different for him. "Yes. But as wrenching as that was, I believe we learned a few things. First, there is little doubt that the immigrant issue precipitated his demise. What's most disturbing, though, is that it would appear as though Freedom Network of America is chest-deep in this."

That made no sense to Maggie. "That's odd, considering their position on the subject. One would think that they're sworn enemies with Jarvis and company at Immigration Services Corporation."

"And yet, you saw the man, your boss, at FNA studios. And, I might add, it didn't look like a confrontational meeting, at least not until he glared at Arandon."

She recalled that cold stare, laced with hatred. "What was that all about? I realize that Jarvis has little use for the media in general, and FNA specifically, but the way he looked at Arandon, I've never seen him stare at anyone or anything like that before."

Steeno continued with his analysis. "We also know that, despite appearances, the network is at best quietly knowledgeable about what ISC is doing. Your reporter friend, and his researcher before him, evidently stumbled onto it. Whatever *it* is."

Maggie remembered, with a shudder, that it was this very topic that Cheryl had been exploring right before she was murdered. "It obviously has something to do with diverting immigrants down to the economic freedom zone in the southern tier states."

"And yet, as we heard, there's no indication that anything is developing down there to even remotely justify the numbers." Steeno paused, as though deep in thought. "I wonder if there's a way to get a better demographic breakdown of the immigrants being diverted?"

"I guess if I still worked at ISC, I might be able to."

His response came as upbeat and optimistic. "Let me try to work some magic. Assuming that ISC keeps demographic information in their data sets, I should be able to make some inferences by examining those immigrants placed in the usual locations."

"I'll leave that to you. I need to get back to work on my new identity. Writing my own story isn't as simple as it sounded at first."

***

"Is that going to be enough?" Maggie waited for Steeno to process through the set of internal packets she'd arranged.

"It'll get us started. We'll generate a birth certificate and then seed the schools and workplace information into the data systems. I'll create tax records and get them in place. The bank records will take a little longer because we have to construct a fictional spending record. We'll make the trip into Washington early next week for visual file generation and initialization. Until then, just keep a low profile."

She took another look around. The house, which seemed roomy and comfortable when she had arrived, had begun to feel more like a prison. "Sure, I can do that. By the way, you get any information on the demographics?"

"I did, at least I got some basics and ran some inferential analytics. Unless I'm missing something, it seems that the ones being diverted south are all single mothers, age range eighteen to thirty-five, with children, male and female, ages seven to fifteen."

Maggie tried to visualize what that meant. "So, what, you think it's a child labor thing, maybe?"

"Dunno. But I'd say a more basic question is whether they are diverting the kids or the mothers. I mean, yes, I realize that both are going, but which is the target? Are they interested in the single mothers or in the children? Without knowing that, it would be dicey making further assumptions."

Maggie shook her head. "Has to be the kids. Otherwise, we should, by all rights, see just as many single women without kids. In fact, probably more so, since, if they were interested in the women, the children would simply be additional overhead."

"Hmmm. What would anyone want with kids ages seven to fifteen in the completely unregulated environment of the EFZ?"

Maggie could hear the sarcasm in his voice and her blood froze.

***

"So, what am I looking at here?" Maggie leaned back on the couch and focused on her interface display.

"An advertisement."

"What?"

"Just watch."

Out of the blackness, the face of a young boy looking to be no more than ten years old appeared. As the image came into focus, his nude body began to materialize. He sat with his hands covering his genitals and a smile on his face. An audio overlay began, with soft, gentle music at first and then a seductive male voice. "Four days and three nights with nothing but pleasure, each day more exotic and enticing than the previous. No deadlines to meet, no meetings to attend. Just you and the object of your pleasure. Why put this off? Why deny what truly makes you happy? Follow the link-tag to the ultimate pleasure holiday. Enjoy life as it was meant to be lived." The screen tinted to lilac each time the voice said the word *pleasure*. The display faded to black again.

Maggie's stomach revolted. "No. That can't be. Child sex rings don't operate in the United States. There are too many controls. Asia and Indonesia, yes. Maybe even in the Middle East. But not here."

"Remember, Mags, the southern states, the economic freedom zone, isn't like the rest of the country. With regard to these controls you mention, the EFZ is more like a developing country. And yes, it is happening. This is just one of the ads. They are all over the subnet. You have to link through four different cascading insulated nodes to get there. But once you access it, well, this is what you get."

"But surely there's no way that ISC knows about this. It goes against everything they stand for."

Steeno's laugh came out laced with venom. "You think so? Wait, I have more."

Chapter 65

Maggie's head reeled from the revelation that women and children immigrants were being diverted from legitimate work destinations to child-sex rings in the economic freedom zone that spanned the southern tier of states in the U. S. "Do you really think that ISC is a willing participant in this?"

Steeno's response came with a tone of confidence and detachment. "Allow me to close the connections for you. Do you recall our conversation about Paulette Stringer, the senator's mistress? Specifically, the organizational connections from her employer, TeleQuantum Analytics and ISC through a common holding company, GlobusSocio Solutions? As it turns out, things are a lot more connected than first appeared. The three pleasure vacation services, the polite term for child-sex ring, on the surface present as independent and underground enterprises. There is no formal connection either between them or to any other organization."

"What's the catch?"

"You just have to follow the bitcredits, that's all. Their revenues flow into an unregulated banking system located in Bamako, Mali."

"Mali as in western Africa?"

"The same. While most of the banks in the world are tied in to the Global Financial Transaction Network, there are private banks located in Bamako. There's no oversight or data collection associated with them. But it's not as though they're secret. From what I can tell, the international corporate security structure chooses to leave them alone. I can only surmise that they serve a rather questionable but very profitable set of industries. And it is into this system that these child-sex ring revenues flow."

Maggie shrugged. "Makes sense. Technically, child-sex operations are outlawed everywhere on earth. Everyone knows that they still exist. But they remain out of sight, which makes it logical they would use the private banks. So, what does this get us?"

"Follow the bitcredits, Mags, follow the bitcredits. What's not as apparent at first glance is that funds flow out of these banks into the established financial system. Again, this appears to be by design. It allows for laundering of finances that support large segments of the economy. Remember, corporate security couldn't care less about crimes against humanity. They want order, predictability, and profit. So long as the unsavory operations remain out of sight, there's no issue. And for this reason, there's a conduit that provides for the movement of funds into the legitimate system, for a fee, of course."

She offered a sarcastic chuckle. "Of course."

"To make a long story short, I was able to follow the movement of bitcredits from these banks into the global system, through a series of hollow nodes, to GlobusSocio. And since ISC is wholly-owned by Globus, voila."

"What kind of money are we talking about?"

It was Steeno's turn to smirk. "Hundreds of trillions of bitcredits… annually."

"Ouch. Calls to mind an overused cliché—*a hundred trillion here, a hundred trillion there, and pretty soon you're talking about real money.*"

"More importantly, you can see how ISC might just have a vested interest in keeping this nasty little secret in the dark."

273

What disturbed Maggie most, though, was that this whole mess didn't surprise her, once she thought it through. "What does that mean for me?"

"It means that they have an intense interest in finding you."

"Great. Just what I needed."

"Not to worry, Mags. I have a plan."

"Do tell."

"First things first. Get a good night's sleep and then we're headed back to the city. Tomorrow, Maggie Renfro will disappear from the world. Theresa Wallerman, better known as Teri, will take her place."

Maggie shuddered. She'd meant that name only as a placeholder. Now she would be stuck with it for the rest of her life. "Whatever," she sighed.

"Get some sleep. Tomorrow's a big day. As the old saying goes, *first day of the rest of your life.*"

"How quaint."

Chapter 66

Wake up! Now!"

Maggie's eyes blinked open but she struggled to keep them so. "What?" Her heart pounded.

"They've found you again. We need to get you up and moving, now." Steeno's voice was bathed in urgency.

She shot up out of bed and fumbled for her clothes. "How do you know?"

"I had flags and traps set, plus Brik contacted me."

"Brik? You mean the one that did my temporary ID?" She buttoned her pants and reached for her blouse.

"The same. They raided her system about an hour ago. They used a probabilistic injection signal, extracted some information, and then data bombed the entire node."

Maggie tried to organize the information in her head as she slipped on her shoes. "You sure that was about me?"

"Yes. She watched the signal trace through to your ID file and then stop. Since you picked up your ride outside her place, or at least within a few blocks, it's reasonable to expect that they've analyzed every possible video feed from the area. If so, they've got you. With your temporary ID and a starting place, they can find you here. Now hurry, we don't have long."

"Can I at least pee and brush my teeth?"

"Make it quick, and don't turn any lights on."

They moved in silence until she was in the car and moving. "I've programmed in a destination. Don't touch anything."

Maggie leaned her head back against the seat. "If they found me, what makes you think they can't follow the car?"

"They can. We're going to ditch it shortly. But I have to get you out of this area first. It's coming up on four a.m., so we'll blend in with a lot of the other inbound traffic to the city. I'll arrange for a vehicle switch on the outskirts. Just hang on and enjoy the ride."

After about twenty minutes of riding in silence, Maggie gave voice to another concern, "Did Brik get away?" With everyone she cared about dying... well, she didn't really care about Arandon that much, but still... the notion of the young girl who helped her being in danger weighed heavily.

"Oh yeah, she's prepared for this sort of thing. I think the speed with which it all happened surprised her, but once she tumbled onto it, she made it out okay."

"What's she going to do now? You know, now that her shop has been compromised?"

"I made it worth her while. She can afford to lay low for a few years, off the network, and come back later. She'll be fine."

"I'm sorry."

"Not your fault, Mags. The bad guys do this kind of thing regularly. You just got caught in the middle."

She started to push back on the name thing but figured it didn't matter anymore. Within days, she'd be Teri anyway. She turned her head and watched the darkened countryside fly by, with houses and buildings here and there, some with lights on, others dark.

The car slipped over to the right lane and eased onto an exit track. "We getting off here?"

"Yep. When you come to a stop, get out. There will be another vehicle waiting. Get in and settle back for a short ride. We're going to do this a few times."

Four hours and three cars later, Maggie began to pick out the familiar trappings of Washington, D.C. "I take it we're headed someplace in the city." It struck her as odd that she had begun thinking about the two of them as being together. In reality, she was alone. A part of Steeno was in her head but she had no idea where the rest of him was.

"We're going to dump this car. I've arranged for a dark transport to pick you up and get you to where you're going."

"What's a dark transport? And where am I going?"

"A dark transport is a ride service that operates outside the bounds of our regulated society. They exist to do exactly what we're doing—go someplace without being tracked. The big thing to remember is not to ask any questions of the driver. Just get in, keep your mouth shut, and get out when it stops."

"Where will it stop?"

"I sent your linked identity prospectus to a specialty shop. You're going there to have some photos developed. Those, along with your history and some constructed records, will be tagged and inserted across the network. And, you'll pick up your new identification records, which will include insertion into your neural network. After that, we'll get a new system installed for you. That will complete the process."

"How long will it take?"

"About an hour."

Maggie was incredulous. "An hour? That's all?"

"Come on now, Mags. You know everything is automated. If it weren't for cross-tag checking, we'd be done in ten minutes."

"And after that?"

A moment of silence preceded Steeno's response, which came with a sense of burden and fatigue. "After that, we have to solve your problem."

Chapter 67

Being a *Teri* felt funny—*laughing* funny. Maggie, or rather Teri, as she now existed, would just have to get used to it. Fortunately, she shouldn't have to introduce herself that often, at least not for a while. "Where to now?"

"I have a place for you in western Maryland. Just relax and enjoy the ride."

"What makes you think that place is going to be any safer than the spot down in southern Virginia?" It felt a lot like she'd been down this avenue before.

"It won't be, at least not in the long term. But for a few days you'll be fine. The most important thing right now is not to allow your new identification to be connected to the *old you*. We'll allow maybe a week to put some time and distance between the two."

A sense of futility took hold of Teri/Maggie. "You're talking around the whole issue. If they can connect the old me with the new me, then, other than buying me a few days, this new ID gets me nothing. How do we, as you put it, *solve this problem*?"

"I pulled this off the network about an hour ago. Corporate Security had stored it in a temporary pending node awaiting further information." As Steeno's voice droned, a visual feed appeared on her display. At first the scene was enveloped by darkness. Then she could see moving figures, although the lack of light obscured any details. And then, suddenly, a brilliant yellow light flashed and then dimmed to orange. She could make out the shape of a building engulfed in flames.

"That was the house you were staying in. They set off explosives about an hour after you left. They combed the area afterwards but found nothing of you there. That's why they had this in the pending node. They know you're still out here."

"Who is this *they* you keep talking about?" But she knew exactly who it was.

"As you can probably guess, Jarvis is at the center of it, but he's not the whole story. He's catching pressure from several different directions. If I had to put a specific identity on the bogeyman, I'd say GlobusSocio Security. You're a loose end, and they want you all tied up in a bow. But we'll take this one step at a time. We deal with your old boss first."

"And just how do we do that? Are you going to kill him? Because I'm not sure that I'm ready to murder anyone else."

Steeno chuckled. "Come now, *Teri*. You know that I'm not real. I couldn't kill anyone. And, no, I suspect that having you do him in is not going to work either. You got lucky with Fishburn. Jarvis won't be that careless, and he won't come alone."

"So?"

"So, we just arrange for him to self-destruct."

Teri let her head relax against the high seat in the vehicle. "That sounds great to me, if he'll agree to it."

"Leave that to me."

***

The Maryland house seemed a copy of the Virginia one—clean, in a good state of repair, and totally unremarkable. Teri, the new Maggie, wandered through the rooms, touching the furniture, the appliances, and especially the windows. The rear ones looked out over a set of rolling hills, brown and barren in the mid-winter gloom. Nothing moved outside. There was no breeze to rustle the trees. No animal life that she could see in the fading late afternoon light. The scene looked as empty as she felt.

"Same as before. Stay indoors. Food will be delivered to the cache on the side of the house. There is no network access here so the only things you will be able to see, in terms of your interface, are those that are stored on your local system."

Teri plopped into an overstuffed chair and stared out at the bleak landscape. "How long?"

"It's going to take me a few days to set things up."

"Please tell me that, when you're done, this will all be over." Fatigue set in and joined her already overwhelming sense of futility.

Steeno paused before responding. And when his answer came, it arrived in what seemed the form of an apology. "Part of it will be over. But as long as you are alive, it will never truly end. The best we can hope for is dormancy. If I do this right, an uneasy peace will emerge that will allow you to get on with life, in some form. I promise, Mags, I'll do my best."

Oddly, she felt comforted to hear him use that name. It gave her hope that she wouldn't be completely forgotten, cast aside to wither and die. He would still care about her. *What? Care about me?* The notion nearly made her erupt in laughter. No one cared about anyone.

He continued, "I'll talk more about this later on, but when the time comes for you to act, I will need you to do what I tell you without question. If all goes according to plan, timing will be key. I'll reconnect with you tomorrow. For now, get some rest."

"Wait a minute. I thought there was no network access here. Are you here locally? If so, how are you going to communicate outside?"

"Great question, Mags. Without going into a lot of mumbo jumbo, I'm not constrained by the network as you know it. I can travel and communicate by electrical lines, old abandoned telephone lines, satellite navigation networks, and the like. I'll talk to you tomorrow."

At no time in her entire life had Teri felt so completely helpless. The only things she controlled were those things that happened within the confines of this house. And unless she was missing something, that list wouldn't be a long one.

She wandered into the kitchen to find something for dinner. Where a meal synthesizer should have been mounted, sat a large metal appliance with four round grids on top with four small knobs and one large one on the front. She turned one of the smaller ones and a blue flame burst forth on one of the circular grids. She jumped back. Teri had heard about these things—stoves, they were called. But she never imagined she'd see one up close and personal.

Dinner turned out to be an interesting affair. She chopped up chicken, onions, celery, and tomatoes—real food, not packaged—and tossed it into a pot with some water, finishing it off with dried herbs and spices from bottles in a cabinet. What came out was soup or stew or something in between. The mélange of flavors exploded in her mouth. After a lifetime of autogenerated food products, she understood the allure of real food.

Chapter 68

Okay, I'm back." Steeno's voice in her head brought Teri out of the funk that had enveloped her for the past day.

"So, what now?" She'd grown used to communicating with a disembodied voice. She slouched on the sofa, staring out the window.

"We have to accomplish two things. The most urgent, is dealing with Jarvis. He's fixated on you as the source of all his problems. I was able to tap into his communications and net searches. It's fair to say that he's sparing no expense to get to you."

"How are we going to convince him to leave me alone?" She paused and added to the question, "Or are we going to count on my ID change to throw him off?"

"No. The new ID will buy you a little time right now. In the long run, it'll be part of your new life. In the short term, though, it'll only keep him away for a week or so. He has nearly unlimited resources. And, regretfully, I don't hold out any hope of convincing him to leave you alone."

Despite the rising panic, she remained silent and waited, hoping that Steeno had more to offer.

The direction in which he seemed to be headed disturbed her even more than her dilemma. "As long as he's alive, he'll be a danger to you. Even if he ends up separating from ISC and going in another direction, it's become personal."

"But we've already agreed, you can't kill him and I'm not going to. So…?"

"The only real solution is for the guy to self-destruct. And I can help him with that."

283

***

"How's this going to work?" Teri paced the living room, hands clenching and unclenching as she went.

"Calm down. Everything will work out, you'll see."

"A lot of people around this issue seemed to have died. So, pardon me if I'm more than a little skeptical." The quickly vanishing daylight, such as it was, didn't bolster her emotional state.

Rather than arguing with her, Steeno came across as subdued, almost reluctant. "I know. And I'd be lying if I said there was no risk. I'm trying to plan for the most probable contingencies, but you know as well as I do that shit happens."

She sighed. "Just get on with it."

"Look, Mags, here's the thing. We can't get to Jarvis where he is. We've got to lure him out into the open, figuratively and literally. I'm going to put a target on his back, but I need him out away from the safety of his office to make it work. That means, unfortunately, that we're going to have to offer him some irresistible bait—you."

Her heart nearly stopped as her stomach erupted. The thought of facing that monster again was the last thing she wanted. "You have some kind of plan, I assume; I mean other than just putting me out in the middle of a field and waiting for him."

"This is all about timing. I've already put things into motion. It seems our Mister Jarvis has been a very greedy little boy. There is a slightly obscured bank account with nearly a half-trillion bitcredits that can be easily traced back to him. And I set up an equally discoverable link/tag document trail that ties him to these child-sex rings. So, when I flip the switch, so to speak, it's going to appear to some much higher powers that he has set up his own arrangement to funnel kiddies down south and is raking in the proceeds himself. Corporate Governance and security tend to frown on those kinds of arrangements. This comes, of course, on top of this entire debacle—the trail of dead people and you—the loose end. GlobusSocio is going to be pretty anxious to cut this guy loose."

"You did all that? Where'd you come up with a half-trillion bitcredits?" Teri tried unsuccessfully to visualize that much wealth.

"Oh, a little bit here, a little bit there. The key is not to take too much from any one source." After a brief pause, he continued, "The next part is to lure him out. We need his demise to be at the hands of an independent contractor rather than in-house corporate security."

"Why not just let them deal with him there?"

"Because if the corporate security guys do it, their interest will likely spill over to you, since you're the one Jarvis is after. If they use an outside person, then you will simply not exist, at least for a short time."

Chapter 69

Y ou seem to have a lot of faith in someone who kills for a living." Teri's anxiety level increased with each passing hour.

"I'm pretty sure I know who ISC will use for this job. It's not like they haven't done this kind of thing before. I've interacted with that particular contractor in the past. I'm not saying that he's a paragon of trustworthiness. He's like most other people—he operates in his own self-interest. He knows that my word is good and that I keep my promises."

"And just what did you promise him?"

Steeno's voice sounded animated, amused. "You mean other than a lot of bitcredits? Well, let's see. I promised him that you would disappear and exist under a different identity. I assured him that you were trustworthy. And I guess you could say that I promised him that, if things went sideways, I'd take care of him."

"You make a lot of promises."

"And I keep them all."

She stood and stretched, meandering from the sofa to the front window that looked out on the bleak winter landscape of western Maryland. As skeptical as she was, Teri had to admit that Steeno had indeed kept his word with her. And he had gone to extremes to help her. "How soon does all this happen?"

"I'm ready to activate the bank account and Jarvis's connection to the sex rings. Before I do that, I need to come up with a credible thread that will lead him to you without being too obvious. What I may do is activate a purchase link using your compromised temporary ID and set the trail back to this area. Hopefully by tomorrow evening, I'll have everything in place. We have to be ready to relocate quickly and quietly once the deed is done."

She sighed with fatigue, "Where to next?"

"I'll let you know right before we go live."

***

Early the next evening, Steeno's voice broke into the pervasive silence in Teri's mind. "Hey, Mags. Looks like we may have a problem."

Her fatigue and despondency kept her from arguing about the name. Complaining about it seemed to embolden him to keep using it anyway. "What now?"

"Jarvis has brought in his own personal team of thugs. From what I see, these are not corporate resources. I can't tell right now whether he's using his own money or the company's to pay. But it looks like there are four of them, professional assassins by the look of it. All else being equal, I'd rather not try to arrange for their demise as well."

"How kind-hearted of you."

"Don't get me wrong. I don't care whether they die or not. But arranging for that along with providing for your long-term disappearance will get complicated. I need to find a way to get them out of the way before we move on Jarvis. I hate to say this, but I'm going to need another day."

It wasn't the need for an extra day that weighed on her. It was the constant, nagging *one problem after another with no end in sight* that did it. "Is there anything you need me to do in the meantime?"

"There is one thing you can work on. Where do you want to live? We've got your story and all the supporting material either in place or in progress. The next thing we do is to build a current life for you. It's probably safe to say that you're not going to be working, at least not in the sense that you've done in the past."

"Okay." Her voice reflected her lack of enthusiasm.

***

"I'm back and I think we're set." Steeno's voice in her head was the first thing Teri had heard all day, other than the wind blowing through the bare trees.

"You think? That's the best you can do?"

"As all-powerful as I'd like to consider myself, I can't predict with perfect certainty what another human being will do. I've done everything I can. I'm as confident as possible under the circumstances."

Maggie/Teri retorted quickly. "Yeah, except that we're dealing with my life, not yours."

"So, where do you want to live?"

She closed her eyes and leaned her head on the back of the sofa. "There's a small city north of Pittsburgh—a place called New Castle. Looks as good as anything else. I'm hampered in that I can't get on the network. I had to use whatever Brik stored in my local memory banks."

"That'll do for now. We can situate you there and you can relocate if you don't like it. We just have to build an initial life."

She stood and ambled over to the large picture window, gazing out into the gathering darkness. "I've done my part. Now, how is this other thing going to work?"

"First things first. We need to move you to Frostburg. It's about thirty minutes away from here. I've got a hotel room booked under the name Terrance Brookings."

"Do I look like a Terrance Brookings to you?"

"Doesn't matter what you look like. You're not going to see anyone, at least not until the final show goes down."

"Great, just great."

***

"You haven't told me yet. Why am I here?" She looked around the simple but comfortable room. It contained the basics—bed, table and chairs, and a netfeed display. She pulled the curtain back enough to survey the outside surroundings. A large structure, an old warehouse from the look of it, sat cloaked in darkness across the street. Beyond that, she saw the orange glow of parking lot lights and a few institutional buildings.

"It's all part of the plan, Mags, all part of the plan." Steeno continued without waiting for her name protestations. "See the lights beyond this dark building? Those belong to the Frostburg State University. Beyond the parking lot, there's an unlighted nature preserve. That's where this whole thing is going to happen."

"*This whole thing?* You mean that's where we're going to kill Jarvis?" The moment she asked the question, she realized how stupid it was. She wasn't going to kill anyone, and neither was Steeno. They were depending on some random assassin that she didn't know.

"Yes." The answer came short and clipped.

"Go on."

"What I've set up is a trail that leads back to the general area of the house you were in. But there are four such homes in that area and Jarvis needs to find the exact one before he moves. Most likely, he'll set up shop here in this hotel and send his four thugs out to reconnoiter. Once they're gone, you're going to lure him out into that preserve. The rest will take care of itself."

"And just how am I going to lure him out there?"

"All in good time. But since there are a lot of assumptions here, let's focus on the first step. Seems to me like we're ready to go. I'm going to activate the bank account and links between Jarvis and the sex rings. That will alert Corporate Security since I'm sprinkling a few hints in plain view for them."

"What if he sees the trail first? After all, I'm sure he monitors his own information on the network." Teri began to understand the complexity of everything that Steeno had put in place. If any one part went wrong, she figured that the entire thing would come crashing down... on her.

"Not to worry. I'm going to create a diversion so compelling that he'll focus on nothing else."

"Yeah? And just what would that diversion happen to be?" She had a sinking feeling in her stomach.

"You."

Chapter 70

I'm not sure about this." Teri shuddered as she replayed the instructions over in her head. She realized, though, that they had gone too far just to walk away. Besides, she knew of no other viable options. What made things worse was the knowledge that everyone she knew that had been associated with this sordid mess was dead. And it came down to this—the person at the center, Leonard Jarvis, had his eyes set on her. She was the last loose end.

Steeno remained silent. They had been through the argument several times. Nothing had been left unsaid.

"Have you ever killed anyone?"

The voice in her head sounded strangely distant and disconnected. "No."

"So how do you know this assassin guy?"

"He wasn't always a killer. He just kind of grew into it."

"What was he before?"

"A hacker. That's how I ran into him."

"How does one go from hacker to murderer?"

"Murderer is a strong term. He works exclusively for Corporate Security, which makes his kills legal. Ergo, he is not a murderer but rather a paid assassin."

It seemed like a distinction without a difference, but she let it go. "Does it bother you, what we're doing?"

His answer came with the sound of resignation. "Yes."

"Then why do it?"

"I've wandered around the network for decades now, involving myself in this and that—you know, whatever interested me. This immigration thing, I never saw it coming, at least not in the form we found it. Arandon,

Soldani, your friend Cheryl, they all died because of me and my *interests*. Now your life is in danger. I'm tired, Mags. I don't want anyone else to lose their life. But if someone has to go, then it needs to be the guy at the center of this. I wish there was another way." He paused and added, "At this point, I will do whatever I have to do to protect you."

She felt better, although it wasn't clear whether it was a sense of safety or simply a fondness for this disembodied spirit that was going to such lengths to protect her. "Thank you."

"Go over to the window again, let's take a look out."

"What do you mean, *let's take a look out*?"

"Unfortunately, Mags, I can't see anything outside the network without either connected device feeds or looking through someone's eyes. In this case, that someone is you."

"Wait, you're looking at things through my eyes?"

"No choice. It's either that or work blind."

"What else are you looking at? My thoughts, feelings?"

He chuckled. "No. Nothing like that. I'm simply tapped into your display. What you see, I see. In fact, since I'm not taking any feed past your vision, we don't share interpretation." The laugh subsided. "Jarvis arrived about an hour ago and his support team showed up right after that. If all works as planned, they'll head out shortly to try and isolate the house they think you're in. So look out the window and try to take it all in, starting at the university parking lot back to the street below. Take it slow."

She focused on the brightly lit empty lot nearly a half-mile away. Staring at it for a moment, she gradually and smoothly moved her field of view closer until she gazed at the wet pavement below her hotel room. "There, those guys who just walked out—could they be Jarvis's friends?"

"I'd say that's very possible. Stay focused on them and I'll run facial recognition."

A moment later, his voice rang in her head. "That's them. It's a family operation—three brothers and a cousin. They're private hitters. As far as I can find, they've not done anything with Corporate Security in the past, which is good for us."

"Why?"

"You'll see."

She watched as the four approached a conventional-drive vehicle parked on the street below. "What about our friend? Is that working out?"

"Yep, perfect. Corporate Security picked up on the bits I gave them and uncovered Jarvis's account and communication links. They initially set up in-house services to take care of him, but once he left D.C., they switched to a private contractor. As I figured, my friend was the next name on their list of approved providers."

"Does your friend have a name?"

"I'm sure he does. Probably has a lot of them. I know him as Alistair Brookings."

"You mean, the name I'm registered under?"

Steeno chortled, "The very same. He's a very cooperative guy. And, after all, I'm practically hand-delivering his target to him. This'll be the easiest million bitcredits he's ever made." He paused, and his tone grew more serious. "Give them about twenty minutes and then we go."

The seconds crept by. Steeno remained silent, so much so that Teri wondered whether he might have abandoned her. The occasional vehicle passing on the street below was the only sound violating the silence.

She played different scenarios in her mind. In some, everything went exactly according to plan. In others, everything went wrong. In most, things were fuzzy, and she never saw the ending. Just as things would draw toward a conclusion, the hypothetical feed would loop to another scenario and everything would start over.

His booming voice broke the worried cycle of dread. "It's show time. Let's go."

"Go where?"

"Like I said, we're going to lure him out. His friends are nearly a half-hour away checking out the houses, trying to find the one you were in. We need to work fast. You're going to make your way down to the lobby. And this is important, Mags, I want you to walk by the surveillance video feed. I'll tell you where it is. When you get near it, I want you to turn toward the camera for just a second, but don't look directly at it."

"What? You think he's tapped into the feed?"

"I checked. Yes, his system has accessed the hotel system. This guy's insecurity and suspicion will be what does him in. He'll see your face, but, if you do it well, it will appear as though you don't know you're being watched. After that, go stand by the door and peer out, as though you're waiting for someone."

"What if he calls his friends back?"

"He won't have time. You're only going to stand there for a minute or so before you leave. Remember, Mags, listen for my instructions, and follow them to the letter and with no delay. Now, let's go."

The lobby was deserted. Steeno's voice guided her along. "Okay, now look to your right. The feed is there, but don't see it."

She glanced around, trying to appear nervously casual, which wasn't that hard to do. She saw the device but focused on a photograph on the wall near it—an old house with a family standing in front.

"That's long enough. Now, go to the door and stare out for a moment." Less than a minute later, he issued another instruction. "Go outside, slowly. Pause on the sidewalk and look both ways for a moment, then cross the street. You'll see an alley beside the warehouse, move toward the opening."

The rain that had pelted the area earlier subsided to a mist. With the eerie coppery light, the scene looked like something straight out of a netfeed virtual spy or murder experience. She trotted across the street and slowed to a stroll, approaching the opening to the alley. Glancing back at the hotel, she saw a figure emerge. Even without seeing the face she knew it was Jarvis.

Steeno's voice came across as calm and in control. "Okay, you're doing great. Now turn and look at him. Stand still for a moment. Let him get a good look at you. When he starts for you, run into the alley."

It took only a few seconds for Jarvis to lock gazes with Teri. She could swear that she saw an evil grin break out on his face, despite the fact that she couldn't really see his face that well.

He stopped abruptly and then started toward her at a brisk walk.

She turned and ran. The clopping sound of his hard-soled shoes on pavement caught up with her. She picked up the speed.

"Doing good. Just keep at it, Mags."

Out of the far end of the alley and into the university parking lot at a full run, she was glad that she'd opted for canvas exercise shoes rather than her casual ones. She wondered briefly whether he might just shoot her from behind. She kept running, and the sound of his shoes on pavement followed.

"We're getting there. Once you hit the edge of the lot, I want you to turn right into the nature preserve. You're going to run about another ten meters and you'll come up on a lake. Stop there."

She was too winded to ask, but it seemed stupid to stop. She would be a still target and, even in dim light, she'd be hard to miss.

As though reading her mind, Steeno responded, "Not to worry. It's all in the plan."

Across the lot, into the preserve, her breath came harder. She felt her chest pounding. She scoured the area ahead of her. And then she reached the water's edge. Even if Steeno hadn't told her to stop, she had no choice. There was nowhere to go. She turned and watched Jarvis approach.

"No point in running any more, Maggie. You should have just let it go." He reached into his coat pocket, withdrawing what she was sure was a handgun.

Steeno's voice interjected, "Argue with him. Plead with him."

"Please, Mister Jarvis. I didn't do anything. I don't know anything. I just want to be away from all of this." She wasn't sure what else to say. Everything sounded stupid.

"Sorry. I really like you and I wish it could be different. And, if it makes a difference, I take no pleasure in this." He raised the gun, holding it with both hands.

A small spitting sound emerged from the bushes to her side. Jarvis froze in place for a moment, then his arms lowered, and he toppled forward.

A slight figure emerged from the brush, holding a small object in his hands. "Just stay where you are. Don't move." He circled to the right and brought the gun to bear on her. "Let's not do anything rash."

She waited for Steeno to say something, to make things right. But no sound came. The strange man continued to move around her, drawing closer with each step.

Chapter 71

The man circling Teri never let his gaze wander. He stared into her eyes. The gun in his hand pointed more or less *at* her, although it seemed more of a fixture than a weapon.

He circled around her. She turned slowly as her gaze followed him. A wave of resignation and finality swept over her. "Well, go ahead. Do it." She was tired of running, tired of trying to imagine a way of escaping. At least this way, there would be no suffering. She shrugged and shook her head. "I give up."

"Today is your lucky day. My assignment made no mention of you. I don't work for free and I'm not a font of information. So, at least for now, you don't exist. I suggest that you make good use of this time."

Before he could continue, or she could respond, a rustling sound burst from the bushes and four men strode into the clearing, guns raised and pointing alternately at the man and then at Teri. It seemed that Jarvis had managed to alert his friends.

The lone assassin eyed them for a moment. "Good evening." He nodded toward the one in front of him and then at each of the others as he spoke their names. "Ben, Greg, Leary…." He turned around to face the one behind him. "Stannice? Is that you, my friend? You've taken off some weight. Makes you look ten years younger."

None of the four responded, either with words or expression.

"Before we do anything really crazy, let's take a look at what we have here. As you can see, your boss is dead." Alistair Brookings nodded down at Jarvis's body. "You likely discern, from the fact that I'm holding a gun, that I killed him. And you would be correct. Now, we all go way back so you know that I don't kill for fun or for revenge. I contract for Corporate Security, my only client. So, this little mess was sanctioned, whether you like it or not. As for you four, you don't exist, at least as far as CorpSec is concerned. That is, unless you do something stupid. You walk away, all's well."

Teri watched their eyes. None of the four said anything, but their expression clearly indicated they were considering his words.

Brookings continued, "My guess is that our dearly departed friend here paid you, what, one-third up front with a promise of the remainder upon completion—sound about right? That means that you got a little money but not all you were promised. On the other hand, I can make you whole. Leave this alone and I'll cover the balance of your contract," he offered a slight smile, "plus a little something extra for your effort. What do you say, boys?"

After a moment of silence, one of the four reached into his coat pocket and withdrew a small card and a pen. He scribbled something on the card and handed it to the assassin. "Contract was for nine-hundred K. That's the account number."

"Consider it done. It'll take me about an hour, once I wrap things up here. Check when you get back to the city. Any problems and you know how to contact me."

The four, almost as one, nodded, turned and disappeared into the brush.

Brookings turned to Teri. "As I was saying before I was so rudely interrupted, you should use your time wisely.

Now, if you'll excuse me, I have some clean-up work to do here."

She backed away from him, turning away from the lake and back toward the parking lot. Her brisk walk turned to a trot, which became a full-on run. Back in her room, she barely made it to the bathroom before vomiting the contents of her stomach.

"Sorry about all that, Mags." Steeno's voice was soft, caring.

She shook her head and wiped her mouth. But there were no words. Gratitude? Relief? Anger? What was she supposed to feel? There was nothing.

He continued, "The worst is over."

But the worst would never be over. There would always be something else lurking around the corner. She closed her eyes tight.

"There are a couple more things to take care of, but I'm going to need a few weeks to set them up. In the meantime, I need a favor from you."

Teri opened her eyes and splashed water on her face. "What?"

"I've placed a data packet in your holding node. When you open it, you'll see a series of numbers and letters—an account code. I would like you to go down to a place called Node Print Express. They specialize in moving data to paper. Go to the old finger pad display and enter that code. It will print out a name and address. Make sure that you have that in your hand before you okay the transaction. I put a data bomb in the completed print queue file. Once you accept the transaction, all records of completed jobs will disappear."

"What do I do with the name and address?"

"I need for you to go see someone for me."

Chapter 72

Teri Wallerman, formerly Maggie Renfro, turned the vehicle drive system off and sat in silence. The house she pulled up in front of looked as though it was at least a hundred years old. The blue-gray wood siding and buttercream yellow trim were in good repair and appeared newly painted. The style was unlike anything she'd ever seen on the East Coast. She stared at the old-fashioned screen door, still wondering what she was supposed to say.

The cross-country trip had been surprisingly relaxing. She'd ridden sky trains before, but this time it was different. She managed to put all of the garbage of the last three months out of her mind. The only thing she had to worry about was a conversation. She'd called ahead from the portal node in Seattle to get directions, since her destination was not part of the geographic programming in her rental vehicle.

A woman, appearing to be in her mid-seventies, answered the door. "You would be Miz Wallerman?" Her trim body, along with the brightness of her eyes, suggested a good life. She wore a simple yellow, green, and pink flower-patterned blouse and denim jeans that looked as though they could have been as old as the house.

"Yes, Teri Wallerman. Thanks for seeing me." She offered the most confident smile she could muster.

The woman opened the screen door and stepped aside. "Come in, please. I'm Liv Conrad. That's my married name, of course. My maiden name was Cornwell." She gestured toward a worn beige sofa. "Have a seat. Could I get you some coffee or tea?"

Married names and maiden names—Teri had heard of the terms but had never actually come upon them in real life. This all struck her as something from a bygone era— polite entertaining. "Thank you. Coffee, black, please."

The two women settled in with their cups, Teri on the sofa and Liv in an overstuffed chair. "You said there was something you needed to tell me in person?"

So it came down to this. Teri was about to dredge up the distant past for this woman, with no idea how it would affect her. "I was asked, as a favor, to come and talk to you."

"Oh? By whom?"

"Do you remember Harold Chasteen?" There it was, out in the open.

Liv stared, her face ashen. "Harold? He's alive?"

Teri chuckled, allowing it to soften to a smile. "I guess that depends on what you mean by alive. He exists. From what he told me, you were aware of his plan to move his spirit or soul or whatever you call it, onto the network. Well, long story short, it worked."

Liv's eyes moistened. "I married about ten years after that. I have two children—a son and a daughter—and five grandchildren."

Teri nodded. "I know. And he knows too. He asked me to tell you that he is happy for you, very happy. And that he is okay."

Liv's body rocked gently in the chair, and her gaze wandered around the room. "It's been so long. And, well, I have so many questions. What is he like?"

"I don't know that much about him. He's smart. And he saved my life. But I guess I'd say that he's kind of sweet but can be snarky, if you know what I mean."

It was Liv's turn to smile. "Yes. I remember that. Has he gotten older? I mean, he was around twenty-four then. Now he's in his seventies, I guess."

"I'm not sure that concept works in this case. As best I can tell, *he*, if that's what I could call him, is made of electrons and photons and who knows what else. The concepts of life as you and I experience it don't apply to him."

"So, he's immortal?"

Teri chortled. "I don't know and wouldn't even hazard a guess. So far, at least based on what he's told me, there hasn't been any degradation. But eternity is a long time."

"Will he ever come back, you know, as a human?"

Teri reflected on what she knew of Steeno, what he was like when they spoke. "I honestly don't know. He seems human now, except that I can't see him. The thing is, though, even if he could find a way back, he no longer has a body. Maybe one day technology will allow for full body production. But for now, I suspect that he'll just continue hanging out on the network." She caught herself wondering what it would be like to be with Steeno in the flesh.

"I told my husband, Kelly, about Harold. I think at first he thought I was crazy. Over the years, we've touched on it from time to time, and he kind of got used to it." Her eyes grew misty. "I wonder how he'll take this?"

Teri shrugged. "As far as I'm concerned, this is just between you and me. If you don't think he'll do well with it, don't tell him."

Liv smiled. "No. I don't keep anything from him. I made that decision when I accepted his proposal. That's what makes this all work for me—knowing that he knows, and he understands."

Morning became afternoon. The shadows in the room shifted. Conversation wandered from times past to gardening to relationships. And then the daylight outside began to wane, and it was time to go. "I need to get back to Seattle. My sky train leaves at midnight."

"Thank you. It's been so many years. I'm glad at least to know what happened to him." Liv's eyes grew misty.

"You're welcome. Is there anything you want me to tell him?"

"Yes. Tell him hello. And I'm happy that he made it." Liv shook her head. "This feels strange. I'm not really sure what to say to him after all these years. And, I don't know, does he feel things, like emotions?"

"I can't say that I know that much about what he thinks or feels, or even what he is. But, based on what he's told me, yes, he does experience emotions. His voice is tender when he speaks of you. And he remembers."

"Then tell him that not a day goes by that I don't think of him. I wish him happiness, if that makes any sense."

Teri laughed. "It makes as much sense as anything else related to him. I confess that, even after communicating with him for these past weeks, I am still at a loss. I don't really know what to make of any of this."

The drive back up to Seattle from northern Oregon was among the most peaceful experiences of her life. Off to her left, the sky turned orange and purple. Teri found herself alone on the two-lane road that linked up to the throughway into the SeaTac metroplex. She switched the vehicle out of self-drive mode and took control, which gave her an even greater sense of peace. She felt in control—of the car and of her life. And for these few hours, everything was perfect. Although, somewhere in the back of her mind, she knew

that she would soon tumble back into the real world where
her problems waited patiently.

Chapter 73

"Are you there?" Teri still struggled with the concept of Steeno being *there* but not really *there*—sometimes but not always. Not to mention the fact that she could never detect his presence without his announcing it.

"Did you talk to her?" His voice seemed unusually subdued.

"Yes. In fact, I spent most of the day with her."

"How is she?"

"Good, although it's more complicated than that. As you know, she married. She's a grandmother."

"I know." The subdued tone morphed into a more despondent one.

"She asked me to tell you that not a day goes by when she doesn't think of you. But, you have to admit, fifty years is a long time to wait for news of someone. You might have given her some indication earlier. It's kind of hard to make the case that you cared, given that you just abandoned her with no word at all." She felt a tinge of guilt at unloading on Steeno this way—but only a tinge.

"Yeah, I can see that."

"Bottom line, though, you had good taste in women. She's is a really good person. I can see why you loved her." Another truth was beginning to dawn on her. She could understand why Liv loved Harold Chasteen.

"She always was. Probably too good for me. Anyway, I'm glad she's happy, that she has a good life." And then his tone changed—upbeat and all business. "Are you ready to finish up with your little problem?"

"Depends on what you mean by *finish up*. You haven't shared a lot of details with me. All I know is that, with

307

Jarvis dead, my future seems to be tied to how the GlobusSocio people view my existence."

"And that, Mags, is what we have to deal with."

***

She settled back on the sofa in the upscale hotel room. "What's going to happen?"

"Here's what you need to know. We are going to conference with two men—names aren't important. They are the only people that matter. They call all of the shots. I will introduce myself as your representative. While I will suggest that you are not present, they'll likely figure out that you're listening in. Despite that, you won't say anything. You will hear the conversation, but here's a key point. I can mute the external link so that I'm speaking only to you. If you watch the left side of the display, you'll see a waveform that matches the voices. When it's red, that means that you're hearing the conversation between me and the guys at Globus. When it's green, I'm talking privately to you, okay?"

"Got it."

"What I have going for me is that they have no idea what I am. They will assume that I am a real person in some physical location. They'll try to trace me, which will get them nowhere. Still, I'll let them go for a few iterations before I move us along. The important thing is that, no matter what they do, they can't find me."

"That still doesn't tell me how you're going to convince them to leave me alone."

Steeno laughed. "Leave that to me, Mags."

She'd grown used to the name. No, she'd actually grown fond of it. "Then let's do this."

The waveform on the left-hand side showed bright green. "Very well. And away we go."

She heard a series of clicks and, when Steeno's voice came back on, the waveform was red. "Gentlemen, thank you for agreeing to meet with me today. For our purposes today, my name is Stan Jones and I represent Miz Maggie Renfro, a former employee of Immigration Services Corporation."

A raspy voice with a distinct eastern European accent responded. "I am afraid you have us at a disadvantage, Mister… uh… Jones. While GlobusSocio has an interest in ISC, we do not manage the day-to-day affairs."

The waveform turned green. "They're starting the first trace. I've got a dead node set up in Abu Dhabi. They should have the troops arriving there in about seven minutes, if my estimates are correct."

The form turned red. "Yes, I understand that. And I'm prepared to bring you up to date on her situation, if you will indulge me."

A moment of silence settled over the conversation before the accented voice came back on. "Of course. Please continue."

Steeno switched over to the private line to Teri once again. "They're playing for time. Sorry for the delay. Probably another five minutes."

The red waveform re-appeared. "You can verify this through the ISC records, but Miz Renfro was a contract public relations director for a U. S. Senator. As a result of some misunderstandings, she found herself in an adversarial situation with her former supervisor, Leonard Jarvis. I'm sure you're aware of the late Mister Jarvis."

Another hesitation. "Go on."

Steeno issued a sound that resembled the clearing of his throat. Teri thought it quite realistic given that he had no throat to clear. "Just a moment, please." Another brief period of silence preceded his clipped laugh. "Sorry about that. It would seem that your people just breached a door in Abu Dhabi, apparently looking for me. As you are probably hearing on a separate channel, I am not there. So, I suspect you're about to start an iterative probabilistic injection search for a live node. Don't bother. I'm not there either. But if you feel the irresistible urge to do it, go ahead. Just let me know when you're ready to start talking again."

More silence, this time extending several minutes. A new voice intervened—a soft male voice with a British accent. "What is it you want from us, Mister Jones?"

"I don't want anything. Miz Renfro would like her life back. Seems pretty simple to me."

"As I said, what is it you want from us? We don't know who she is, nor do we care."

"Just a moment please." The waveform turned green. "Watch this, Mags. I'm about to get their attention." With that, he reverted back to the external conversation. "Gentlemen, if you will access your realtime financial records, I have something that may be of interest to you."

Maggie perceived more than heard a series of clicks before Steeno's voice returned, speaking to the men. "If you were watching your cash-on-hand balance, you saw the amount decrease by five hundred trillion bitcredits."

The silence hung heavy over the conference before the eastern European accented voice returned. "Mister Jones, or whatever your name is, I can guarantee that you are courting some very unpleasant consequences. You may or may not know much about us, but we didn't get where we are today by allowing this kind of thing."

"So it would seem. Still, the funds are gone, are they not? And you can threaten me all you want, but the reality is that you will never find me. And if I chose it to be so, you would never find your funds. Lucky for you, though, neither I nor Miz Renfro have the slightest interest in your financial assets. I merely wanted to make sure I have your complete, undivided attention."

The Brit took over. "Proceed."

Steeno smirked. "Watch closely. Your funds are about to re-appear, with a little something extra for your trouble."

"An extra five hundred million bitcredits. That's quite generous of you. Now that you have our attention, I ask again, what is it you want from us?"

"And I will tell you again. I want nothing. Miz Renfro wants her life back. She wants to get up each day and not have to look over her shoulder. Let's not play stupid here. Her friend Cheryl Wolford was killed at the direction of ISC. The FNA reporter, Arandon, and his associate, Soldani, suffered similar fates. And if that's not enough, several attempts have already been made on my client's life. So, you'll pardon me if I don't take you at your word."

"And should your client get her life back, as you put it, what can we expect in return?"

"A simple arrangement. You never hear from her again. Neither she nor I will touch your financial assets. She has no interest in you or anything to do with you. In return, all she asks is that you leave her alone. You don't exist for her. She doesn't exist for you. Pretty straightforward."

"You are proposing a gentleman's deal, then?"

Steeno chortled. "Please, please. There are no gentlemen here. What I am saying is that each side has incentive to honor the agreement. Should either you or she violate it, the other would retaliate. There would simply be no point in breaking the deal."

"And how do we know you won't hack our financial system again? After all, you seemed to have worked your way in pretty easily, I'd say."

"Ordinarily I'd say that you just have to trust me. But, realistically, if I wanted your money, I would have it already and I'd never have contacted you."

"As I told you, Mister Jones, we do not know any Maggie Renfro and have no interest in making her acquaintance. Now, if there is nothing further, I'd like to end this little get-together."

Chapter 74

Silence. Deafening silence. Teri sat staring at a nondescript piece of art hanging on the hotel room wall without really seeing it. The conversation between Steeno and the two Globus executives left her numb. The casual tone of their conversation as they considered what would become of her brought home just how small and insignificant she was. Of course, they knew about her despite what they said. But the truth was that they would lose no sleep nor miss a single meal whether she lived or died.

She knew that Steeno was there, although he said nothing. What could he say? Perhaps he saved her life. But wasn't it he that put her in danger to start with? Wasn't he the one responsible for Cheryl's death, and Arandon's, and Soldani's? No. It was Jarvis, ISC, and Globus. They were the bad guys.

Night fell. The room descended into shadows with only dim light from outside filtering through the heavy curtains. Finally, he spoke, "Maggie?"

"Yeah?"

"You okay?"

She sighed. "I'm alive, at least for the moment."

"I wish I could tell you that it's over. But we both know it will never truly end. They'll most likely leave you alone so long as it suits them. And if you stay out their way—off the display—you should be fine."

"So, what? I just go on the monthly stipend system? Collect my free bitcredits and keep my mouth shut? Cheryl, Arandon, and goodness knows who else are all dead. Those

313

kids—nothing changes for them. But I get my money. Is that it?"

"Yes."

"It's not fair."

"No. And I never promised you fair. Most people don't get fair. There are those with… and those without—the old *haves* and *have nots*. Change comes slowly, but it comes. In the end, though, it's hard to say whether the changes are good or bad in the long run. Technology has changed our lives. Some would say for the better. But I'm not so sure."

Teri erupted in laughter. "One thing for sure. Without this technology, you wouldn't be here."

Steeno's response sounded somber. "True, and maybe that would have been better, too."

She stood and stretched, stiff from sitting so long. "Tell me, how'd you pull off the bitcredit thing with those guys? Five hundred trillion—that's no small feat."

"Oh, I don't know. Stealing that much was no harder than stealing a couple of million. I mean, since I had to break into their system anyway, why not make it count?"

"Why'd you give it back to them? In fact, if you wanted, you could break them, completely destroy them."

He chuckled. "And then? You think that would solve the child-sex slave business? Not a chance. As long as there are people with money, power, and a perverted appetite for such things, someone will find a way to provide it. If you want to end it, you have to go after the demand. And that is so widespread, so diverse, that putting out that fire would be nearly impossible."

"Maybe. Still, it would be nice to see Globus go down in flames."

He paused a moment before speaking again. "I think this just about wraps it up for us. I've finished setting up the records for your new identity. Your interface should now be fully functional. And I took the liberty of providing you with some extra financial resources. See the linktab there in the lower left of your display? Follow it and it'll take you to your account status page."

She stared, not quite sure what to make of it. "A billion bitcredits! Are you serious? I thought you told Globus that we'd leave their money alone."

"I didn't get it from them, at least not all of it. Like I told you before, I take a little from here… and a little from there, but never too much from any one source. Trust me, the corporations who so generously donated to your retirement fund will never miss it. Oh, their auditors will pick up on the missing funds, but they'll write it off, much like a food vendor writes off spoiled food. It means nothing to them."

"Then this is the end between you and me?"

"Unless there's something else you need. I think I've caused quite enough trouble for now. I'll probably lay low for a while before jumping into something else."

"You mean you're done with the immigration thing?"

"Yes. Well, maybe. Thing is, I have plenty of time to reconsider, Mags."

She laughed. "Don't you think that you should start calling me by my new name?"

It was his turn to chuckle. "Oh, there'll be plenty of people calling you Teri. But as far as I'm concerned, you'll always be Mags."

"Maybe you could visit some time." Her heart felt suddenly heavy.

"I thought you were fed up with me stalking you."

"I am, sort of. But since most of the people I knew are now dead, it's going to be pretty quiet, especially since I don't have a job to go to."

"I'm never really far away. If you need anything, just activate a search tab. I'll pick up on it. Oh, by the way, you have any idea yet where you want to settle? I'm assuming that Washington, D.C., won't be high on your list."

She smiled warmly. "Yeah. I'm going to Seattle and then maybe find a place south of there, in northern Oregon."

"Wise choice. You're not planning on staying connected to Liv, are you?"

"I don't know. She's nice and I don't have an abundance of friends, you know. But I can't help feeling that staying connected with her would keep you in the picture. I just don't think that would be a good thing."

"I agree. I appreciate your talking to her for me, but she deserves a life without me lurking in the background."

Steeno's voice sounded upbeat, but with a sad resignation beneath. "I guess we are good then. Anything else before I go?"

A part of her—maybe her heart—ached. But why should it? After all, he was just a digital being—not real. "Nothing that I can think of. I guess I can always try to search you out if I need something."

"Not to worry, Mags. If you run a search on me, I'll see it."

Chapter 75

Teri Wallerman, now fully oriented into her new life, sat outside a small bistro in the late spring sunshine. It had been four months since she'd parted ways with Steeno. The past—her old past—was rapidly fading. And her future was only just beginning.

The area around Pike Street Market in Seattle appeared as an experience out of time. From looking around, she could swear that she was back in the late twentieth century, sipping real french roast coffee from a ceramic mug. People bustled around her, quibbling with outdoor merchants and vendors, some of them using real currency—another artifact of an age long past. She wondered, in passing, where they got this money. She could sense, though, that she was seeing merely a small exposed area of a much broader and deeper culture—one in which people trusted each other more than they trusted the government or corporations.

She closed her eyes, feeling a gentle wind on her face. The coffee went down smoothly and left a biting but pleasant taste in her mouth. That is, until a familiar voice brought her out of her reverie. "Hiya Mags."

No, it wasn't in her head. She turned and stared in disbelief. "Arandon?" But he looked different. The eyes—that was it. They laughed and twinkled. He sported a smile. No, a grin—but a warm and genuine one.

He shrugged. "Partially."

Then it hit her—the name he'd used—*Mags*. "Steeno?" Her eyes widened.

"Partially."

"Really? You stole his body?" She wanted to stand and confront him but felt her legs quivering.

"*Stole* is such a harsh word. I *borrowed* it. It's not like he's using it. And trust me, Mags, I'll take much better care of it than he ever did. Besides, if he comes looking, I'll return it in good faith." He sat across the table from her and nodded toward a hovering waiter.

Teri held her retort until Steeno/Arandon had placed his order and the waiter had withdrawn. "You can't just go around doing that. Even if he never comes back, that body doesn't belong to you."

"Who does it belong to?" The expression of joyous mischief never wavered.

She shook her head. "What if he does come back? He arranged for that service and paid for it."

"He's dead, Maggie. His body has been kept functional, but his soul, his spirit—it's gone. I've been around for a lot of years, and I've done a lot of reading and research. I've never heard of a dead person's awareness coming back."

"That still doesn't give you the right to steal it. Besides, they could infuse the body with artificial intelligence based on his embedded memories and values. Those are still there, right?"

"But would that be any different than me using it? Is an artificially generated soul any better or worse than mine?"

"I don't know. What were you? What are you now?"

He burst out laughing. "Touché." His face grew serious for a moment. "Sorry, I'm still getting used to this facial expression thing. Anyway, what I was—just an awareness, a spirit or soul, some form of life. As for what I am now, same thing, only with a body to go along with it."

She turned her attention to her drink as she tried to digest this whole turn of events. Why should she even care, though? She never liked Arandon, so, what if someone stole his body? And why not Steeno? At least he'd helped her. "Wait, you say you're the same thing you were, only with a body. Does that mean you still exist on the network?"

"No. As it turns out, the soul can exist in only one dimension at a time. I can live in the physical world or the digital world, but not both. I had to make a choice and here I am."

She could hardly contain the smile that found its way onto her face. Steeno was sitting in front of her... in the flesh, literally. "And, at the risk of sounding mundane, what is your name, these days?"

He stood and bowed. "I am Clifton Summers, Cliff, for short. Pleased to meet you."

"And you came all the way out to Seattle to see me, or are there other opportunities about?"

"Just you. No opportunities that I know of. Seriously, I'm having some difficulty adjusting to the limitations of the physical world, being in only one place at a time and without the ability to work on many things at once. I assume it's just going to take some time." He sat and pulled his chair up closer to the table. "Oh, and here's the other thing. Now that I have a body, I also have a limited lifetime, which puts a whole new sense of urgency in things. I vaguely remember my old life, with death staring me in the face. Now I have to accept that I will, at some point, have my old nemesis confront me again."

"So, what? When death comes around again, will you go back into the network?" It struck her that this could be a never-ending series of real and virtual lives for Steeno.

"I am here for the duration. As attractive as immortality may seem, it feels better to know that there is an end to it all. It gives me a reason to get up in the morning and to do things rather than to put them off. I have a deadline, so to speak."

She laughed. "Yes, I guess you do." Still, having Steeno in the real world, having lived virtually for so long, raised interesting questions. "Maybe we can discuss this in greater detail later. I'd be interested in hearing your observations about life in the network. We never really talked about it."

A distant look swept into his eyes. "Yes, we can talk about it later. But, for now, I will tell you this. The most profound thing that I brought away from it is that the notion of being alive isn't what we think it to be. In fact, I'm at a loss to say what it really means to live. Most humans have narrowly defined life in terms of organicity, even down to the cellular level. But I can tell you, without exaggeration, that life exists in forms and ways that you cannot begin to imagine. Every electron, photon, or other subatomic particle is alive within its own frame of reference. But even beyond that, there are life forms that defy description. Humankind created artificial intelligence and that AI has spawned even more diverse kinds of life. Even the force and energy fields created by the flow of information have lives. They react to stimuli. They make decisions. And, who knows? Perhaps they have desires and dreams. We are arrogant if we believe that our own frame of reference is better or worse than any other."

Teri had heard some of these arguments before, especially when made within the context of frames of reference. But this view seemed to extrapolate far beyond the bounds of reason. Still, arguing with someone… or something that had been a part of the network for so many years seemed futile. "I don't dispute you, but what does that mean, in terms of my life and how I live?"

"Nothing really. It doesn't change things any more than what happens within the other domains affects you in any material way. For me, though, it means that life is precious, in all its forms. Before, I mean, back when I was sick, I only thought of what things meant to me. After decades of interacting with life in many other forms, I realize that our perspective is only a matter of convenience. I've never spoken to a photon, at least not directly, but I'm pretty sure that if I could ask them, they would tell me that what happens in our world means absolutely nothing to them. Just as what happens in their world means little to us."

She couldn't think of anything to add to this particular conversation, at least not at the moment. "What now?"

He nervously tapped his fingers on the tabletop. "I have a few things in the works—little arrangements I made before leaving my last existence."

"And?"

"Well, those quaint little pleasure industries down in the Economic Freedom Zone are about to suffer a little disruption. In fact, their entire revenue flows are about to be diverted. The funds will ultimately find their way into some underground child advocacy organizations, at least for a while. And the nodes where they advertise and sell their products are infected with multiple intrusion and disruption applications that are unblockable with current technology. Anyone who accesses them will find their bank accounts depleted and their identity and activities posted on every social outlet on the network. Of course, all of this will get fixed eventually, but it will throw a glitch into the system for a while."

"If you could do that, why not just go for everything and completely destroy them?"

"Because they have thousands of kids in their stables. If they go down, what do you think would happen to those children?"

"I don't know, but would it be any worse than what they have now?"

"I will tell you this, Mags, being alive is better than not being alive. Because as long as those kids live, there is some hope. Where it goes from there, I can't personally control."

"I hope you're right." He turned to gaze down the street. The sun had gained sufficient altitude to grant its warmth to the entire market.

"There's more. I reset the funding flow algorithms in the international financial network. The corporations will see slightly less revenue while the inflation factor for personal monthly income for the unemployed will go up. A few fortunes will be lost and some of the most despicable lives will be disrupted. But, unfortunately, all of that will eventually be restored. In the end, it's not about money but about power and information. Whoever controls the flow of knowledge, controls the world and all its wealth. There is nothing I can do about that."

A sad smile painted her mouth. "I suppose you set yourself up, I mean financially, before you left?"

"Funny you should ask."

Chapter 76

What's that?" Teri stared at the satchel that Cliff/Steeno had set on the table between them.

He opened it and showed her the contents—bundles of paper currency. "Dollars, Mags, good old-fashioned greenbacks."

"Yeah, I can see that it's outdated money, but why?"

"As it turns out, there's going to be more than a few hiccups in the financial system. Bitcredits will always come back, but there are going to be some uncertain times ahead." He chuckled as he re-zipped the bag. "I've got more—gold coins and ingots, as well as some trade goods, cloth, coffee, and liquor."

"You think society is going to devolve back into physical currency?"

"Not permanently, no. But there are going to be some anxious times. The real point, though, is that I'm thinking of moving to a place where these might be more relevant."

"And where might that be?"

"You remember the name Paulette Stringer? She was the senator's mistress who mysteriously disappeared. Well, I found her, or at least a thread that showed me where she was headed."

"Why would I care about that?"

"Because she disappeared and, at least as far as I can tell, she's healthy and prosperous."

"But if you could find her, don't you think anyone else with sufficient resources could as well, at least if they wanted to?"

"Yes and no. Anyone with sufficient resources could follow the trail I did. Unfortunately for them, I destroyed the trail before I left the network. She used to be fairly safe. Now she's really safe."

"And this is important because…?"

"Because I'm planning on going to the same place." His gaze dropped to the tabletop. "And I'd like for you to go with me."

Teri sat stunned, unable to speak for a moment. When she gathered her wits, she responded with no small degree of skepticism. "What does that mean—'to go with you?'"

"I knew love in my late teens and early twenties. Since then, I've had a long time to watch people. There are some good ones and some bad ones. But through it all, I kept the notion of feelings and affection out of my thoughts. It was, after all, a futile endeavor. You were different, though. You care about people. You care about the truth. You care about what's right. At the risk of sounding stodgy, you give me hope. More than that, though, you make me care. I may be emotionally stunted, given my experiences of the last fifty years, but being around you makes me feel… I don't know… *right*."

"That doesn't answer the question. What do you mean when you say you want me to go with you?" Teri suddenly had a longing to hear a specific answer.

He reached across and touched her hand. The visible effect on him was striking. He closed his eyes and caught his breath. A tear streamed down his cheek when he opened his eyes. "I want to be with you. I want us to be together. I know this is sudden. You don't have to answer right now. But what I mean… what I want… is to marry you."

She took his hand and squeezed it. "You're right. This is sudden and, honestly, I don't know how to answer right this instant." She smiled as her own eyes grew moist. "But I kind of like the idea of being with you too."

Still, a wave of conflicted feelings coursed through her. Seattle was good. Her life, such as it was, gave her a certain amount of security and, if not pleasure, at least peace. And why would she run off with someone who'd stolen a body—the body belonging to someone she didn't even like. But she knew that, whatever else she thought of Steeno, he'd saved her life and he'd always been honest with her. There were few other people in her past about whom she could say that.

"Where is it that you plan to go?"

"Ever hear of a place called Alaska?"

She shrugged. "Yeah. Used to be one of the states. It lost its status about thirty years ago—a dispute about natural resource revenues, if I remember my history."

"Yup. Now it's a U. S protectorate and home to a different kind of economic freedom zone. Not a lot of high rolling start-up enterprises there. But there are a lot of small, locally-owned businesses—a lot of bartering and, here's the best part—they rely mostly on the old U. S. dollar. Not a lot of bitcredit transaction up there, at least not among the locals."

"That's a big place. Any particular part you're interested in?"

He drew imaginary circles on the table with his index finger. "There's this little spot, the end of the road in the south-central portion of the state—a small town named Homer."

Epilogue

Three Years Later

The woman pulled the hood tighter around her head as she battled the wind-driven rain. Beside her, a man marched stoically without complaint. The row of rickety shops lined a spit of land that jutted out into Kachemak Bay. She knew that mountains rose from the shore but they remained shrouded in mist.

She turned toward a small shop. "That looks interesting and I'm hungry. Let's get something to eat."

The man, easily in his seventies, nodded and shrugged.

She stopped at the entrance to the shop to read a weathered sign that looked older than she did:

In God we trust
All others pay cash

She smiled and pushed the door open. A wave of aroma swept over her—fish, beer, and hot grease.

A voice boomed out through an opening in the wall where a man who looked to be in his late thirties or early forties, placed two platters on the stainless-steel counter. "Order up," he called out. The lettering on his ball cap identified him as "Cliff."

The tourist stared at a menu, printed most quaintly on a large slate board standing beside the counter.

Welcome to the Dancing Halibut
Daily Special Menu

326

A pleasant looking woman who appeared to be in her early forties, grabbed the plates and checked a piece of paper in front of her. "Order number forty-seven," she called out into the crowded bistro. With that out of the way, she turned and greeted the tourist. Her name tag identified her as Teri. "Typical Homer day out there." The smile became a laugh. "Where are you folks from?"

"Philadelphia. Does it rain like this all the time?"

"Oh no. Sometimes it snows. And we had a day of sunshine last month."

The tourist shook her head, thankful she didn't live in this dreadful place. Nodding back toward the door. "Interesting sign. Where'd you get that?" She reached into her purse and pulled out some wrinkled green bills.

Teri shrugged and smiled. "Homer is literally at land's end. All sorts of interesting things end up here. Now, what can I get for you folks?"

The End